coffee

will

make

you

black

coffee

will

make

you

black

.

APRIL

SINCLAIR

HYPERION

new york

For information address

Hyperion, 114 Fifth Avenue, New York,

New York 10011

Library of Congress

Cataloging-in-Publication Data

Sinclair, April.

Coffee will make you black : a novel /

by April Sinclair.

p. cm.

ISBN 1-56282-796-0

1. Afro-American women—Illinois—

Chicago—Fiction. 2. Young women—

Illinois—Chicago—Fiction.

3. South Chicago (Chicago, Ill.)

—Fiction. I. Title.

PS3569.I5197C64   1994

813'.54—dc20   93-13271   CIP

10   9   8   7   6   5   4   3   2

For my mother,

JULIANNE SINCLAIR

And in remembrance of my maternal grandmother,

JULIA BELL GUNTER

"If I should live forever and all my dreams come true,

my memories of love, will be of you."

ACKNOWLEDGMENTS

"It takes a village to raise a child," according to an African proverb. It took the love, support, and wisdom of many people to write this book.

Thanks, first and foremost, to Susan Holper, my manuscript consultant, for walking me through the creative process with sensitivity and insight.

A special thanks to all of the people who encouraged me at readings from my work in progress throughout the San Francisco Bay Area and in Garberville, California.

I am grateful to three fantastic teachers, James Frey, Allie Light, and Irving Saraf. And also to the Ragdale Foundation, Urban Gateways, and the crew at the Alameda County Community Food Bank for their support.

Thanks to Winifred Golden and the Margret McBride Literary Agency: the best agent and agency any writer could hope for. And much gratitude to Leslie Wells, my brilliant and supportive editor, and the rest of the wonderful staff at Hyperion Press.

The enthusiastic backing of my family in Chicago and Florida and my friends in the San Francisco Bay Area kept me going. Thanks especially to Kimberly Rosa and Judy MacLean for their help with the manuscript. And sincere appreciation to Wayne Jenkins for buying me dinners at a time when I could hardly afford groceries.

PART ONE

spring
1965

.

summer
1967

chapter 1

"**M**ama, are you a virgin?"

I was practicing the question in my head as I set the plates with the faded roosters down on the shiny yellow table. When Mama came back into the kitchen to stir the rice or turn the fish sticks or check on the greens, I would ask her.

This afternoon at school a boy named Michael had passed a note with "Stevie" written on it; inside it had asked if I was a virgin.

My name is Jean Stevenson but the kids at school all call me Stevie counta there's been this other Jean in my class since the first grade. Now I am eleven and a half and in the sixth grade.

So, anyhow, I was really surprised to get this note from a boy like Michael Dunn, who's tall with muscles and has gray eyes, curly hair, skin the color of taffy apples, and wears Converse All-Stars even though they cost $10 a pair.

I'm not saying I look like homemade sin or anything. It's just that I'm taller than most of the other girls in my class and half of the boys. Mama says I'm at that awkward age, and that soon I won't just be arms and legs; I'll need a bra and a girdle. I can't picture myself needing a bra, as flat-chested as I am now. And to tell you the truth, I'm not too hot on having my behind all hitched up in a girdle. I have to help Mama into hers on Sunday mornings, and I feel sorry for her, all squeezed in so tight you wonder how she can even breathe.

I stirred a pitcher of cherry-flavored Kool-Aid. I loved Daylight Saving Time; it was after six o'clock and still light outside. The sunshine pouring in through the ruffled curtains made the flowers on the wallpaper look alive.

I studied my reflection in the pitcher of Kool-Aid. It wasn't like I wasn't cute. I had dimples and my features seemed right for my face. My straightened hair was long enough to make a ponytail. My skin was the color of Cracker Jacks. But most negroes didn't get excited over folks who were darker than a paper bag.

"Jean, turn off the oven!" Mama shouted from her bedroom. "Okay."

I stared out the kitchen window at the row of gray back porches and dirt backyards. We had been in the middle of Social Studies when I had gotten Michael's note. I had lifted the lid of my wooden desk and felt behind the bag of old, wet sucked-on sunflower-seed shells and pulled out my hardcover dictionary. I'd snuck a peek inside and looked up the word "virgin." I'd seen the words "pure" and "spotless" and "like the Virgin Mary, mother of Jesus." I thought I was a good person for the most part. I didn't steal and I tried my best not to lie. I went to Sunday school, and when I stayed for church, I always put my dime in the collection plate. But I wasn't about to put myself up there with Jesus' mother. It seemed like Michael was asking me if I was a goody-two-shoes or something.

So I'd had no choice but to answer the note with the words "Not exactly" and pass it back to him. I wondered what Michael thought of my answer, I hadn't seen him after school. I hoped he would say something to me on Monday. I knew it wasn't my place as a girl to say anything to him. I would just have to wait and see what happened, I told myself.

Mama returned to the kitchen. She looked glad to be out of her girdle and work clothes. She was wearing her oldest print housedress, and the extra pounds showing around her waist didn't make her look fat, they just made her look like somebody's mother. Mama had tied a scarf around her hair so she wouldn't sweat it out, and she was wearing Daddy's old house slippers. It struck me how different Mama looked from June Cleaver or Donna Reed on TV, not just because of her pecan-colored skin but because they practically did their housework in pearls!

I turned facing Mama, and folded my arms across my chest. I watched her take the pan of fish sticks out of the oven and set them on a plate.

I cleared my throat. "Mama, are you a virgin?"

Mama lifted the top off the pot of collard greens and breathed in the steam. She glanced at me and turned off the gas. I could tell by the look on her face that she was trying to think up a good answer.

"Jean, where did you pick up that word, at church?" Mama asked, rearranging the pressing comb and the can of bacon grease on the stove.

I stared down at the yellowed gray linoleum.

"Well, no, not exactly . . . at school."

"Mrs. Butler brought it up?"

I pulled on the tie of my sailor blouse and twisted it around my fingers.

"No, Mama, Mrs. Butler ain't brought it up, this boy asked me if I was a virgin."

I had the nerve to glance up at Mama. Her large dark eyes were arched up like she had seen a ghost.

"Don't say 'ain't'! Didn't I tell you to never say 'ain't'? I can run from 'ain't.' "

In my opinion, this was not time for an English lesson, so I just hunched my shoulders. "Mrs. Butler *didn't* bring it up, this boy asked me if I was a virgin." I repeated, correcting my English.

"Well, Jean Eloise, you should have told him he'll never get the chance to find out." Mama frowned as she stirred the rice. "Humph, you stay away from that boy; he's got his mind in the gutter." Mama pointed her finger in my face. "All men are dogs! Some are just more doggish than others. Do you hear me?"

"Mama, the dictionary said something about the word 'virgin' meaning pure and spotless, like the Virgin Mary. I don't understand why you say Michael's got his mind in the gutter then."

" 'Cause he's a dog, that's why! I just got through telling you that."

I stuffed my hands into the pockets of my blue pedal pushers and looked Mama in the eye. "Mama, am I a virgin or not?"

"Lord, have mercy, I forgot about the cornbread!" Mama opened the oven door and took out the pan of cornbread. It looked fine.

Mama let out a big breath. Maybe it was hard having a daughter at an awkward age, I thought. "Jean, all unmarried girls should be virgins."

"Mama, Michael knows I'm unmarried."

"You haven't even started your period yet, of course you're a virgin."

I stared down at my brown penny loafers. "Mama, what happens when you start your period?"

Mama patted her cornbread. "I don't think you're ready for this kind of discussion."

"Mama, I'll be twelve in four months."

"Jean Eloise, I'll tell you everything I want you to know when the time comes. Now, call your daddy and the boys for dinner, the fish sticks are gettin cold."

I groaned as I left the kitchen. Boy, I could've gotten more out of Beaver Cleaver's mother.

✳

It was Saturday morning and Grandma was visiting; my Aunt Sheila and my Uncle Craig had dropped her off in their shiny, new '65 Buick. They didn't have any kids yet, and they lived downstairs from Grandma in her two-flat building. Grandma owned a chicken stand down on 47th Street in the heart of the South Side. It was named after her: Mother Dickens' Fried Chicken. I was proud of her. My mother's youngest brother, Uncle Franklin, and his wife, Aunt Connie, helped her run it. My uncle Arthur worked on the railroad. He lived in Orlando, Florida, with his wife and twin boys. Grandma said she wasn't rich, but she'd come a long way from Gainesville, Florida.

I buried my face in Grandma's big chest. I could smell the peppermint candy that she kept in the pocket of her cotton housedress. Grandma held me close as she rocked me in the sunny kitchen. I traced her fudge-colored arm with my finger. Mama says Grandma spoils me. Grandma says I'm her heart. Mama can't stand to see me up in her mother's lap; it really gets her. But I can't help myself, Grandma's lap is my favorite place in the world. Unless maybe if I had a chance to go to Disneyland, but that's all the way in California and Grandma's lap is right here on the South Side of Chicago.

"Grandma, how come your skin's so soft and smooth? Do you use Ivory liquid?"

"Chile, good black don't crack." Grandma smiled. Grandma carries herself like a queen. She's tall and big-boned and wears her gray hair in French braids. She has what she calls laughing eyes and she says she's proud of her large nose and full lips.

I took color from my mother's side of the family, 'cept I've got a lot of red in my skin. My daddy's grandmother was a full-blooded Cherokee Indian. All of Daddy's sisters live in Oklahoma, where he's from. I've never met them. His mother and father are both dead. Mama says she wishes I'd gotten more of Daddy's lighter color and especially his curly hair. She says she prayed that if I was a girl I'd have good hair that didn't need to be straightened. Mama says one reason she married Daddy was cause she was looking out for her children. She says it was almost unheard of for a colored man to marry a woman darker than himself. Mama says she was lucky.

Anyway, Mama says she doesn't know where I was when they were handing out color and hair. She says I let my nine-year-old brother David get ahead of me in the hair line and my six-year-old brother Kevin get ahead of me in the color line. But at least I've got nice features, she's thankful for that, Mama always says. In other words, she's glad I don't have a wide nose and big lips like Grandma and some other colored people. And Mama likes that I have high cheekbones, of course.

My brother David is tall and slim, with Daddy's features and Mama's color. Kevin is short and chubby but otherwise looks like Daddy spit him out. David and Kevin are the regular type of brothers that you want to keep out of your face as much as possible. But otherwise we get along pretty okay.

I would describe Mama as looking like Dr. Martin Luther King's wife dipped in chocolate. They have similar features and they both seem to have serious looks on their faces most of the time.

Daddy, on the other hand, smiles a lot, but you still know you'd better not cross him. He's big and tall with muscles and narrow eyes like the Indians who are always getting killed on TV. His skin is the color of peanut butter, just like my little brother Kevin's.

"Jean, if you don't get off of your grandmother's lap, you better." Mama had sneaked up on me in her furry slippers.

I looked up at Grandma. Her eyes were closed; she had dozed off.

I got up, mainly because I didn't want to hear Mama's mouth.

"You oughta be ashamed of yourself, a big girl like you having the nerve to be in up somebody's lap."

Maybe Mama was right, I thought, maybe I should be ashamed, maybe there was something wrong with me.

"Lord have mercy, Evelyn, why can't you let the child be?" Grandma always took up for me.

"No, I won't let her be, Mama. Now, I'm not going to have it this year. Jean Eloise will be twelve in September. Jesus began preaching at twelve. Now she's too old to be up in somebody's lap. How's she gonna learn to be a responsible adult? She needs to get out with girls her own age." Mama let out a sigh. "Ever since that Terri moved away she's stayed cooped up in this house feeling sorry for herself." Mama stood over me with her arms folded.

Grandma didn't argue with Mama, she just reached in her apron pocket and handed me a peppermint. Mama started putting the dishes away, Grandma picked up the quilt she had been working on, and I sucked my candy.

I sat down at the kitchen table and laid my head on top of my arms. Terri used to be my best friend, but she moved away last fall, right after we both got our applications from the Peace Corps in the mail. Me and Terri had planned to join the Peace Corps and teach in Africa together when we grew up.

I felt like crying just thinking about Terri now. We had been best friends since kindergarten and we used to do everything together.

Mama turned away from the dishes she was putting up in the cabinet.

"Jean, I told you, you should've never had a best friend in the first place. Always have a group of friends, then you won't be so dependent."

I kept my head on the table.

"Mama, I didn't set out to have a best friend, it just turned out that way."

"Why don't you call one of the girls from the Methodist Youth Foundation?" Mama asked.

"I'll see them tomorrow at Sunday school. They're church friends. There's nobody I really want to hang out with that much anymore. Unless they were really cool or something."

"You seem awfully particular for somebody sitting up in the house by yourself on a Saturday afternoon."

My secret wish was to be popular, to have all the cool people flocking to be my friends. This girl in my class named Carla Perkins is popular. When she had her birthday party last month, kids practically begged her to invite them. Me and Carla don't know each other 'cept to speak, but I had secretly hoped that a miracle would happen and I would get invited to her party. But of course when Carla had passed out her invitations, there hadn't been one for me.

I wondered what it would feel like to have a bunch of friends to walk with and give you Valentine cards and invite you to all the cool birthday parties. Being popular must feel different from making the honor roll or having your poem published in the school newspaper, or even having a best friend, I thought. Then I remembered Michael's note. Maybe he wanted me to be his girlfriend. I would really be something then.

Mama dumped a fat brown paper bag on the kitchen table in front of my face. She tore it open. It was full of fresh string beans.

"If you're going to stay cooped up in here, then you can just make yourself useful. Steada lying around here like a May snake, you can start snapping these beans."

I sat up and began popping the ends off the bright green beans and breaking them in the middle. I liked hearing their snapping sound.

Grandma looked up from her quilt.

"You know, Evelyn, I suppose every mama wants her child to be popular. I remember one time, you must've been along in age with Jean Eloise, you had to stay home from school, counta you twisted your ankle. What made it so heartbreaking was it was Colored Day at the Carnival and your class was all set to go. I hated to have to leave you home alone that morning, but I ain't had no choice. I was working for a new family on the other side of Gainesville and your Daddy was doing day labor on a farm. Neither of us could take a chance on missing a day. When I got home that night you and the rest of the kids was asleep. I ain't get to talk to you face to face till that next evening."

"Mama, why do you have to use 'ain't'? I had to get after Jean yesterday about saying 'ain't.'"

"Anyways," Grandma continued, ignoring Mama, "you told me half the class had come by to see you, they had even brought you by some pink cotton candy, don't you remember? Yassuh, I was so happy to hear that I didn't know what to do. Like I said, I s'pose every mama want her child to be popular. But I'll never forget that you told me this other girl, by the name of Lillie Mae, had been out sick the same day as you and didn't nobody even ast about her, remember?"

"Didn't nobody?" Mama frowned.

Grandma ignored her again. "Your exact words was 'I'll never forget them so long as I know Jesus,' you said. 'Nobody cared about Lillie Mae, they ain't care whether she lived or died.' Them was your exact words, remember? My heart went out to Lillie Mae just as though I'd give birth to her."

Me and Mama were quiet; all you could hear was the snapping of our beans.

"Somebody colored's on TV!" Kevin yelled from the living room.

"Well, I sho hope it ain't that Stepin Fetchit fellow again," I heard Grandma say as I followed behind her and Mama.

I was hoping I wouldn't end up like Lillie Mae.

chapter 2

It was Sunday after church and Mama was standing at my bedroom door with these two girls from the other sixth-grade class. I was shocked that Denise and Gail seemed to be here to see me. It wasn't like I had older brothers to get next to or anything. Mama looked surprised too. Denise and Gail were fast girls who wore their hair in French rolls and liked to crack their gum. Gail already had two big bumps sticking through her shell top, and they both had hips holding up their cutoffs. I knew Mama looked down on people who wore shorts before Memorial Day, even though it was warm and humid outside.

"Jean, didn't you hear me calling you?"

I shook my head. I'd been playing with my yo-yo.

I nodded at Denise and Gail and they nodded back. I tried not to seem too surprised by their visit.

Gail was no bigger than a minute but she had a shape. She had delicate features like a Siamese cat, and her skin was the color of an old penny. Denise had some meat on her bones, large eyes, a wide nose, full lips, and was light-skinned. Mama would call Denise "yellow-wasted." That's what she called light-skinned people with hair nappy enough to be straightened and/or African features.

Mama leaned against the wall with one hand in her apron pocket. I motioned for Denise and Gail to come into my room.

"Well, girls, we just got in from church not too long ago." Mama frowned at my Sunday dress and petticoat bunched up in the chair. "Twenty minutes earlier and you wouldn't have caught us."

"Gail, you can sit on this chair," I grabbed my dress and petticoat. "Denise, you can sit on the bed here," I scooped up the stack of Archie comic books, and looked around my small, junky room for a place to stuff them. Denise and Gail eyed the matching white bedroom furniture that Mama and Daddy had bought at a house sale in the suburbs.

"When did your churches let out?" Mama asked as the girls sat down.

"I ain't went to church this morning. I ain't got up in time." Denise answered.

"I ain't got up in time either."

Mama closed her eyes, and made a face like she'd just eaten something that tasted bad. "You ain't got up in time?"

"No, my mama and them was playing cards last night, kept us all up late," Denise explained.

I turned away from the closet and gave Mama a look that begged her to shut up. But there was no stopping her.

"Girls, listen to yourselves, you're butchering the English language!"

Denise and Gail looked at Mama like she had just landed here from Mars.

I sat down on my bed and stared into the quilt Grandma had made me. I was sick of Mama. It was bad enough she had made Daddy paint my room pink. She knew blue was my favorite color.

"Girls, you should have said, 'I *didn't* go to church this morning because I *didn't* get up in time.' And you shouldn't be kept up all night because of your mother's card playing. I hate to think some people would put card playing ahead of church services. And by the way, have you girls ever heard Dr. King speak?"

Gail and Denise hunched their shoulders. I couldn't tell if they were saying no or that they didn't care. I remembered how Mama and Daddy had called me and David in from playing to watch Dr. King give his "I Have a Dream" speech on TV, two summers ago. When Dr. King said the part about having a dream that one day he would live in a country where his four little children would be judged not by the color of their skin, but by the content of their character, I looked over at Mama and she had tears running down her face. It was the only time I'd ever seen her cry except at her father's funeral when I was five. David had asked Mama why she was crying. Mama had answered, "Because he makes me proud to be a negro." Next thing we knew Daddy's eyes were wet, and by the time Dr. King ended with "Free at last, Free at last, thank God Almighty, we're free at last," shivers were running down my spine.

"If you ever get a chance to hear Dr. King speak, pay close attention to his command of the English language," Mama continued.

I cleared my throat as I sat on the bed, hoping Mama could take a hint. It was obvious that Denise and Gail didn't want to be bothered.

"Well, I've got a chicken to cut up. You girls have fun this afternoon and, Jean, as soon as your company leaves, clean this place up. You should be ashamed for anyone to see your room looking like this."

Denise and Gail rolled their eyes when Mama hit the door.

"Dog, is she always like that?" Denise wanted to know.

"No," I lied. I felt embarrassed to even be connected to Mama.

"Well, that's good, is she a English teacher or something?" Gail wrinkled her forehead.

"No, she's a bank teller."

I forgot about Mama and went back to wondering why Denise and Gail had come over in the first place.

"Do you all want to play Monopoly?"

"No, not today." Gail smiled.

"Jacks?"

Denise shook her head. "Some other time."

"Barbie dolls?" I asked, willing to forget I'd ever been a tomboy.

"Stevie, did you know that me and Michael are cousins?"

I looked at Gail's face to see if they favored each other. They did, sort of.

"No, Gail, I never really knew that."

"Well, we are. Anyway, dig up, I hear you been talking to Michael."

"Well, he just passed me a note, we didn't actually talk yet."

"We knows all about the note. Do you call yourself digging Michael or not?" Denise jumped in.

I wondered if Denise was his cousin too. I couldn't tell from their faces if I was supposed to dig Michael or not. I felt like I was on Perry Mason.

"Well, I think he's cute, and I think he's really cool. I'm not sure if I know him enough to dig him or not. We've never really had a conversation. The note was a big surprise. I didn't even know he was paying me any attention."

"When he sent you that note asking you if you was a virgin, you put down 'Not exactly,' " Denise reminded me.

I stared down at my quilt and ran my fingers along the different patches.

"I didn't think I met the definition of the word totally," I said, glancing up at Gail and Denise. They both looked interested. "I'm not completely pure and innocent. I've done a few things," I admitted, remembering the time I picked some cherries off some people's tree without asking, and other stuff along those lines.

"So who's the boy you messed around with?" Gail asked.

"Huh?"

"Okay, you ain't gotta give his name, but what did y'all do, just play with each other's thangs?" she asked.

I remembered the time me and my brother David had played doctor when we were four and six. "Yeah," I nodded, trying to seem cool.

"Did he stick his dick inside you?" Denise wanted to know.

I raised my eyebrows. He was only four years old, I thought to myself.

"Just rubbed it against you?" Denise continued.

"I'm too embarrassed to talk about it," I said, swallowing.

"I understand, we ain't mean to get all up in your business," Gail cut in. "But ain't no sense in me lying, I was surprised when Michael told me about you. All this time I had you figured for a L7," Gail drew a square in the air.

I shook my head and tried to look surprised. Me an L7? No way.

"Well, we just wanted to check you out, see what your story was." Denise said.

"Hey, any girl my cousin talk to, I make it my business to check out. 'Cause don't nobody get next to Michael without coming through me," Gail pointed to her chest.

"We'll be in touch," Denise said, getting up.

Gail stood up too.

"Well, thanks for stopping by, it's been really boss. I mean, feel free to drop by the crib anytime." I tried to sound hip.

Monday was cool, damp, and gray, but I was walking home with guess who? Gail and Denise. I had been surprised to see them waiting for me when our class let out. Me and Michael hadn't crossed paths all day long. I still didn't know what he thought. But I wasn't about to say anything to him, so I'd just have to wait. Michael must be interested or Gail and Denise wouldn't be giving me the time of day, I figured.

I usually walked home with Linda and Melody. They were nice but square. So, when I saw Denise and Gail waving to me, I told Linda and Melody to go ahead on.

Denise and Gail were all the way cool, and if I was walking home with them, people would figure I had to at least be half-way cool. I hoped that my ponytail and pleated skirt fit in okay with their French rolls and tight, straight skirts. At least all three of us were wearing pullover sweaters.

The three of us walked through our neighborhood, past the rows of two-flat brick buildings and occasional bungalows, cracking our gum as loud as we could.

"Niece, you got any more of that red-orange fingernail polish, girl?"

Denise shook her head and cracked her gum.

"Where'd you get it from anyways?" Gail asked.

"I copped it from Walgreen's that time, remember?"

"Oh, yeah, that's right."

I almost swallowed my gum. I had to bite my tongue to keep from saying, "You mean you stole it?" Gail didn't bat an eye.

I decided to try and change the subject. We weren't that far from Walgreen's now; I didn't want them to get any ideas.

"Mrs. Butler asked me if I was gonna write a poem for the school paper again this year."

Gail and Denise just went on cracking their gum.

"Have either of you ever thought about writing anything for the paper?"

"Humph, that's the last thing I would wanta do, write something," Denise groaned.

"Yeah, " Gail agreed. "Why you bringing up school stuff? It's bad enough we got to sit up and look at the teacher all day long, now we gotta listen to your ass."

I stared down at the new blades of grass and the tulips about to bloom in front of a house.

"Mrs. Butler mentioned it to me on the way out, so it was kind of fresh on my mind, that's all. But I think I'll let it go this year. It ain't no biggie."

"Sho ain't," Gail agreed.

"Not unlessen you a square." Denise laughed.

"Thank you," Gail stretched her hand out and Denise gave her five.

I cracked my gum and shook my head to let them know that I was at least halfway cool.

"Oooh!" I shouted, feeling a hand grabbing my behind, through my skirt. I slapped the hand away and turned around and saw Michael standing there grinning. This other boy, Calvin, was feeling on Gail.

"Leave me alone!" I shouted, backing away from Michael. "Don't touch me like that again!"

For some reason, Michael started dancing around, doing the Mashed Potato.

"Oh, you know y'all like it." Calvin smiled as he ran his fingers through his greasy, processed hair. He was just too cool, with a do rag tied around his head and wearing a black leather jacket, gold knit top, burnt-orange pants, and cockroach-killing shoes.

"No, I don't," I answered. I could still feel Michael's hand on my butt, and it was a creepy feeling.

Calvin draped his tall, skinny body around Gail, resting his head on her shoulder and holding her waist. "Girl, you know you crazy 'bout me."

"You a lie," Gail said, smiling.

"You another lie."

"No, I ain't. Get away from around me, nigger, you overdrawn at the funk bank." Gail pushed Calvin's arm off her and broke away.

Denise laughed real loud, maybe 'cause nobody was paying much attention to her. Michael was kicking a rusty can. I had to admit that he looked cute in his White Sox baseball jacket, his khaki pants, and his high-top Converse All-Stars.

"Niece, what you laughing at?" Calvin wanted to know.

"You black nigger, you!"

"Who you calling black, little girl?"

I didn't like Denise throwing Calvin's color up in his face. A person couldn't help being dark. Calvin's smooth skin reminded me of the eggplant that Alice, the Chinese girl, had brought for Show and Tell in first grade. I knew that Calvin was hurt; I could see the pain in his narrowed eyes.

"Look in the mirror and you'll see," Denise answered Calvin. Calvin scrunched his face up until his top lip almost touched his bunny-shaped nose.

"Shut up talking to me, little girl. I bet you still pee in yo bed."

"Nigger, you pee in yo bed so much the rats and roaches gotta wear raincoats." Denise laughed.

"Doon, baby, doon!" Gail shouted and held her hand out and Denise gave her five.

"That's okay, Calvin, man, cause you know Niece and them so po, man, I was at they crib, and I stepped on a roach, man, and Niece mama yelled 'Save me the white meat!' " Michael said, laughing.

Calvin gave Michael five.

"Forget y'all forgot y'all never thought about y'all," Denise sang.

"Shut up, bitch, just shut yo ass up," Calvin shouted as he and Michael ran away laughing.

"Yo mama!" Denise yelled as the boys turned the corner.

"If they touch us like that again we should report them to somebody," I said.

Denise and Gail stood looking at me with their mouths hanging open.

"Are we supposed to like it?" I asked, confused.

"Course, fool, you just s'posed to act like you don't dig it," Denise said, rolling her eyes like she couldn't believe how dumb I was.

I didn't really appreciate her calling me a fool.

"Nobody felt on you, Denise," I reminded her, wondering if she knew how icky it felt.

"You ain't got to rub it in. Michael's felt on Niece's booty plenty of times before, right, Niece?"

"Damn straight!" Denise put her hand on her hip and stuck her behind out. "Michael's felt on my booty plenty of times!"

I didn't know what to say so I just cracked my gum.

Another Saturday had come already. I was in the backyard hanging up clothes. The sun was shining but the wind was blowing through my T-shirt and jeans. They didn't call Chicago the Windy City for nothing, I thought, chasing a dish towel that had blown out of the clothes basket.

Me and Gail and Denise had walked home together for a whole week now. Michael still hadn't said anything to me about the note, although yesterday he and Calvin had run up to us again. Michael had walked between me and Denise and put his arm around both of us. It had been exciting walking down the street all cool with somebody fine having his arm draped over you—as long as I didn't run into Mama or Daddy or one of my tattle-tale brothers.

I pushed a clothespin down on Daddy's big, white undershirt. I liked the smell of the clean clothes.

"Stevie!"

"Girl!"

"Stevie!"

I turned away from the line and watched as Gail and Denise kicked open the metal gate and burst into our yard. Their eyes were all stretched out like something big had happened.

"Girl, we got something to tell you!" Gail said, all out of breath.

"What?"

"Don't tell me she ain't heard!" Denise said, huffing and puffing and raising her eyebrows.

"What, heard what?"

"Gail, I thought sho she'd heard by now!"

"I haven't heard nothing. Tell me."

"Girl, Carla Perkins saying she gon kick yo ass! Counta you been talking to Michael," Denise explained, pointing her finger at me.

I swallowed hard. My head was swimming. Carla Perkins was going to kick my ass for talking to Michael? I hadn't even ever been alone with the boy; we'd never had a whole conversation. He'd felt my behind once and put his arm around me, but that had been it.

"I didn't even know Carla liked Michael."

"Girl, we know," Denise continued. "Everybody knows you and Michael been talking for a whole week now. I don't know where that bitch Carla is coming from."

"Shoot, Michael's probably fixing to ask you to go with him any day now. What yo answer gon be?" Gail put her hands on her hips.

I picked up a pair of Kevin's jeans and started hanging them on the line. "Gail, I don't know now. I just don't want to get in any mess. I don't even know Carla, 'cept to speak to her. I had no idea she even liked Michael."

Gail reached in the clothes basket and pulled out Mama's slip and started hanging it up. "You can't let her take yo man away from you, girl, without putting up no fight though."

I kept on hanging up clothes, trying to block out what they were saying.

Denise picked up my paddle ball off the ground and started pounding the little red ball in the air. Like I wasn't already starting to get a headache.

"Stevie, I hear you, girl: don't start no bull, won't be no shit. Excuse my French, honey, but the shit done already started," Denise said between bats.

"The girl done started talking about yo mama!"

"Don't tell her that," Gail interrupted.

"No, Gail, she may's to well hear the truth." Denise pointed with the paddle. "I would want somebody to come tell me if somebody was out there talking about my mama, now, wouldn't you? Otherwise how could they call theyselves your friend?"

"I s'pose." Gail nodded and picked up a pair of Mama's panties and put them on the line. I wasn't sure Gail knew me well enough to be handling my family's underclothes.

I tried to sound casual. "So, what did Carla say about my mama?"

Denise threw the paddle ball down on our old barbecue grill.

"Girl, she say yo mama . . . she say yo mama so black that when she sweat she sweat chocolate!"

I cleared my throat, "My mama's so black that when she sweats she sweats chocolate!" I folded my arms.

Denise nodded and pulled on the plastic clothesline.

"Look, I ain't said it, Carla the one said it."

"Look, Stevie, she just telling you what the heifer said. It ain't like she and her people's 'zactly light-skinned theyselves."

"Yeah, she got her nerve," I mumbled.

"Hey, if'n it was me, hey, something would have to jump off! It'd be me and her, 'cause don't nobody talk 'bout my mama and get away with it!" Denise shouted.

I reached in the basket and pulled out my sailor blouse and hung it on the line.

Denise grabbed the clothesline. "You gon jump on her, Stevie?" Her eyes were as big as silver dollars.

"Niece, you think I should fight her?"

"Hey, is fat meat greasy? Damn straight! Sides, you ain't got no choice. She say she gon kick yo ass if she catches you!"

"Oh," I said, feeling like my knees might give out.

I held on to the clothesline for support. "Maybe me and her could just stay outta each other's way. She sits two whole rows away from me in class. I mean, I haven't had that many fights before. And I never fought over a boy."

"Look, you can't let somebody just push you around, talk about your mama, take away your man, uh uh, not if you wanna hang with us," Gail said, shaking her head.

"If you run from her, people will walk all over you the rest of your life, girl!" Denise shouted.

"Are you sure she said she's gonna jump on me if she sees me?"

"That's exactly what the hoe said. Don't tell me you scared of her 'cause she's taller than you and already twelve. Don't let them long fingernails she got scare you neither," Denise continued, glancing down at my short nails.

"Look, Stevie, you ain't got nothing to be scared of. Carla might be taller, but y'all got 'bout the same mounta meat on y'all's bones," Gail pointed out.

"I guess you're right." I forced myself to smile.

"Could you believe Carla told me that Michael's gonna ask her to go with him? Michael ain't thinking about that gap-toothed hoe!" Denise laughed.

"So what you want us to tell her?" Gail asked. "You say you ready for her anytime, anyplace, right? You say y'all can duke it out!"

"Tell her you say, Come awn, baby, come awn!" Denise cut in.

Gail and Denise didn't wait for me to answer; they put up their fists and pretended to box. I tried to act like I was having fun watching them.

"Jean! Jean!"

"What, Mama?"

"Don't what me, come in here and see what I want. Your daddy needs you to go to the store."

"See you, Stevie." Gail patted my shoulder.

"Don't worry, girl, we'll be watching out for you." Denise winked.

"Yeah, girl, we got your back," Gail added.

"Thanks." I let out a big sigh as I walked toward the house.

chapter 3

Mama was standing in front of me trying to push a dollar into my hand.

"Here, run to the store and get your daddy some Ex-Lax, run on now."

"Mama, can't Kevin or David go? They're not doing nothing but watching TV." I sure didn't want to go out now, if Carla was looking for me.

"Don't tell me who to send, I'm sending you. Now get going."

"It's not fair, I'm the one who has to do everything around here just because I'm the girl. They don't have to wash dishes, they don't have to hang up clothes, they don't have to clean the bathroom, they don't have to lift a finger!"

"You forgot to mention that you were the only one who got a new Easter outfit last month. And I didn't hear the boys complaining then. Funny you never complain about being the only one who doesn't have to share a room with anybody. Now the boys are watching a baseball game, it would be unfair to make one of them go to the store. You know how it is when you're involved in something. You could've been halfway to the store by now steada standing here arguing with me."

"Mama, I can't go . . . "

"Don't make me have to whip you." Mama tried to hand me the dollar.

Instead of taking the money, I ran to my room. I fell on my bed and buried my face in my pillow.

"What's wrong with you, Jean Eloise? Do you want me to call the asylum? Have you lost your mind?" Mama shouted from the doorway.

"No," I said, staring at my pillow.

"Then get up or I'm going to get a belt and wear you out!"

"Nothing's the matter," I said, sitting up.

"Well, if there's nothing wrong with you then I'll let you explain to your daddy why you can't go to the store, that is, if you'd rather deal with him than with me."

Mama started folding my clothes on the chair and putting them in the dresser.

I decided I'd rather deal with Mama; at least she wasn't constipated.

"Mama, this girl says she's gonna beat me up if she catches me."

"What for? What she want to fight you about?"

"Over Michael, she likes Michael and she knows I like him too."

"Now, that's stupid, two girls fighting over some old, stanky boy." Mama groaned and sat down in the chair.

"Jean, come here and pick these marbles up out of the floor."

"Mama, she says Michael is going to ask her to go with him."

"To go where?"

"Oh, Mama, you know," I said, putting my marbles in their pouch.

"No, I don't. Where are they going? They're not going anywhere. How much has he spent on her? I bet he hasn't so much as bought her a Tastee-Freez. Humph. All he can do is get her in trouble. Thought I told you to stay away from that boy anyway. Going together! You better go with some schoolbooks! You got no reason to fight anybody."

"She said something about you too, Mama. Carla Perkins said something bad about you."

"About me? I don't want you fighting anybody counta what they said about me. They don't even know me. What do I care what somebody out there in the street says about me. They're not First National Bank; they don't sign my check."

Mama pointed to the floor. "Look, if you're not going to finish that puzzle then put the pieces back in the box." I got on my knees and started breaking up the Empire State building.

"So, what did she say about me?"

"Oh, nothing."

"First you want to fight over a boy, then just over plain nothing."

I looked up from the puzzle. "It wasn't just nothing, Mama, it was bad!"

"She doesn't even know me, how bad could it be?"

"Real bad."

"Girl, you done started, so you may as well finish it. Out with it now!"

I stared at the puzzle pieces. "She said—she said you so black when you sweat, you sweat chocolate." I looked up at Mama out of the corner of my eye.

"Is Carla Perkins that gap-toothed child across the alley? Her mama does hair at No Naps Beauty Salon; they came over here passing out cards a year ago?"

"That's her." I nodded.

"You scared of her? She's nobody to be scared of, aren't you bigger than she is?"

"No, not anymore, she grew."

"Well, you can't stay cooped up in this house forever. You're going to have to face her sooner or later."

coffee will make you black

Daddy walked into the room, and I sat down on my bed. "You back from the store? Where's my Ex-Lax? What's going on here?"

I glanced at Daddy standing in the doorway in his gray janitor's uniform. He didn't look too happy. I just stared down at my quilt. I decided to keep my mouth shut and let Mama do the talking.

"Ray, she's scared to go out 'cause some girl says she's gonna beat her up over some boy," Mama said, sucking her teeth in.

"What!" Daddy folded his arms and leaned back against the wall. "Look, if anybody messes with you, you pick up something—a brick, a rock, whatever—and say, Come on, you think you bad, I'll show you who's bad, come on! If you don't see anything to pick up, take your fist and bust them dead in their mouth!"

For a minute I saw myself being tough just like Daddy said, and I couldn't help but smile a little.

"Ray, listen how you sound. You'll have somebody out there getting hurt."

"Yeah, and it won't be her. Evelyn, she's got the right to defend herself. And if knocking somebody upside the head is the only way people will leave her alone, too bad. I was a red nigger in Oklahoma, remember. Now g'on girl, get outta here and get me my stuff."

I could hear my brothers clapping and yelling. "Home run, jack! Home run, jack!"

"All right!" Daddy shouted, rushing toward the living room.

"Jean, sometimes you have to stand up to somebody before they respect you," Mama said.

"Evelyn, bring me another beer!"

I let out a breath as I took the dollar from Mama and stood up to go.

I had made it to the store in one piece and was on my way home with Daddy's Ex-Lax in my pocket. I had been careful not

27

to pass Carla's building and I would be able to reach my gate without passing her yard if I cut through our alley. I checked to see if the coast was clear. I let out a breath; there were only a couple of little boys playing with a big red ball. Hey, maybe by Monday Carla would've forgotten all about me, I thought as I walked down the alley. I could relax, I was almost home now.

"Hey, y'all, there she is!" One of the little boys yelled. All of a sudden a bunch of kids came running out of Carla's yard toward me. I immediately recognized Carla, Denise, Gail, and Michael with his White Sox cap on backward, in the crowd.

I felt really scared all of a sudden. I was afraid my legs would give out or I would pee on myself. It was like I was a runaway prisoner that the hound dogs had captured in one of those movies. It crossed my mind to try and make a run for it as the crowd made a circle around me, rubbing their hands together, screaming for a fight. How would it look to run home like a scared rabbit, though? Forget how it would look, could I beat them to the gate?

"Humbug! Humbug!" A boy named Andre yelled, slapping his fist and jumping up and down. I could tell he'd be very disappointed if I started yelling for my mama and she came out and rescued me. Carla walked toward me looking mean. I searched for Denise and Gail, but neither of them would meet my glance. My heart sank. They were supposed to be my backup. How could they not be on my side now?

What was I going to do?

Maybe Carla wasn't as unreasonable as she looked. I opened my mouth to try and explain things to her, to let her know she could have Michael, I didn't want him. Then Andre shouted, "Okay, the baddest one hit my hand!" Of course Carla hit his hand. Andre slapped my shoulder, "Okay, she hit you, come on, duke it out, y'all."

"Give them some space now!" another boy yelled.

I didn't move. Carla was so close I could smell Cheetos on her breath.

"She hit you, hit her back," a girl named Peaches screamed as though she'd paid money for this. Like we were Cassius Clay and Sonny Liston.

"You can't run from no fight!" Gail shouted.

"I ain't gonna let her run!" All of a sudden I felt Denise push me into Carla. Carla pushed back, and I almost lost my balance.

"I didn't even know you liked Michael. You can have him," I said, trying to keep from crying.

"Bitch, I ain't stuttin' Michael!"

"Ooh, she called you a bitch! Doon, baby, doon!" Andre yelled.

I couldn't believe my ears. If Carla didn't want Michael, then what were we fighting about?

Before I could ask her, Carla grabbed my shoulders and pushed me into a tall chain-link fence. I could feel the cold metal digging in my back. Carla took her right hand and yanked my ponytail loose. The rubber band fell in my face.

"Ooh, you let her do you like that!" Peaches yelled.

"That's for talking about my mama, don't nobody talk about my mama and get away with it!" Carla shouted, holding her hand up like a claw. She looked ready to rake her nails across my face at any minute.

I knew I hadn't said anything about her mama.

Tears were starting up in my eyes and a hot anger took over me. I stomped on Carla's foot. Ouch! I had taken her by surprise. She bent down and I grabbed her shoulders and pushed her into the dirt and concrete. I was mad at Denise, Gail, Carla, Michael, all of them. I couldn't believe it. I had Carla on the ground. Years of wrestling with my brothers was about to pay off. All of a sudden Carla looked scared. The crowd seemed quiet and excited at the same time. Most of them didn't care who won, I thought, they just wanted to see a fight.

I held Carla down, sitting on top of her stomach and pinning her arms to the ground. "Carla, I never said nothing about your mama!"

"You a lie, you said my mama so black when she sweat she sweated chocolate."

"Ooh, ooh." Somebody laughed.

"Look, Carla, I never said any such thing. That's what Denise said you said about my mama!"

Carla looked confused, then she looked mad for being in this position. "Niece, you know I ain't said nothing about this girl's mama, why you tell that lie on me?"

Denise was quiet.

"Let me up, girl. We gon get to the bottom of this shit."

I was glad to get up, glad the fight was over.

Carla dusted off her T-shirt and jeans. You could tell she had hated being on the ground. Gail stood between Carla and Denise.

"Stevie was trying to take Michael away from Niece. Niece and Michael was talking way before Stevie came into the picture."

"I wasn't trying to take anyone away from anybody. Michael's the one who came up to me. I was minding my own business." I faced Denise. "You never even told me you liked Michael."

"Player, Michael man, you a player." Calvin stretched his hand out and Andre gave him five.

"Well, why did y'all drag my name into it, I ain't had nothin' to do with it." Carla gave Denise an evil look.

"Niece wanted to see Stevie get her ass kicked, to teach her to leave somebody's man alone," Gail explained.

"Which one do you dig, Michael? You got to pick," Peaches insisted.

Michael hooked his thumbs in his belt loops. "Hey, I ain't in it, it's between them two. Baby, I ain't tied to nobody."

"Neither am I," I said loudly.

"Ooh, she said neither is she!" Andre yelled.

"Didn't nan one of y'all tell the girl that Niece liked Michael, then how she s'posed to know he yo man?" Carla folded her arms and stuck her mouth out.

"Yeah, how was I s'posed to know?" I folded my arms too.

Neither Gail nor Denise had an answer.

"Niece and Gail, I don't 'preciate y'all dragging me into this bullshit! Don't ever bring no shit like this to my door again. What kind of fool do y'all take me for? I ain't fighting y'all's battles. Y'all must think I'm a new kind of fool."

I remembered my Daddy's Ex-Lax. "I don't got time for this shit either," I said, surprised to hear myself cuss.

I cut my eyes at Gail and Denise; they looked away. I turned to go.

"Say, Stevie, you don't need people like them," Carla said.

I looked at Carla. "Neither do you," I said.

Carla looked surprised, but she couldn't help but smile a little.

There was something about Carla that I liked. I had a feeling that she felt the same way about me.

It was Sunday evening, and I'd just finished telling Grandma about the fight yesterday. I was washing the dinner dishes and she was sitting at the kitchen table working on her new quilt.

Daddy had gone to Walgreen's last night and bought half a gallon of Neapolitan ice cream, my favorite, to celebrate my victory. My brothers were mad that I hadn't sent anybody to come get them to watch the fight. Daddy, David, and Kevin had talked about the fight till Mama made them shut up. But I could tell that Mama was glad that I had stood up for myself too. She said she knew Gail and Denise were no good the first time she'd laid eyes on them. Mama said she hadn't liked the idea of me hanging out with two no-churchgoing Baptists anyhow.

I had finished the dishes and was sitting in Grandma's lap. Daddy was in the bathroom; a day later, the Ex-Lax was finally working. We could hear Mama getting after David and Kevin in the living room.

"Give me the water gun! I don't care who it belongs to! I'm not going to have you running through my living room like heathens, jumping on my furniture. We work too hard for things. And David, put a shirt on, I don't know where you all think you are. You act just like a bunch of savages. I don't blame white folks for not wanting to be around you. I wish I had somewhere I could go myself sometimes. Now, boys, if you're going to watch *Bonanza,* sit down in front of the TV and watch it!"

"You think you and that girl Carla will turn out to be friends?" Grandma asked as she held me in her lap.

"Maybe. I don't think we'll ever be tight like me and Terri were."

"Life is funny, you never know about life," Grandma said.

I could never see Carla joining the Peace Corps, I thought.

"Here comes Mama." I rolled my eyes.

Mama walked into the kitchen with her apron on. She frowned when she saw me in Grandma's lap.

"Evelyn, you peed tonight, like the old folks used to say, you peed with that dinner. Chile, you a true Dickens, cause you sho can fry you some chicken," Grandma bragged.

"Mama, you sound like somebody in the backwoods. Don't talk like that. You'll forget one day and say that out somewhere."

"I'm like Salem cigarettes, y'all took me out the country but y'all ain't took the country outta me. You dragged me away from the Baptist church to the African Methodist Episcopal, but I still miss the singing. I'm sorry, child, but every now and then I've got to just tell it like it is."

Mama shook her head and started sweeping the kitchen floor. "Mama, you used to say the world was no place for anybody soft and colored, but now every time you look around, you got Jean up in your lap."

I looked at Mama, but didn't move. Something told me not to get up this time.

"Evelyn, let me enjoy my only granddaughter. We're not hurting nobody."

"It's all right to spoil *her,* mighty funny you didn't have that attitude with any of us."

Mama cut her eyes at me. I knew she still expected me to get up. She looked mad enough to spit. "Jean, get down from there. If you don't get down from there, you better!"

I didn't move.

"Mama, just push Jean Eloise out of your lap." Mama almost sounded desperate.

Grandma didn't move a muscle and neither did I. I wondered if Mama would come over and drag me out of Grandma's lap, or worse, go get a belt and start whipping me. Instead, she just went back to her sweeping.

"You raised us to be tough. I remember having to get myself dressed, help little Sheila and the boys get ready, fix breakfast, make Daddy's biscuits. Sometimes we went out wearing mismatched clothes, hair half combed, looking like ragamuffins, 'cause you'd left before day to go take care of some white family."

"Evelyn, you know I had to do whatever I could to make a honest dollar," Grandma said quietly.

"Yeah, that's why we never had Thanksgiving dinner on Thanksgiving, 'cause you had to cook and serve *their* dinner." Mama swept the floor harder.

"Chile, when I would be cooking them dinners, I'd be thinking about how good the leftovers was gonna taste. We might not have ate good on Thanksgiving, but, chile, we sho greased the next day, remember that?" Grandma smiled.

"It still wasn't fair; we needed you. When I fell down and skinned my knee once, I remember crying for you and nobody was there to put a Band-aid on it and to say it'll be all right. Even the good times—I got a hundred on a test once and ran home all excited and didn't remember till I hit the door that you weren't there to tell." Mama was sweeping up a storm now.

"I'm sorry, baby, I wanted to be there all them times. I know it was hard on y'all. Me and your daddy, may his soul rest in peace, wanted y'all to have the best of everything. But when you're colored the deck is stacked against you, you know that. I couldn't never afford new clothes for y'all but I kept my eyes open for the best hand-me-downs I could find. I wished I could've been there to give y'all castor oil every time y'all was sick. I guess that's one reason it was such a comfort to hear that half the class come by to see you that time you twisted your ankle."

Mama stopped and leaned on the broom handle and stared off into space. "I was a new girl, nobody cared about being my friend. I was by myself practically all the time. Nobody to walk home with, nobody to play in the schoolyard with. Franklin and Arthur had each other, and Sheila was too young; besides she had her own little friends."

"Yeah, but those kids surprised you, 'cause when you twisted your ankle that time you found out different. Half the class come by to see you, remember?"

Mama kept staring into space. "Nobody came by to see me."

"What you mean, nobody came by to see about you? I never forgot that you said, Mama, it was so many they couldn't all fit. They had to come in two shifts. I know my memory is still intact." Grandma tapped her forehead with her finger.

"They didn't care whether I lived or died."

"That's what you said about Lillie Mae, remember? You said, 'Mama, nobody cared whether Lillie Mae lived or died.' "

"Look, Mama, I was there, nobody came by to see about me, okay, nobody!" Mama set the broom against the wall and folded her arms like she was cold all of a sudden. I could hear my heart beating. I was almost afraid to breathe. I felt Grandma's body stiffen.

"When I went to school the next day, that's when I found out Lillie Mae had been out too, upset stomach, and that half the class had gone by to see her. Even took her some pink cotton candy from the Carnival. I pretended to myself that they had come by to see me. I went home and told you that half the class had come to visit me so you would think I was popular."

Mama turned around and looked at Grandma, her dark eyes soft and watery. I had never seen this side of Mama.

"So you wouldn't have to feel guilty about not having been there to take care of me," Mama continued.

I let out a big breath. "All these years Grandma's heart was going out to Lillie Mae steada you," I said, looking at Mama. "Humph, I used to want to laugh every time your grandmother said that. Lillie Mae had everything going for her. She was light enough to pass, with long, good hair and green eyes. Everybody wanted to be her friend. None of them cared whether I lived or died." Mama's voice sounded shaky.

I felt Grandma's thigh muscles moving and I stood up. She walked over to Mama and put her arms around her.

"Baby, I wouldn't trade you for all the Lillie Maes in the world."

I went over and hugged Mama from the other side.

"Mama, I wouldn't trade you neither," I said.

"Oh, get outta here." Mama reached in her apron pocket and pulled out some tissue and blew her nose.

"You all are too much," she sniffed, "but I wouldn't trade you either."

I felt close to Mama and it was a good feeling, maybe as good a feeling as any virgin could expect to have.

chapter 4

We were outside at recess, playing Squeeze the Lemon. It was February and stomp-down cold. The wind was calling names and kicking tails, as my daddy would say.

I raced a bunch of kids for the warm corner. A whole mess of bodies, in winter coats and wool hats and scarves, were squashing me half to death. I could hardly breathe; I was the lemon. It felt great!

The bell rang all loud and the warm bodies rushed away. I felt the hawk again, full blast.

I was back at my desk studying my spelling words. The wooden door creaked open. In walked Carla Perkins, grinning, carrying a pass and a little booklet so everybody could see it. We all knew she'd been to the nurse. Every girl knew Carla had gotten her period today and every girl who hadn't gotten hers yet wished she was in her shoes, including me. Carla handed Mrs. Cunningham the pass with a big smile on her face.

Mrs. Cunningham frowned at Carla and sucked in her teeth as she took the piece of paper.

"Take a seat now and turn to your spelling lesson." Mrs. Cunningham was a tall, large brown-skinned woman from Jamaica, who wore her hair in a bun.

I tried to give Carla a smile as she passed my desk. I wanted to congratulate her later on, but I couldn't think of anything to say that wouldn't make me sound like a square. I wished that I had my period too, then we'd have something in common.

It would be a year in May since me and Carla had the fight. Everybody knew it had happened on account of a misunderstanding. I could tell Carla wasn't still tripping on it. We always spoke when we ran into each other. I would always smile, but Carla would just nod and keep stepping. She didn't hate my guts or anything like that; she probably could just take me or leave me. At this point I could never see us being tight. But for some reason I couldn't help but like Carla. I knew that Mama would think Carla was loud and ignorant, but I thought she was fun and all the way cool. Here Carla's birthday was coming up in two months and I probably wasn't getting invited to her party again.

I still missed my old best friend, Terri. I wished she'd never moved away. I wondered if she was still friends with Mary Beth. Mary Beth lived next door to Terri now, and they'd gotten to be friends. Terri had called me on my birthday last September and told me about her. The problem was Mary Beth was white and she wasn't allowed to play with negroes. So she and Terri had to sneak around and stuff. I wondered if Mary Beth's family had finally sold their house.

I hung out with other girls—it's not like people treated me like I had the cooties or something. It's just that I was still not really tight with anybody, and that bothered me, sort of.

"Class, you are out of order!" Mrs. Cunningham's Jamaican accent jumped into my thoughts.

"Who is keeping up that noise?" Mrs. Cunningham looked around the room with her eagle eyes. The class got quiet. Mrs.

Cunningham was the kind of teacher who didn't take no stuff.

"Class, February is Negro History Month, you know."

Half the class mumbled or nodded.

"This year we are selecting young ladies and young gentlemen from the seventh- and eighth-grade classes to sing at a program for the Children's Hospital."

Daddy was a janitor at Children's Hospital. Maybe he'd get to hear me!

"Close your lesson books and sit up straight now. I'm going to select four students from our class, two ladies and two gentlemen."

Lots of kids sat up straight to the point of looking ridiculous. They folded their hands on their desks in front of them. I tried to act normal. I sat up a little straight and halfway folded my hands. I wanted to get picked like anybody else, but I didn't want to get my hopes up.

"Bernice Tyler," Mrs. Cunningham pointed. Bernice couldn't help but grin. Everybody knew that she could sing; she sang in the junior choir of a sanctified church that was on the radio every Sunday. Mrs. Cunningham would've been a fool not to pick Bernice.

"Anthony Jones."

"Tony, man, all right." Calvin patted him on the back.

"Pick me, Mrs. Cunningham, pick me, I wanna sing!"

I turned around. I was surprised to see Carla leaning out of her seat, practically begging, out and out gripping, as they called it. I felt sorry for her because I knew it wouldn't work. Mrs. Cunningham would never pick somebody jumping out of their seat, especially not somebody like Carla—although she was a good singer; Carla's voice stood out even when we sang "The Star-Spangled Banner" every morning. Carla was going to feel like a fool, though, when Mrs. Cunningham smiled her evil smile and picked somebody else.

"Jean Stevenson."

I couldn't believe Mrs. Cunningham had said my name.

"Me?" I asked, pointing to myself.

"Dog! She can't even carry a tune!" Carla shouted.

I felt my face getting hot. Some kids busted out laughing.

"Carla Perkins, you keep yourself quiet, do you hear me!"

I turned and looked at Carla; she was cutting her eyes and had her mouth all poked out.

"You just better put your face good, young lady, or else you can march to the principal's office!"

Now I could really kiss my birthday-party invitation goodbye, I thought.

"Roland Anderson." Mrs. Cunningham had picked the second boy. There were a few groans because Roland is a square.

I raised my hand.

"Yes, Jean?"

"Mrs. Cunningham, I don't want to be in it."

Mrs. Cunningham looked surprised, and the whole class came to attention.

"What is this you are saying to me, Jean? What kind of foolishness are you talking about?"

"I want Carla to have my spot, she is a better singer than me."

"She is a better singer than *I*," Mrs. Cunningham corrected me.

"She is a better singer than I and I think she should be in the chorus."

Mrs. Cunningham looked like she was in shock. I turned around and glanced at Carla. Her mouth was hanging open like she was surprised too.

"Wait a minute, you want Carla Perkins to have your spot? Is that what you are saying to me? Do I understand you properly?"

"Yes," I nodded.

"I can't believe what I am hearing!"

Mrs. Cunningham walked over to my desk and stood over me with her arms folded.

"How could you sit there and have the audacity to tell me after I have made my selection that I must give your spot to Carla?"

I didn't know what audacity meant. It wasn't one of our spelling words, but it didn't sound good. I couldn't think of anything to say. I just stared down at the hole in my wooden desk that used to hold ink bottles in the olden days.

"In the first place, nobody tells me what to do. In the second place, you don't have a spot!"

"It was just a suggestion," I mumbled.

"Jean, don't give me any back chat. I don't need your suggestions. Let me tell you something, Jean Stevenson. You don't tell me who to choose to represent our class, our school, our people. Now, since you didn't appreciate the opportunity that you were given, I will choose a more deserving young lady. Angel Walker, you will be the second girl." Angel nodded and smiled without grinning. Angel knew that this was no time to grin, no matter how happy she might be.

Mrs. Cunningham let out a sigh as she walked toward the front of the classroom. I knew that I was on her bad side now and it would be a long time before she would forget what had happened today. But I had a feeling that I had finally gotten Carla's attention, and to me that was more important.

I was walking home from school with Melody and Linda in the butt-kicking cold. Linda was about my height and weight. She was cute, but too dark to be considered pretty by a lot of people. When we went to the Museum of Science and Industry back in third grade, Peaches had refused to hold Linda's hand. Our teacher, Miss O'Connor, had asked Peaches why she wasn't holding her partner's hand. Peaches had said, " 'Cause she too black." A bunch of kids had laughed. Miss O'Connor had turned red, counta she's white. Linda had looked like she was going to cry, and I'd felt sorry for her. I'd remembered the time me and Mama were leaving Sears and I'd stopped to tie my shoe. I was rushing to catch up with Mama when a white woman was coming in the door with her daughter. The woman had said, "Becky, wait and let the nigger get out." I had felt worse than if somebody had slapped me. Anyway, Miss O'Connor had ended up holding Linda's hand.

Melody was short and chubby with a round face. She was a safe color, not light enough for people to call her yellow or so dark that somebody wouldn't want to hold her hand.

Me, Linda, and Melody turned up my street. I had my long, red wool scarf wrapped around my neck, covering my mouth. My fingers felt like they were frozen inside my gloves, it was so cold.

"Say, Stevie! Say!"

"Stevie, guess what? Carla Perkins is calling you, girl."

"Yeah," Melody added. I could hear the surprise in their voices. I was surprised too. I slowed down, but I refused to come to a dead stop.

"Stevie, hold up, girl, hold up!"

I turned around and watched Carla with Tanya and Patrice, two cute, popular girls from the other seventh-grade class, running to catch up with me. I made believe that the three eager brown faces belonged to reporters running to catch up with a star. Like I was one of the Supremes or somebody.

Carla Perkins was breaking her neck to catch up with me on the same day she'd gotten her period!

"Girl, thanks a lot for being in my corner like that today. I really 'preciate what you tried to do. Stevie, you all right," Carla said, pounding my back.

"Yeah, that was real boss," Tanya cut in. I smiled; I figured Carla had told Patrice and Tanya everything.

I pushed my scarf down so I could talk.

"Carla, you welcome. But Mrs. Cunningham should've picked you anyhow. You gotta voice and a half."

Carla smiled. I could see both of her dimples.

"Stevie, I ain't mean what I said about you not being able to carry a tune. That heifer had just made me mad, that's all."

"That's okay." I hunched my shoulders.

"Hey, I bet Mrs. Cunningham's face was cracked, though, when you told her to let Carla be in it, huh?" Patrice asked.

"Her face sho was cracked." Linda tried to sound cool even though she wore glasses and was always on the honor roll.

"My girl say if Carla can't be in the shit, then she don't want no parts of it," Carla bragged.

I liked hearing Carla talk about me like we were really tight.

"I bet neither one of y'all would've gave up y'all's spot for me, and we s'posed to be Ace Boon Coons." Carla raised her eyebrows and turned to Tanya and Patrice.

"It wasn't no big thing," I cut in. "Besides, Mrs. Cunningham didn't let you in it anyway." I didn't want to start out on the wrong foot with Tanya and Patrice.

"Yeah, but it's the thought that counts, just like with Christmas presents. And you still lost out, on accounta you stood up for me, Stevie. I'll never forget that, sho won't."

We were in front of my house now. Carla rested her elbow on my shoulder. "Stevie, I'm so glad you ain't let that stupid mess that happened last year come in between us."

"That's right, I had forgot all about that fight," Tanya said.

"What fight?" Linda asked.

"You heard about that fight, remember . . ." Melody began.

"Let it go! It's dead now, so why y'all bringing it back up?" Carla shouted.

"Don't Niecie and Michael go together now?" Patrice asked.

"Will y'all let me finish, shit! Anyway, like I was saying, Stevie, I'm glad you ain't let that stupid mess come between us, 'cause you know me and you go all the way back to kinnygarten."

"Yeah, you got that right," I said, glancing over at Linda and Melody. They were looking at me with new respect, I thought.

"See you tomorrow, Stevie. Check us out at recess, okay?" Carla yelled.

"Sure, see y'all."

"Check you later," Tanya said.

"Yeah, check you later," Linda and Melody chimed in.

"Why it got to be so cold? Damn, it's cold out here! Do anybody know if the groundhog seen his shadow?" Carla shouted as I ran up the steps. I hoped David was in the window and had seen me walking home with such a cool crowd.

It looked like everybody had beat me home except Daddy; he was working swing shift at the hospital. I could hear my brothers playing with their GI Joes in their room. Mama was standing at the living-room window looking out. She'd probably gotten a ride home from one of the other tellers at the bank.

I sat on the floor and began pulling off my snowy boots.

"Who were those girls?" Mama called to me in the hallway.

"Linda and Melody?" I asked, walking into the living room in my sock feet.

"I know Linda and Melody, I'm talking about those *other* girls."

"You mean Tanya and Patrice and Carla?" I asked, plopping down in Daddy's big bronze vinyl chair, and digging my feet into the dark green carpet. I glanced up at the mantel. Daddy had gotten a new bowling trophy.

Mama was sitting on the couch. She had changed out of her bank clothes into a blue duster. She frowned as her finger felt a tear in the plastic slipcover where gold material was showing.

"I thought that was Carla Perkins. Why does she have to be so loud? I could hear her mouth all the way in here. I've never understood why negroes have to be so loud." Mama leaned forward and straightened out the *Ebony* and *Jet* magazines on the glass coffee table. She glanced at the smiling white faces on the covers of *Woman's Day* and *Life* magazines. "And you wonder why white people don't want their children to go to school with you." I hunched my shoulders and headed toward my room, carrying my books.

"What are you doing walking home with Carla anyway?" Mama asked, hot on my trail. "After that fight, I thought you'd had enough of her."

"That's dead, Mama. How much you wanna bet we don't end up being friends? How much you wanna bet, Mama?"

"You know I don't bet," Mama said, passing my door and heading for the kitchen.

"Jean, get a knife and cut up this green pepper for the meat loaf," Mama said as soon as I walked into the kitchen. "Wash your hands first."

"Guess what, Mama? Carla got her period today!"

"I suppose it won't be long before she'll be pushing a stroller."

I turned away from the sink. "Why do you say that, Mama?"

Mama frowned as she took stuff out of the refrigerator.

"Don't both of her older sisters have babies now?"

I nodded, surprised that Mama was so up on the 'hood.

"Neither one of them could keep their dresses down. So how can you expect any better from her? She'll do well to make it through eighth grade." Mama chopped away at the onion.

"Oh, Mama, she'll make it way past eighth grade. Carla's popular but she doesn't even have a boyfriend right now."

Mama closed her eyes to avoid the onion. "Time will tell," she said.

"Anyway, Mama, I bet Patrice and Tanya have already started their periods too."

"So what? Everybody gets her period sooner or later."

"I hope I get mine sooner. Mama, how old were you when you got yours?"

"I was older than twelve, I'll say that. In my day girls didn't develop as early."

"How old were you, Mama?"

"What difference does it make? Can't you find something else to talk about? Getting your period is nothing to celebrate. Why do you think they call it the curse? It's just the beginning of a lot of mess, you'll see. It's nothing to get excited about, believe me."

"What kind of mess?" I dumped the cut-up green pepper in the bowl with the onion and ground beef.

Mama poured a can of tomato sauce into the mixture.

"It's messy to take care of. It's one thing to smell a man, it's another to smell a woman," she continued. "Nobody wants to smell a woman's period on her."

"What does it smell like, Mama?"

"Let's put it this way, people would rather smell a dead fish. Now hand me my spices."

Boy, Mama sure could take the fun out of things, I thought as I watched her shape the meat loaf.

It was the next day and I was standing on the playground with Carla, Tanya, and Patrice. Carla had seen me and waved for me to come over. They were giggling like girls do when they talk about boys.

"I don't know who it was, but I swear I felt something up against me when we were playing Squeeze the Lemon yesterday." Tanya giggled.

"What you feel, girl?" Carla giggled too.

"I swear I felt . . ." Tanya couldn't talk without laughing.

"Come on, girl, tell it," Patrice said.

"Okay, okay, I swear I felt somebody's you know what!" Tanya laughed.

"Somebody's thang?" Patrice asked.

"Some boy's dick?" Carla laughed.

Everybody giggled. I tried to giggle too, although I hated giggling. Maybe I just wasn't good at it. Probably it helped to have older sisters.

"How you feel somebody's thang up underneath all them coats and stuff?" Patrice wanted to know.

"Must've been your 'magination, girl," Carla said.

"Yeah, girl, must've been your 'magination," I agreed, wanting to at least say something.

APRIL SINCLAIR

Tanya looked at me sort of surprised, like I didn't know her well enough to be jumping on the bandwagon.

"It couldn't have just been my 'magination, cause guess what happened." Tanya raised her eyebrows.

"What?" we asked.

"Promise not to tell nobody?"

"Cross my heart and hope to die," Carla said.

"I'll keep it a secret," I said, ready to hear it.

"My lips are sealed," Patrice squeezed her mouth together.

"Okay, well, I know it wasn't my 'magination, cause my love came down!" Tanya whispered.

"Your love came down!" Carla said, raising her eyebrows.

"Ooh, girl!" Patrice scrunched her face up and sucked in her breath.

"Oh, wow!" I said, wondering what the heck they were talking about. One day I would have to ask Mama. I was glad that I hadn't crossed my heart and hoped to die like Carla.

chapter 5

I'd seen a robin on the way to school this morning. Mama called spring the growing season. She was right because all of a sudden I had breasts. It felt strange to have two bumps sticking out of my chest. Mama had taken me to Sears to buy me my first bra. It was a size AA. She said if I took after her, one day, I'd be wearing a D cup. That was hard to imagine.

Anyway, I felt grown-up wearing my new bra, but I also felt fenced in, like I was giving up something. Now, I could never walk around the house without a shirt on. I couldn't run or jump without a bra because my breasts would bounce. Young men on the corner who had never noticed me before were saying, "Hey, mama," or "Hey, baby." I always spoke and tried to smile so they wouldn't call me a bitch. But I got tired of jokers asking me how I was doing or if they could walk with me. When I complained to Mama, she said, "It's all part of being a female. Men like to meddle, always have, always will. So long as they don't put their hands on you, just smile and keep stepping. Wait until you hit thirty-five, you'll be glad to get a little attention then," she added.

I still thought breasts might be more trouble than they were worth. Growing up reminded me a little bit of Hide and Go Seek. When it was your time to grow up, Nature said, "Here I come, ready or not." And Nature could always find you.

Carla's thirteenth birthday was coming up right after Easter. She was definitely having a party and I was definitely invited. Carla had asked me what boy I hoped I got to kiss when we played Spin the Bottle. I'd told her I didn't know what boy I wanted to kiss, but I could sure think of a few boys I *didn't* want to have to kiss. Linda and Melody had worried me to ask Carla if they could be invited too. When I brought their names up to Carla she'd said, "Sho, if they're friends of yours, okay."

It wasn't cold enough to play Squeeze the Lemon anymore. Now it was Double Dutch weather. Last week Carla had asked me to be her Double Dutch partner. Of course I'd said yes. Tanya and Patrice were going to be partners too, and we even let Linda and Melody play. I had taken my allowance money last Saturday and bought a brand-new plastic clothesline for us to jump with. I knew a lot of girls looked up to me now on accounta my rope.

We were on the playground jumping Double Dutch at afternoon recess. Linda and Melody turned the rope and sang as me and Carla jumped. Patrice and Tanya stood waiting for us to miss.

"Fudge, fudge, fudge, boom, boom, boom, call that, judge, boom, boom, boom, boom. Mama's got a newborn baby, boom, it's not a girl, boom, not a boy, boom, just an ordinary baby, boom, wrap it up in toilet paper, send it down the elevator, kick out." Me and Carla kicked our feet out. "Shirley Temple went to France to teach the girls the Watusi dance, first on the heel then on the toe, then split the rope and around you go."

I felt something wet on my thigh that I could no longer ignore as I crisscrossed my legs. There was a strange heaviness in my stomach as I tripped on the rope.

"Y'all missed!" Tanya shouted.

"Y'all ain't missed, Stevie missed." Carla groaned. "How come you messed us up like that, girl? We usually get all the way to I like coffee, I like tea, I like the white boys and they like me. What happened?"

"She missed, that's what happened. Here, hurry up and give us our turn before the bell rings." Patrice handed Carla the rope.

My panties felt wet. Suddenly it hit me that I had started my period.

"I think I just started my period!" I felt happy and scared at the same time as I watched the smiles on the other girls' faces.

"Don't worry, you can't see nothing. But you better go straight to the nurse," Carla warned.

I tied my sweater around my waist to be sure.

"She's lucky it ain't summertime and she wasn't wearing white pants, you remember Peaches and them white pants, don't you?" Tanya asked the others.

"Who could forget Peaches and them white pants?" Carla answered.

"Yeah, who could forget Peaches," I heard Linda agree.

I headed for the nurse's office. I wondered how come I didn't remember Peaches and them white pants.

The nurse, Mrs. O'Malley, had taken care of everything. She'd given me a brand-new elastic belt and shown me how to tie the ends of a Kotex pad to it and which side to use. She'd told me I could expect to bleed three to five days every month. If I got cramps, I could come to the sick room and lie down with the hot-water bottle. The nurse was a cross between Mrs. Santa Claus and Hazel, the maid on TV.

I marched into Mrs. Cunningham's room with a pass and a little booklet that said I had become a woman and was part of the mystery of life and stuff like that. I didn't hide the booklet or shove it up in people's faces. I just held it so anybody could see it if they had a mind to. Mrs. Cunningham took the pass without smiling or frowning. I tried to walk normal with this bulky thing that seemed to have a mind of its own in between my legs. I looked for Carla, and she gave me her dimpled smile. I felt proud as I took my seat, no matter what Mama said.

"You don't need me to tell you anything, it sounds like the nurse told you everything." Mama sounded like she was relieved.

We were in the kitchen and she was about to fry the pork chops. I was mashing the potatoes.

"Oh, that blue box in the bathroom cabinet is where the Kotex are. Let me know if we run low."

I nodded. "Mama, are you gonna tell Daddy?"

"No, he doesn't need to know about this."

"What about Grandma?"

"I might mention it to her, but it won't be the first thing that comes out of my mouth."

"Oh."

I wanted to hear about the juicy stuff. Mama had never really sat me down and told me the facts.

"Mama, what happens when your love comes down?"

Mama dropped a pork chop into the hot skillet and jumped away as it splattered.

"What are you talking about, Jean Eloise?"

"Somebody said that her love came down. What does that mean?"

I added a little more milk to the potatoes.

"Who said some mess like that? I bet it was that Carla Perkins, wasn't it?" Mama wrinkled her forehead.

"It wasn't Carla."

"I bet she was there, I bet she had something to do with it!"

"Well, what does it mean, Mama?"

Mama turned a pork chop over with the long fork.

"It means that whoever said it has her mind in the gutter, that's what it means. The devil is everywhere these days. Well, I won't have you talking that trash in my house. Whoever said it, you need to stay away from her. You need to stay away from that whole Carla Perkins crowd."

I would just have to find out stuff from other people. Mama wasn't getting up off of nothing, I thought. Besides, Carla's birthday was less than two weeks away and I didn't want to push Mama now. I knew I had to lay low for a while.

We were in the coatroom getting our sweaters and stuff for morning recess. I reached for the jump rope hanging from my hook.

"Forget it, Stevie, we ain't jumping today," Carla said.

"How come? It's not raining, the ground's not even wet from last night."

"Just be cool, Stevie, just be cool. We ain't jumping today, okay? Just follow me."

I followed Carla into the auditorium, which didn't make sense to me, because we were supposed to be on the playground during recess.

"Carla, we're not supposed to be in here. What are we going to do in an empty auditorium? What if we get in trouble?"

"I told you to just be cool, you'll see."

I followed Carla past the rows of empty seats to the back. I could hear giggling. I was surprised to find Tanya and Patrice all hunched over a book.

"Here, Stevie, you've got to read it. It's my sister's diary, girl, you gotta read it!" Tanya handed me the smooth blue book with a flap hanging from it. I flipped over to the cover. It said ONE YEAR DIARY. It had a place for a key.

"Tanya, won't your sister be mad? Isn't it sort of personal?"

"Who cares, with all the dirt she's done to me all my life? Besides, I'm gonna take it home at lunchtime; she'll never know I found it. It's her fault for forgetting to lock it."

"Go 'head, Stevie, don't be no square. It ain't no harm in it. Her sister Annie Pearl's the one that did it, you just reading about it." Carla elbowed me.

"Besides, how else we supposed to find out about stuff?" Patrice wanted to know.

I thought she kind of had a point.

"Why should I be the one to read it?"

" 'Cause you on the honor roll, I don't want nobody stumbling over they words at a time like this," Carla explained.

"Read about the part when her love came down! Turn to March 22," Tanya insisted.

I sat down with the book. I figured this beat trying to get something out of Mama.

" 'I know I'm in love, don't care what nobody say, 'cause ain't nobody ever made me feel this way,' " I read aloud with Carla, Patrice, and Tanya sitting on both sides of me.

"Dog, your sister's a poet," Carla declared.

" 'Derrick just look at me and I go to melt. I can't keep my mind on nothing else. Seem like everything be Derrick and Derrick be everything.' " I let out a sigh. You couldn't help but be affected.

"Yo sister sho do have a way with words," Carla cut in, again.

"I wish I had me a Derrick," Patrice added.

"Keep reading, Stevie, hurry up and get to the good part!" Tanya said.

" 'When he be kissing me, I don't never want him to stop.' " Patrice let out a couple of giggles. " 'Last night when he rubbed his thing up against my thigh . . . ' " I had to come up for air; this was getting juicy. I could hear my heart beating. I could tell that the others were hanging on every word. Carla elbowed me, "Don't stop now, keep going, girl."

I continued, " 'My panties was wetter than they ever was before.' "

"OOH WEE, see, I told you her love came down," Tanya whispered. I swallowed hard. This stuff really was something!

" 'I know the reason I be scared is 'cause we don't have no protection and I don't want no baby.' " I wondered what protection was. It didn't sound like it was a gun or a German shepherd.

"Hurry up 'fore the bell ring!" Carla shouted.

"Okay. 'Derrick say he gonna buy some rubbers before the next time he rub his dick against me.' "

Why would he need boots? I wondered.

"Stevie, be cool." Carla elbowed me again.

"Carla, why are you stopping me now? It sounds like it's really about to get good."

"I know, Stevie, but there go Mr. Davis and Mrs. Robinson standing right behind us."

I turned my head and saw the principal and the music teacher staring at us. They were two red-looking white people. Patrice and Tanya let out big sighs.

"Mrs. Robinson, let me know if the piano needs tuning for the assembly. Remember, it needs to be in tiptop shape for the graduation in June."

Mrs. Robinson nodded. We sat like statues.

Mr. Davis leaned over and snatched the diary out of my hand. "You girls follow me."

I cut my eyes at Carla. That's what I got for following her. I could tell from the sound of Mr. Davis's voice that our gooses were cooked!

Carla, Tanya, and Patrice were suspended from school for three days. Mr. Davis had talked to our teachers and they had decided not to suspend me because I was on the honor roll. Mr. Davis said that Tanya could have her sister's diary back if her mother came up and got it.

Mrs. Cunningham told me that I couldn't return to school without my mother. There was no way I could have Mama miss work to come up to school about me, when Carla's birthday party was this Saturday. No way, I thought.

Me and Carla were walking back to our class with Mrs. Cunningham.

"I don't know when I've been so disappointed. Jean, you are one of my brightest students. No one expects anything from Carla, but you have really disappointed us."

Carla rolled her eyes as Mrs. Cunningham continued.

"We have an old Jamaican saying, 'Every tub must sit 'pon its own bottom,' Jean. You can't go through life following behind other people; you have to have a mind of your own."

"I didn't say it was anybody else's idea," I reminded Mrs. Cunningham.

"Look, I wasn't born yesterday, you know. I don't believe you did this without being influenced. I've been teaching for a long time now. I know my students."

"Okay, okay, I dragged her into it! Satisfied now! Hey, I'm suspended anyway, what do I care if you know. Stevie . . . Jean ain't know nothing about it till we got in the auditorium. And then we had to twist her arm, okay!" Carla blurted out as we reached the door.

"Clean your desk before you leave," Mrs. Cunningham said coldly.

I was at home washing the dishes. To top everything off, we'd had liver for dinner tonight. On *Gunsmoke,* at least they always gave you your favorite food before they sent you to the gallows. We couldn't have had fried chicken or spaghetti. No, we had to have liver.

I had been quiet during dinner, barely touching my food. Mama had let me get away with it because she knew I couldn't stand liver. I just couldn't bring myself to tell her what had happened today, not with Carla's birthday party three days away.

My hands shook as I washed dishes now. I had almost broken two glasses.

*

It was the next morning and I still hadn't told Mama what had happened. Carla had called me last night and brought me up to date. She said none of them had told their mothers they were suspended. In fact, she, Patrice, and Tanya planned to hang out at her crib and watch the stories all day. Carla's sister, Marla, would cover for them because Carla would be able to babysit her "rusty-butt boy" and tell her what was happening on *The Edge of Night*. Carla's sister was even going to sign their mothers' names to the suspension notices. Carla said it was no sweat, they had it made in the shade. It wasn't like she had never been suspended before. Everything was cool. Carla was trying to get her sisters to let her borrow their 45s so we could dance at the party. Everything was set. It seemed like I was the only one in trouble. Carla said that even Annie Pearl had kept her cool after Tanya said if she hit her, she would tell her mother what was in the diary.

I knew I was pressing my luck as I walked into Mrs. Cunningham's classroom alone, without Mama.

"Jean, where is your mother? Is she talking with Mr. Davis?"

Dog, Mrs. Cunningham couldn't even let me get the Pledge of Allegiance out before jumping in my face.

"No, she's home in bed. She was too sick to come out. She's got the flu. That bad flu that's going around."

"Okay, Jean, I'm going to give you until tomorrow."

"It's a bad flu, Mrs. Cunningham, a real bad one."

"What about Mr. Stevenson? Can he come in tomorrow?"

No way, I thought. Daddy hit harder than Mama.

"He's got the flu too, Mrs. Cunningham."

"Okay, Jean, I'm going to let you stay today because we're having a math test. But you either show up tomorrow with one of your parents or have them call me. Do you understand?"

"Yes, Mrs. Cunningham."

If I could just stall one more day, I'd have it made. Tomorrow was Friday. If I could just hold Mrs. Cunningham off one more day, I could go to the party on Saturday. Mama had already made my hair appointment at No Naps Beauty Salon. In fact, Carla's mother was the one who was going to do my hair.

I had made it! It was Friday afternoon and I was on my way home from school. Mrs. Cunningham had been out sick today and we'd had a substitute teacher. I had totally lucked out. The substitute had barely been able to keep the class from going crazy, let alone figure out I was supposed to bring my mother up to school. I couldn't believe it: nothing was gonna come between me and going to Carla's party now. I knew that chickens would come home to roost, as Mama always said. But let them roost on Monday, that's all I asked. Besides, a lot could happen between now and Monday. The Russians could attack. We could be invaded by Martians from outer space. Mrs. Cunningham could fall and hit her head and lose her memory. Anything could happen.

chapter 6

David met me at the door. I could tell something was wrong, because his eyes were so big. David grabbed my arm and started pulling me toward my bedroom. He was a head shorter than me and two years younger, but he was strong.

"David, what are you doing? What's wrong? Why are you grabbing on me?"

"Jean, you better change out of that dress and put on some long pants! Mama's talking to your teacher on the phone! I can tell you're in trouble just by how her voice sounds. Jean, you're really gonna get it!"

I set my books down on my bed.

"How long has she been on the phone?" My voice was shaking.

"Long enough. I think they're fixing to get off. I heard Mama thanking Mrs. Cunningham and saying she was sure she wouldn't be having any more problems with you. Jean, you better hurry up and put a couple pair of pants on. I think I just heard her put the phone down!"

I could hear Mama's loud footsteps coming toward my room. She was still wearing her bank shoes. I looked at David; we both knew it was curtains now. The TV was blasting in the living room. Kevin was watching the Mickey Mouse Club. I would've given anything to be a Mouseketeer right now. Why couldn't I be Annette Funicello, instead of Jean Stevenson?

Mama stood in the doorway with her arms folded, looking mad. She hadn't changed out of her navy skirt and white blouse.

"I talked to your teacher and she told me everything! I'm not going to have it, Jean Eloise! I'm not going to put up with it!"

David picked up my yo-yo off the chair and started playing with it.

"David, put that stupid yo-yo down and go pick me a switch! And, boy, you better bring me something I can work with, cause I'm gonna tear her legs up!" David ran out.

"How could you be so low? How could you be so low? Reading out of some slut's diary!" Mama shouted.

I sat on my bed, frozen. Mama's eyes looked like they were on fire. I was scared. I knew David would be back with a switch soon.

"I told you that Jezebel would be your downfall. Mrs. Cunningham said Carla Perkins and her gang were behind everything! To think you could've been in the chorus, singing at the Children's Hospital, knowing your father worked there. Jean, how could you cheat your poor, hard-working father out of being able to point and say, 'That's my daughter'?" Mama walked toward me and shouted, "How could you've been so selfish? I feel like knocking you down! I'm so mad I don't know what to do!" I moved back against the wall to get further away from Mama, but I knew there was no escape.

"Why would you want to let somebody like Carla have an opportunity you should've had? And then to read that filth, when you knew you had no business there in the first place." Mama continued, "Jean Eloise, I've tried to show you right from wrong. I don't know what is going to become of you. I'm just going to have to beat the devil out of you! I don't know what else I can do!" Mama said, pointing her finger at me.

David came back in the room carrying a switch. Kevin was with him. They looked like they felt sorry for me. I felt sorry for me, too. But I knew begging or crying wouldn't help. Mama had made up her mind to whip me. She snatched the switch from David's hand.

"Get over here, Jean! You boys get out of here. This is between me and your sister. Go back and watch TV."

"No!" I said, moving back toward the wall.

"Don't you tell me no!" Mama reached across the bed and dragged me by the arm and stood me up. She started hitting me with the switch. My legs felt like they were on fire, the switch was stinging me so much. I couldn't stand up anymore and fell to the floor. Mama was hitting my behind now and shouting, "Jean Eloise, you brought this all on yourself! You brought this all on yourself!"

I hadn't cried yet, although I had wanted to. I knew my brothers were listening for me to cry. We all knew that Mama never stopped whipping you until you cried. Besides, I couldn't hold the tears back any longer.

I finally screamed and the tears came out like a flood.

"This is for telling that lie about me having the flu." Mama hit me again. I just broke down and busted out sobbing with my face against the bare wood floor. The crying seemed like it was coming from way deep in my stomach. I felt as if once I started I'd never be able to stop.

"Now you want to act like somebody's beating you half to death! Well, if you don't shut up, I'm going to really give you something to cry about. I thought you'd had enough."

I was still lying on the floor, with Mama standing over me. I tried to force myself to stop crying. I knew it only made Mama madder. She wanted me to cry just enough to show that she had hurt me, but not so much that it would seem like she was cruel.

"Those tears aren't going to sway me one bit. Don't even

think of going to Carla's party, now. Don't let the thought even cross your mind!"

I got up off the floor and sat on my bed. The room looked different. It was like going outside after a movie.

I wiped my eyes, my dress was all wet in the front from my tears. Somehow, Mama saying that I couldn't go to Carla's party made me mad. I had taken my whipping; that should be enough. In fact, I felt mad enough to spit.

"You just want me to end up like you, without any friends!" I yelled as Mama walked out of my room.

Mama ran back into the room carrying the switch. She stood over me.

"How dare you have the nerve to talk back to me after I just finished whipping you! Do you want me to tear your behind up again?"

I looked at her as evilly as I could.

"You should see how ugly you look," Mama said, frowning.

I kept right on looking ugly. I was mad.

Mama folded her arms, still holding the switch. "You couldn't pay me to say such a thing to my mother. One of the Ten Commandments says, 'Honor thy mother and father and thy days will be long.' That's the only commandment with a promise."

Mama looked down at me to see if she'd gotten to me. She hadn't. I wasn't in an honoring mood. I was still mad.

Mama sat down in the chair across from me. She reached over and set the switch on top of the dresser.

"I don't see how you could say that I don't have any friends," she continued. "I've got plenty of friends. I do unto others as I would have them do unto me. I love my neighbor as myself. I was the first colored teller at the bank to be voted teller of the month. So I don't see how you could even make your mouth say that I don't have any friends."

"How come nobody ever calls or comes over to visit you except Grandma and Aunt Sheila?" I blurted out.

I knew that I was skating on thin ice, but at this point what did I have to lose?

Mama stood up, but instead of picking up the switch, she pointed her finger at me.

"I've never been one to sit on the phone all day or to run in and out of people's houses or have them running in and out of mine. Besides, I don't need a lot of friends. I have a family to take care of. That's one reason I wanted a daughter. A son is a son until he takes a wife, but a daughter is a daughter all of her life," Mama recited.

I still didn't want to end up like Mama, I thought.

Mama sat back down in the chair. I could tell she was about to make one of her "Jean Eloise speeches." She had whipped me, she wasn't letting me go to Carla's party, and now I had to listen to one of her sermons. Why couldn't she just leave me alone?

"Jean Eloise, I don't want you to be just like me."

Good, I thought, at least we agree on something.

"You think I don't remember how it was to be young? Thirty-five is not as far away from twelve and a half as you might think. There were parties I would've given anything to have been invited to and Valentine cards that I wanted to get. I know what it feels like to want to fit in, to want to be popular. You never stop wanting people to like you, no matter how old you get."

"Mama, the reason I wanted Carla to have my spot in the chorus was because I saw how bad she wanted to be in it and I knew she was a better singer than me."

"A better singer than I," Mama cut in.

"Anyway, I knew that no matter how much Carla wanted to be in the chorus and no matter how good a singer she was, Mrs. Cunningham wasn't going to pick her, just because she didn't like her. Remember when my poem was published in the school newspaper that time?"

"Of course, you know I kept it and sent copies to everybody I knew. It's still on the refrigerator."

"Well, what if they hadn't published my poem because they didn't like me, even though it was a good poem?"

"Well, that wouldn't have been fair."

"That's what I mean. I didn't think it was fair to Carla. I know how it feels to be on the honor roll, to have my poem published in the school newspaper, and to be picked to be in the chorus. But, Mama, I never knew how it felt to be part of a crowd before, to be popular. I thought for somebody like Carla being part of a crowd, being popular, was everything. I didn't know that something was missing for her, until I saw how much she wanted to be in that chorus. I wanted to see her get what she wanted. It's like with Christmas presents, Mama, every year you say it's better to give than receive. I wanted to give something to Carla."

Mama stood up and started hanging up the clothes that were on the back of the chair.

"Well, I suppose we should be glad that a girl like Carla wants to be a part of something worthwhile," Mama said from the closet. "Jean, pick up those papers off the floor, why do you think I got you a desk?"

"Mama, in a way we're all like Carla." I stooped down and picked up a pile of school papers.

"What do you mean?"

I sat back on my bed. "Remember last year when Terri called me on my birthday and told me she'd gotten to be friends with this white girl named Mary Beth, who wasn't allowed to play with negroes? Her family was one of the last white people left on the block and they were still trying to sell their house?"

Mama leaned against the closet door. "Yes, I remember that."

"And as soon as they see Mary Beth's father's car drive up, Terri's gotta cut through the bushes and hide."

Mama nodded.

"Well, Mary Beth's parents won't give Terri a chance, just because she's colored. I don't think it's fair not to give people a chance, do you, Mama?"

Mama didn't say anything. She was just staring into space. I stood up. "Mama," I said walking toward her.

Mama looked around the room. "I hope you're not going to wait until the last minute to look for something to wear to the party."

"What party?" I asked, confused.

"How many parties are you invited to tomorrow? Have you suddenly become *that* popular?"

I couldn't believe my ears, but I was afraid to say anything.

Mama folded her arms, "Look, I don't know if I'm doing the right thing or not, but I'm going to go ahead and let you go to Carla's party, Stevie."

Mama had said I could go to Carla's party, and she had called me Stevie! Mama had never called me Stevie before. I wasn't mad anymore. All of a sudden I wished Mama had a party to go to.

chapter 7

So this is what it's like to be at Carla's party, I thought, glancing around the basement filled with girls in party dresses and boys in dress shirts and pants. Nobody really looked happy, they just looked cool. Maybe we were having fun and I was just too square to realize it. The boys stood around the food table gulping punch and stuffing themselves with potato chips and hot dogs. I overheard them say, "Man, this" and "Man, that" between bites. The girls were all bunched up on the other side of the room.

I sat next to Patrice and Tanya drinking Hawaiian punch, balancing a paper plate with a half-eaten hot dog and some potato chips on my lap. Carla was standing nearby talking to Joyce and Bernice. Melody and Linda were playing with Carla's little niece and nephew, Malcolm and Lakisha.

"Look, that's her second hot dog," Patrice said.

"Who?" I asked.

"Her," Tanya said pointing to Joyce, a chubby, light-skinned girl. "If Carla had known she was gonna make a pig out of herself she wouldn't have invited her," she added.

"Look, a lot of boys are on their second hot dogs," I pointed out.

Patrice shook her head and sighed. "Stevie, boys are different. They can eat as much as they want and people will think it's cute. If a girl does that, people will talk about her like a dog. Girls can't get away with the things boys can, don't you know that?"

"Yeah, but that doesn't make it right."

"There go Stevie's man, y'all," Tanya teased, pointing to a boy that looked like a groundhog.

"No, it isn't, I don't even know him."

"You know that's your nigger, girl, you ain't got to be shamed." Tanya laughed.

"I never seen him before in my life."

"Well, you better grab him, cause there go you last chance, girl," Tanya insisted.

"Carla, who is that over there? The dufus-looking one with the bifocals," Patrice asked.

"That's Marc's brother, Sherman. I didn't know he was going to bring him," she said, hunching her shoulders.

"I knew that wasn't none of Stevie's man. I knew you was lying." Patrice smiled.

"Well, you shouldn't have let him in." Tanya laughed as Carla walked away.

Patrice elbowed Tanya. "Remember how we used to stick our arms out to see who was the lightest, remember?"

"Yeah, let's do it."

"Put your arm out. Stevie, Tanya, Cassandra, have y'all's palms facing up. Come on, Tessa, Renee, let's see who's the lightest. Peaches, Joyce, Melody, Linda, all y'all come over here. We gonna see who's the lightest!"

"Carla, bring your arm in here, too," Patrice shouted.

I looked at my arm against the bunch of other ones. Mine was in the middle, but closer to the dark ones than the lighter ones.

"Tessa's arm's the lightest. No, check out Peaches' arm."

"Mine is light as Peaches'," Joyce insisted. "Linda's arm is the darkest. Look at her arm next to mine. It looks black!" she added.

Linda looked embarrassed.

"Why are we doing this?" I asked, pulling my arm out of the pile.

"Cause y'all girls! And girls are stupid!" Michael shouted as Tyrone gave him five. The group of boys laughed.

None of the girls answered my question. "Do you think that it makes somebody better 'cause her arm is lighter?" I asked. Everyone was quiet.

"Stevie's right, this game has played out," Carla said, pulling away. "Besides, I ain't gonna let nobody put none of my guests down." Everyone began shaking their arms out and turning away.

I sat in a corner eating my second hot dog, tuning out the chatter of the girls around me. Melody and Linda were dancing with Carla's niece and nephew. They were the only ones who looked to be having any fun. "It's twine time, ooh ahh," Lakisha and Malcolm shouted over and over as they threw their chubby little arms and legs from side to side. I knew that tomorrow everybody would brag about how cool and happening Carla's party had been. And the ones who hadn't been invited would think they'd really missed something. I knew, because I used to be one of them.

Carla turned off the record player and dimmed the lights. She sent Lakisha and Malcolm back outside to play. She stood up waving an empty wine bottle. "It's time! Everybody sit on the rug, make a circle, y'all. We fixin' to play Spin the Bottle!"

The girls moved faster than the boys toward the big piece of gray carpet in the center of the floor. I realized that I didn't want to have any of these boys slobbering on me. What if I got stuck with a boy who had bad breath? I'd never been kissed before and I didn't want my first kiss to be with just anybody. I wanted to save my lips for somebody special.

"Where you goin'?" Carla asked as I slipped out of the room.

"The bathroom."

"Well, hurry back, we're fixin' to play!"

"Okay," I answered happily from the stairs.

You could only hide in the bathroom so long. I headed for the kitchen to talk to Carla's mother. She was frosting Carla's birthday cake while drinking a can of beer and smoking a cigarette.

She wore a tight, black miniskirt and a black and white polka-dot blouse. Mama had said Mrs. Perkins was too dark to have a red tint in her perm and too old and plump to wear miniskirts, after we ran into her shopping at the A&P.

"Stevie, where you at?" Carla's mother asked as I walked into the kitchen.

"Huh? I'm right here."

"It means, how you doing, or how you be, that's what they say in New Orleans."

"Oh, are you from New Orleans?"

"No, I hail from Little Rock."

"Little Rock, Arkansas?"

"That's right. You're so smart."

"Thanks."

"Stevie, I'm so glad you and Carla got to be friends."

"Is it okay if I sit in this chair?"

"Make yourself at home, Stevie, set yourself down."

"Can I help you with anything?"

"Not right now, you can just keep me company. You are so polite. My two other daughters only ran around with riffraff. I tell Carla all the time, Be like Stevie, she's going to amount to something."

"You tell Carla that?"

"Sho do, I preach to her all the time. Carla is my last hope."

"Carla has a good singing voice."

"Stevie, most negroes can carry a tune. I want her to get something in her head. I don't expect my kids to discover the cure for cancer. I just want them to do something with their lives, so my struggle won't have been in vain."

"Well, Carla is really cool. I always looked up to her."

"Cool! Don't make me lose my religion! Cool don't pay the rent! Cool don't pay the bills. The only thing cool do is rhyme with fool! Do you hear me?"

"Yes, ma'm."

"I wish you *would* mention cool to me again, I'll whup you and Carla both! Do you hear me?"

"Yes ma'm." I was having second thoughts about my decision not to play Spin the Bottle.

"Don't get me started," Mrs. Perkins continued. "I have struggled to raise these three girls to the best of my ability, with no help from nobody. Do you hear me?"

I nodded.

"I would shovel shit in a barnyard to feed my children."

I raised my eyebrows. I wasn't used to hearing grown-ups curse.

"I've done damn near everything but steal and sell tail to keep a roof over their heads. Stay in school, I tell them. Education is something that nobody can take away from you," she said, smashing her cigarette out. "Don't end up like me. Look like the only rest I'm gonna get will be in my grave. Stevie, promise me something."

"What?"

"Promise me you'll never put your trust in no man."

I didn't know what to say. I trusted my father and my uncle. Maybe Mrs. Perkins meant other men. Carla's mother didn't wait for me to answer. She just took a drag off her cigarette and threw her head back, and emptied the can of beer into her mouth.

"There is nobody out there for you," Mrs. Perkins shouted

and pointed with her knife. "If you make it in this world you're gonna have to make it all by your lonesome. Do you hear me? Cinderella was not written about the negro woman. Do you understand?"

"Yes, I think so," I said, edging back a little from the knife. She was really getting worked up.

"Your Prince Charming ain't never gonna come! Do you hear me?"

"Yes, ma'm," I said. But I still planned to wait and see what would happen.

chapter 8

"**Y**ou can tell Yusef Brown is nasty, huh? You can tell where his mind is just by the way he looks at you, huh?" Carla yelled so I could hear her over all the cussing and carrying on. We were hunched over our bicycles, watching these boys playing basketball in the park. It was a sunny Saturday afternoon at the beginning of June. Carla took a big suck off of her orange Popsicle.

"Look how his skin shines when he sweats; it looks just like hot fudge," I said.

"Yeah," Carla agreed. "Tyrone skin remind me of gingerbread, make me wanna eat him up," she added.

I let out a big sigh and bit off a piece of my Popsicle and sucked on it hard. The cold, cherry-flavored hunk melted in my mouth.

"Yusef Brown is cool, you gotta hand him that, though," I added.

"Course, Yusef Brown is cool! He wear khaki pants, don't he? He gotta black leather jacket, don't he? He pitches pennies, don't he? And he even got nerve enough to keep a Kool cigarette behind his ear." Carla put her hands on her hips. "Now, if that ain't cool, then I don't know what is!"

I sloshed a piece of Popsicle around in my mouth while I thought. Yusef didn't seem to know I drew breath. Outside of school, we might as well live in two different worlds. Here I was thirteen and fixing to graduate from eighth grade, and I still had to come in when the street lights came on. When I was going in was probably when Yusef was just going out sometimes. I sloshed another piece of Popsicle around in my mouth.

"I hate it when you do that, it sounds so nasty!"

"Carla, if my mama would let me go to the dances down to the Baptist church, I might be able to get me some play, you know," I said, continuing to slosh.

"Yeah, Yusef be at them all the time. Why your mama so strict? The dances be at a church."

"My mother says church and dancing don't mix, in her book."

"What book is that? My mama say, 'The Lord say make a joyous noise'!"

That's probably why Carla's mother was Baptist and mine was an African Methodist Episcopal, I thought.

Carla had never met her father. He had gone to the store for a pack of cigarettes two weeks before she was born, and had never returned.

Carla's voice jumped into my thoughts. "The Graduation Tea is coming up soon, and there'll be dancing there. You better make your move or you'll end up holding up the walls. Or worse, dancing with Rolaids."

"His name is Roland, Carla."

"Whatever his name is, he still ain't got no behind."

Roland was a square, skinny boy who wore glasses and was good in math and science. He called himself liking me. According to Carla, his biggest drawback was that he had no behind.

"And after all that time I spent last Saturday, teaching you that new Bop, too." Carla shook her head sadly. "If it wasn't for me you'd still be doing the Twine. No, actually you'd probably still be doing the Twist." She laughed.

"Ha, ha, very funny." I watched Yusef dribble the ball. He could be a dancer, I thought.

"Maybe I'll drop my books again," I mumbled.

"Drop your books? You ain't told me you dropped your books."

"Yeah, last week, I guess I forgot."

"Well?"

"Well, he stooped down and picked them up for me. He practically had no choice, since I dropped them on his foot.

"Oh. Well, did y'all talk?"

"Yeah, I told him I was sorry and I thanked him. And he said, 'Cool.'"

"That was nice. I likes that, cool."

"Oh, Carla, he didn't really pay me any attention. I could've been any girl."

"Well, if you drop your books again he'll probably just think you're clumsy. Hey, at this point you'd practically have to drop your draws to get Yusef Brown to notice you!"

"Very funny." I frowned.

Carla didn't have to worry: she was practically going with Tyrone. Besides, she was the kind of girl lots of boys liked. Not that she looked any better than me, according to Mama, but she just had this way about her. Sometimes around boys I felt like I was in a play but didn't know my lines. Where was I when they handed out the scripts?

Carla's eyes never left Tyrone. He looked like a young Muhammad Ali running with the ball in his new Converse All-Stars.

"I just can't help it, I just gotta weakness for bowlegged niggers." She sighed.

Tyrone threw Yusef the ball. I watched his strong body jump up and do his famous dunk. Tyrone gave him five.

"You can tell he done done it before," Carla said, sucking on her Popsicle sticks.

"You mean you think Yusef's had sexual intercourse?" I whispered.

Carla looked confused. "I don't know nothing about them fancy words. I just know he done stuck it in somebody before, I just bet he probably has."

"For all you know, Yusef could still be a virgin," I said.

"Don't make me laugh. You can tell by the way he walks, the way he pimps." Carla put one hand behind her back and strutted.

I laughed and turned my back to the fence. "Carla, don't forget how he's all the time bending backward and sticking himself out."

"Yeah, and I swear his hand never be far from his dick," Carla said, giggling as I grabbed at my crotch. We both fell out laughing. A chill suddenly ran down my spine. I felt kind of scared and excited at the same time. I didn't want to like a dog like Yusef Brown, but I just couldn't help myself.

"Y'all so into basketball, maybe y'all should join up with the girls' basketball team next fall. My sister, Johnnie Mae, she the captain."

It was Willie Jean, a tall, flat-chested, tomboyish girl who'd moved here last year from Mississippi. Carla said she gave new meaning to the word "country."

Carla rolled her eyes, which I knew meant she didn't want to be bothered with Willie Jean.

"I play basketball with my brother sometimes; I've gotten pretty good." I tried to be nice.

"They always looking for new girls and you 'bout tall enough, I reckon," Willie Jean said.

I rolled my Popsicle sticks in their paper, and tossed them into the trash.

"Hot dog!" Willie Jean shouted. "Good shot!"

I blew on my fingers and proudly rubbed my chest.

"You better watch it. Next thing you know, you'll be getting muscles and nobody'll want you, not even what's his name," Carla warned.

"Forget you! Somebody will always want me." I stuck my tongue out at her.

"I take that back." Carla laughed. "No *man* will want you. I'll put it that way."

"My sister go out on plenty of dates," Willie Jean cut in.

"Yeah, yeah, but how much you wanta bet she don't go out on half as many dates as the head cheerleader?" Carla climbed on her bike. "You see, Willie Jean, we ain't so much into basketball. We really into basketball players, right, Stevie?" Carla said as she began pedaling away.

"Yeah, sort of." I jumped on my bike. "So long, Willie Jean." I turned around to get one last look at Yusef's sweaty body.

"Hey, Stevie," Carla yelled as we picked up speed. "A girl with a name like Johnnie Mae ain't gonna get but so many dates!" Carla laughed as we rode out of the park.

It was Sunday morning and me, Mama, my brothers, and the minister were standing on the steps of Faith African Methodist Episcopal Church. Reverend Sawyer stood head to head with Mama, which meant he wasn't tall for a man. But Reverend Sawyer wasn't little. He looked to me like he could come out of his robe and kick some butt if he had to. "Reverend Sawyer, that sermon was just beautiful. I wished I could've taped it, so my husband could hear it," Mama said, grinning.

"Well, thank you, Sister Stevenson, I sure wish we could get Brother Stevenson to join the flock."

"Reverend Sawyer, you're sounding like a Baptist preacher."

"Don't tell me my roots are showing." Reverend Sawyer laughed, wiping sweat off his forehead with his handkerchief.

Kevin called Reverend Sawyer "bean head" in private because his bald head reminded him of the coffee bean a boy had brought to Show and Tell once. Kevin worried he'd go to hell because of it.

"Your husband doesn't work on Sunday morning, does he?"

"No, he's home in bed. Mama couldn't wake him up. Daddy's gotta hangover!" Kevin explained.

I knew Mama felt like strangling him. Instead, she went on and tried to cover it up.

"Uh, that's right, Reverend Sawyer, my husband has a headache. He strains his eyes, doesn't read in enough light. Come along, children, there are other people in the congregation besides us."

"I'll remember you in my prayers," Reverend Sawyer called out.

Mama grabbed Kevin's arm. "Nobody was talking to you, boy. Speak when you're spoken to! You got one more time to embarrass me like that!"

We walked smack dab into Roland. Mama slapped a smile on her face; she liked Roland. He was smart and polite. His people were members of Faith like us. Both of Roland's parents were teachers. His father was a deacon in the church, and his mother sang in the choir. His oldest sister was a freshman at University of Illinois Circle Campus. Deep down Mama was especially proud of dark-skinned people who did well in life. So in her eyes Roland could do no wrong. The fact that he wore horn-rimmed glasses, was a total square, and had almost no behind didn't seem to faze her.

"Good morning, Mrs. Stevenson, Stevie, David, Kevin. Nice to see all of you."

Me and my brothers nodded.

Mama perked up. "Good morning, Roland. How are your parents?"

"They're fine, thank you. My father's inside helping to count the money, and my mother's changing out of her choir robe."

"Roland, you enunciate so well. So many of our young people underestimate the importance of good diction."

"Thank you, Mrs. Stevenson. As you know, my mother is an English teacher."

David made a face. He and I would crack up later and say

how we'd wanted to throw up, or how badly we'd needed a shovel. But now we had to keep a straight face or else Mama would be reading us all the way home.

"Stevie, I wondered if I could walk you home?" Roland stood there with a goofy smile on his face.

I didn't want to be bothered with Roland on a Sunday, and yet Mama might not be through yelling at Kevin. I was caught between a rock and a hard place. I decided to go with the devil I knew. I was used to tuning Mama out. Forgive me, God, I didn't mean Mama was a devil, I said in my head.

"Sorry, Roland, some other time. I just want to be with my family right now. I was hoping that my mother and I would have a chance to go over the sermon together."

David started to hoot, but he pretended like he was coughing. Kevin's eyes were big as saucers, but he didn't dare say anything. Even Roland looked like he was caught by surprise. Mama smiled; she was tickled to have any excuse to discuss religion.

"Well, okay, some other time then." Roland tipped his stupid cap and we said our goodbyes.

"What profit a man if he should gain the world but lose his own soul? Now I take that to mean . . . " Mama started.

Mama was one of the few people who could make a body look forward to Monday.

Daddy walked into the kitchen carrying an empty rat trap. Mama had seen a rat while she was doing the laundry in the basement. Daddy put the huge trap on the table and sat down across from me.

I looked up from my homework.

"Daddy, if X plus Y equals Z, then Z minus Y is equal to X, right?"

"What are you talking about?"

"The new math."

"Is two plus two still four?"

"Yes, of course."

"Good. That's all I want to know. Now get me a beer."

I frowned. The idea that Daddy could get his own beer was probably as foreign to him as the new math.

"Jean, bring me a piece of cheese, while you're at it."

I stood over Daddy, holding a can of Hamm's, watching him mash a piece of cheese into the brand-new trap.

"Thanks, just set it on the table."

"You know, I've heard peanut butter works better."

"Who's doing this, me or you?" Daddy tried to sound mean, but his smile gave him away.

"It was just a suggestion," I said, going back to my homework.

"Girl, I was trapping rats before you was born."

"Did y'all have them when you were growing up?"

"Sho did." Daddy sipped his beer.

"The first rat that I can remember showed his behind on a cold winter night. It was almost Christmas. It was going to be another hard-candy Christmas."

"What's a hard-candy Christmas, Daddy?"

"A Christmas when you ain't getting nothing but hard candy, 'cause that's all your people can afford."

"Oh. Must've been a dumb rat to pick you all's house, huh?"

"Well, times was hard. Anyway we set a trap that night and it went off while we was asleep. The next morning, my father told my mother that I had to take the rat off the trap before I went to school."

"How old were you, Daddy?"

"Younger than Kevin. I couldn't have been more than seven."

"Weren't you scared?"

"Course I was scared. I told my mama that I didn't want to take no rat off no trap. I had tears running down my face and everything."

It was hard to imagine my big, strong father as a scared little boy with tears running down his face.

"So what did your mother say?"

"She said, Just run on to school, boy. See to it later."

"Couldn't you just tell your father that you were scared?"

Daddy pretended to choke on his beer. "Girl, please! You must be kidding! My father believed that a boy should be tough as nails. He'd buy my sisters ice-cream cones and wouldn't buy me nan."

"How come?"

"My mama asked him the same thing."

"What did he say?"

"He said, 'Let him go out and hustle. Nobody's gonna give a man nothing.' My mama reminded him that I was just a child. But that didn't make him no never mind."

My grandfather had died of a heart attack when I was seven. I'd met him when I was a baby, but I didn't remember him.

Daddy drank some beer, and stared out the window into the dark night. "And it didn't make me no never mind when he died, either," he whispered.

I swallowed, I remembered my father saying he was only going to his father's funeral for his mother's sake. Now I understood why.

"Daddy, did you end up having to take the rat off the trap?"

"My stomach was in knots all day long. When I come home from school that afternoon, Mama told me to run quick to the hardware store to buy a new trap. She'd thrown the rat, trap and all, into the furnace."

"Did your father ever find out?"

"No, and over the years, we bought a number of traps too. Some mamas used to have pin money. My mama had trap money."

I laughed.

"Jean, I wished you could've known my mother. She was really special," Daddy said, wiping his eye with the sleeve of his work shirt.

He always got teary-eyed when he talked about his mother. The only time I'd seen my father cry was when I was nine. His sister called and told him that their mother had died from TB. He was sobbing by the time he hung up the phone.

"Daddy, were your mother and father close?"

"What do you mean, close? They had five kids." Daddy said, finishing his beer. "Mainly, my mother and father just stayed out of each other's way. They were on their own separate missions."

Sort of like you and Mama, I thought.

"You think your parents were happy?"

"They didn't have time to worry about being happy. Besides, happiness isn't what's important in life."

"It's not? Well, what *is* important in life, Daddy?"

"Raising a family, making a living, that's what's important. Any fool can be happy."

I didn't argue with Daddy but I thought that there was a lot to be said for just being happy.

"Daddy, are you gonna make Kevin take the rat off the trap?"

"Nope, we've got a furnace."

chapter 9

I was sitting at my desk Monday morning. Mr. Cox was giving us a history review. My eyes were glued to Yusef Brown out in the hallway, jumping up and down pretending to make baskets. Mr. Cox had sent him out there, counta he had his hat on in the class and plus he'd been chewing gum.

"Jean, do you know when that took place?"

I jumped and looked up at Mr. Cox's balding white head and beady blue eyes. I stared down at my history book.

"Eighteen sixty-five," I heard Willie Jean whisper from behind me.

"Yes, Mr. Cox, in eighteen sixty-five," I said just as cool as you please.

The class snickered.

"Eighteen sixty-six?" I asked shyly. The class broke out into hoots and hollers.

"I asked you if you knew when the last fire drill took place." Mr. Cox shook his head.

I swallowed. "Oh, it was around Valentine's Day," I said, as the recess bell rang.

I huffed and puffed as I made my way out into the hallway. Who did that heifer think she was? What was she trying to pull, I thought to myself. I had never done anything to her.

"Wait till I catch up with her," I mumbled on my way down the stairs.

"Say," Carla came up from behind me. "Don't let that bitch get away with that. There she is, jack her up, Stevie."

"Willie Jean, that was really cold-blooded!" I shouted. Me and Carla followed Willie Jean onto the playground and so did a bunch of other kids. I didn't want a crowd around us, because I knew a crowd meant a fight.

Willie Jean turned around. "It was just a joke, Stevie."

"Ha, ha, well, it was so funny I forgot to laugh."

"You don't know her that well." Carla cut her eyes and put her hands on her hips.

"Oooh, doon, baby!" Tanya shouted. "She say you don't even know her that well!"

"This is between us, Willie Jean, let's talk over there." I pointed to a far corner of the playground. Willie Jean nodded. "We don't need no crowd," I explained.

Me, Carla, and Willie Jean walked away from the others.

"Willie Jean, why did you try to make me look like a fool?"

"You look like a bigger fool, trailing behind a no-good boy the likes of Yusef Brown!"

I raised my eyebrows. "What business is it of yours?"

"Yeah, what business is it of yours?" Carla sounded like an echo. "Don't tell me you wanna get next to him, 'cause I know he ain't thinking about you." Carla sucked her teeth. "Shoot, your chances are slim and impossible and, honey, slim just left!" Carla laughed.

"I don't want none of Yusef Brown. He don't move me and

he don't groove me. I just think Stevie can do better for herself, that's all."

"What do you care?" I asked. Me and this girl weren't even tight or nothing.

"When Stevie's holding up the walls at the graduation tea, what can you do for her but hold up the walls with her?" Carla added.

"There ain't no law saying that two girls can't dance together," Willie Jean answered all calm.

"Yeah, but everybody feels sorry for them. They know they dancing together 'cause they can't get no man." Carla folded her arms.

"Sometimes a boy will cut in if two girls are dancing together. He'll say something like, Y'all two ladies ain't got to be dancing together. I saw that happen at my Aunt Sheila's birthday party," I explained.

"Yeah, it be's that way sometimes, if you happen to luck out," Carla agreed.

"I don't know if I'd call that lucking out myself." Willie Jean turned and walked across the playground toward the volleyball game.

"She don't know if she'd call that lucking out." Carla shook her head. "Is she fully clothed and in her right mind?"

"What is she trying to say?" I asked.

"Stevie, I think she's trying to say she funny."

"Carla, you think she's really that way?"

"I ain't wanna say nothing before, cause you know how I hate to talk about people. But the girl told on her own self. I could tell she had some boy in her, from jumpstreet. Nine outta ten of them P.E. types do. Her sister's probably all crossed up too."

"Here comes Roland." I hunched my shoulders.

"From the pitiful to the pathetic. I'm gonna go and see if I can find Tyrone."

"Hey, Roland."

"Hi, Stevie." Roland stood there grinning, looking even goofier than usual.

"Stevie . . . uh . . . I was thinking . . . maybe . . . you know ah, would you mind if I kind of walked you home from school today?"

"I guess." I forced myself to smile. "Well, Roland, I gotta go play volleyball. You need to wipe your glasses off, they're all steamed up."

"Oh, okay. Well, see you after school." He grinned.

During lunchtime, me and Carla sat in the swings on the playground and ate our fried-bologna sandwiches. A few minutes ago, Tyrone had come by and dragged Carla away, laughing and screaming.

Now I just sat in the swing and let it rock me gently back and forth. The sun was in my face and I just let my feet drag through the wood chips that they always put on the playground.

I felt somebody's hands pushing up against my back. I started moving forward and I grabbed onto the swing's chains. I turned around. I couldn't believe it: Yusef Brown was pushing me!

I liked the way his hands felt against my back. And the rubber swing felt good up under my butt.

Yusef grabbed the swing and brought it to a halt.

"I heard about you." Yusef bit back his bottom lip. He had what Grandma called laughing eyes.

"Heard about me, what did you hear about me?" I asked, surprised. I wasn't the kind of girl that boys usually heard about.

"In class this morning, eighteen sixty-five." Yusef burst out laughing.

"Oh, that," I said, not sure whether I now thought it was funny.

"You cracked everybody up! 'Eighteen sixty-six.' " Yusef laughed some more.

I still wasn't crazy about Yusef laughing at me, but I figured it beat being invisible.

"Stop making fun of me." I punched at his arm playfully.

"Okay, okay." He smiled, holding his arm. "Look, I wasn't making fun of you. I just thought you was so cool counta the way you took it, didn't get bent outta shape or nothing behind it. They said you was cool to the end, just said, 'Around Valentine's Day, Mr. Cox.' "

"I have to really hand it to Willie Jean, though; she's the one who whispered eighteen sixty-five." I decided to go along with Yusef.

"Yeah, that was really slick."

The afternoon bell rang and I picked up my stuff. I hoped that Yusef would walk me back to class. I wanted everybody to see us.

"Oh, Stevie, they told me the reason you got into trouble in the first place was counta you was checking me out making jump shots in the hallway." Yusef winked as we walked toward the building.

"I suppose maybe I glanced out there once or twice. Who is 'they'?"

"That's for me to know and for you to find out." Yusef had the nerve to reach over and poke my nose. I felt so dizzy I could barely stand up. The halls were crowded with everybody rushing, but I hoped somebody had seen that. Yusef Brown had talked to me. Yusef Brown had pushed me in the swing. Yusef Brown had played with my nose! Yusef Brown was walking me to the classroom door, and all on accounta Willie Jean. Carla was never gonna believe this.

I would always sit in that middle swing and I would only eat fried-bologna sandwiches in it. I smiled goodbye to Yusef and took my seat.

It was afternoon recess and we were out on the playground. It was the first chance I'd had to talk to Carla about Yusef.

"It was right here, he came up right behind me. You couldn't have been gone more than five minutes. Just started pushing me."

"I can't believe it, after all this time. Yusef talked to you and all on accounta her. Tell it to me again, I swear I can't believe it."

"Carla, that's what you said the first two times I told you."

Recess was over and I was back at my desk. I tried to sneak a peek at Yusef without being too obvious. I didn't want to get into trouble with Mr. Cox again. I wondered if Yusef would start giving me the time of day from now on. Things could never go back to the way they were before, I told myself. I knew that my life would never be the same. I had half a mind to write a poem.

"Stevie, Stevie!" It was Carla. "Girl, everybody done gone. Ain't you heard the bell? School's out."

"Oh." I started grabbing my stuff. The afternoon had flown by or else I must've been in another world. I followed Carla out of the room.

"Stevie."

I turned around, surprised to see Yusef standing in the hall, with his hands stuffed in his khaki pants.

"Yeah, Yusef?"

"Can I walk you home?"

"Oh . . ."

"Sure," Carla finished my sentence. I guess she could see I was practically in a daze. "Stevie, y'all two go head on, I can catch up with some peoples." She winked at me.

I stumbled down the steps with Yusef walking on the outside. I had to grab hold of the banister on account of my weak condition. I felt like I'd died and gone to heaven, or at least like those women who used to be on *Queen for a Day*. I can't believe it, I said to myself as we walked out into the sunshine. I just can't believe it.

Then I saw Roland coming toward me, like he'd come to

wake me out of my dream. Oh, brother, I thought, I'd forgotten that I'd told him he could walk me home from school today. No way, there's no way I'm gonna give up this heaven, I told myself. Maybe he'll get the message; even he couldn't be that stupid.

"Hi, Stevie . . . Hi, Yusef."

"Hey, Roland.

"What's happenin', man," Yusef said automatically.

"Well, bye, Yusef, come on, Stevie, let's go," Roland had the nerve to say.

I couldn't believe it. I couldn't believe it. He didn't have the sense he was born with. If he messed this up he was gonna be sorry. I would hate him forever!

"Oh, y'all got some sort of plans?" Yusef asked.

"Yeah, Stevie and I are . . . "

"Going to discuss a math problem *later, on the telephone.*" I grabbed Yusef's arm and steered him away. "Bye, Roland, I'll talk to you tonight on the phone."

I left Roland standing there with his mouth open. Surely even he had sense enough not to push things any further.

"Slow down, Stevie, why you walking so fast?"

"I always walk fast, it's good exercise."

"Hold up, let me carry your books."

"Okay." I slowed down; we were far enough away from Roland now.

I felt so special walking with Yusef, I was waving to practically everybody. It seemed to me that all kinds of people were looking at me differently because I was with him. Yusef, who was wearing khaki pants and Converse All-Stars gym shoes, Yusef who'd rather walk home with me today than pitch pennies. Yusef who was now lighting a Kool cigarette and smoking it. I couldn't believe I was walking down the street with a boy who had nerve enough to smoke a cigarette less than two blocks from the school. I just hoped we didn't run into my mother or father.

We were standing in front of my house. Yusef had put his cigarette out a block ago, thank goodness.

"Well, I better be getting in. Thanks for walking me home."

"Sho," Yusef handed me my books. "Well, see you later, alligator."

"In a while, crocodile."

I skipped up the stairs three at a time, I was so excited.

I was watching TV with my brothers in the living room. Mama stood in the doorway. "Jean, telephone!"

"Who is it?"

"It's Roland Anderson. Now get up and go to the phone."

"Mama, tell him I'm watching Andy Griffith."

"The show is over, Opie and Andy are carrying their fish home. Jean Eloise, if you don't go to that phone, you better."

"All right," I groaned. When Mama called me Jean Eloise she meant business. I wondered if mothers gave their children awful middle names just so they could torture them.

I picked up the phone and sat down in an avocado high-backed kitchen chair.

"Hi, Roland."

"What's the meaning of what you did this afternoon?" I felt kind of taken aback: I wasn't used to Roland coming on like gangbusters. I didn't know he had it in him, to be honest.

"Stevie, I really think that was rotten!" Roland continued.

"Okay, okay, look I forgot that I said you could walk me home. I'm sorry. It just slipped my mind."

"Okay, let's say you forgot, seeing how forgettable I am. When I reminded you, you could've at least had the decency to tell Yusef you'd made a mistake." Roland's voice was shaking.

I felt bad, but at the same time I felt as if whatever way I went Roland was going to be hurt, sooner or later. I decided to get it over with.

"Roland, I'm sorry, I mean you're one of the nicest boys in our school. I know what I did was wrong in a way."

"In a way?" Roland cut in.

"Yes, in a way, because you see, Roland, I did what I wanted to do. It might sound cold and maybe you can't understand it, but I couldn't pass up the chance to walk home with Yusef Brown just to walk home with you."

I bit my bottom lip, I hadn't meant it to come out that way. I couldn't hear anything on the other end. I wished Roland would say something, cuss me out, anything.

"Roland, are you there? Roland, I'm sorry, I didn't mean it to come out like that. I'm sorry."

"Stevie, I have homework to do. Goodbye." I had never heard Roland sound so mad.

"But, but," I said as I heard the receiver click.

I sat there with my mouth open. I didn't know if I was happy or sad. I felt like they were both mixed in together. At least now maybe I could concentrate on Yusef. Nothing was in my way.

It was the fourth day in a row that Yusef had waited to walk me home. Every time I'd seen him leaning up against the building, I had needed to convince myself that he was waiting for me. Carla was going crazy. She couldn't believe that Yusef was up in my face every day either, but she was happy for me.

Me and Roland really hadn't run into each other since we'd talked. Luckily he was in Mrs. Verducci's eighth-grade class, so I'd been able to avoid him without too much trouble.

Because it was the fourth time that Yusef was walking me home, I felt like I could start up a conversation.

"So, Yusef, you gonna go out for the basketball team next year?"

"Course." He smiled. "Then I'm getting a basketball scholarship and play at a big-time college. Then I'm gonna play for the NBA. Then I'm gonna be another Lew Alcindor and Wilt the Stilt, all rolled into one."

"Wow, you got it all planned out."

"Definitely. What about you? Are you gonna try out for junior cheerleaders next year?"

Actually when Yusef said, "What about you?" I was ready to

tell him about how I planned to get on the school newspaper and major in journalism in college and be a newspaper reporter.

"I'm not sure, I know Carla wants me to, 'cause she plans to be a cheerleader. But I guess I'm not so sure I can make it. I hear it's a lot who you know, and I'm not so sure I'm the cheerleader type."

"Don't sell yourself short. If you have a dream, stick to it. Just practice doing the splits and learn the cheers. And keep hanging with Carla; she'll clue you in on what you gotta do."

"Yusef, did you know they have a girls' basketball team at Southside?"

"Naw, I s'pose I ain't never thought about it."

"Well, they do, Willie Jean talked to me about going out for the team. Her sister Johnnie Mae's the captain."

I looked up into Yusef's face as we turned the corner, trying to get a clue as to what he thought about me playing basketball. I was hoping that at least he wouldn't bust out laughing. This was the longest conversation we'd had so far.

"I don't see why a girl would want to play basketball. I mean what would be the purpose? She can try to go with a basketball player and get to wear his jacket, without having to break her nails. Why sweat if you ain't got to?"

I took a deep breath. I wanted to make Yusef understand why a girl might want to play basketball, but I didn't want him to not like me anymore, to think I was a freak or something.

"Yusef, I think a girl can like playing basketball 'cause it's fun, same as a guy."

"I can see a girl like Willie Jean wanting to play basketball, 'cause, shoot, she ain't nothing but a tomboy from the getgo. I mean, excuse me, but some of them act like they got a dick bigger than mine. I'll put it this way, I wouldn't want a lady of mine playing on nobody's basketball team. Understand, kemo sabe?"

I groaned inside. Maybe Yusef wasn't all that great after all. But maybe if you wanted to have a boyfriend you had to go along with certain things. Nobody was perfect, and after all, basketball wasn't that big a deal. It wasn't like I was a boy and dreamed of playing for the NBA. I decided to just let it slide. Yusef had talked like I was gonna be his lady. I reminded myself of that.

"So, Yusef, what else are you gonna join next year?"

"I might join the chess club, if I have any extra time."

"The chess club!" I couldn't hide my surprise. I never would've guessed in a million years that Yusef played chess. I was almost surprised that he knew what it was.

"My uncle taught me how to play. Me and him play every time we get together. What you think, everybody in my family is a thug?"

Yeah, more or less, I thought. After all, Yusef's older brother Ricky was a known gangbanger. His name was spray-painted on buildings and everything: RICKY BROWN WAS HERE.

"For your information, my Uncle Marvin graduated from Morehouse College," Yusef said proudly.

"That's nice." I pretended not to be surprised. "Yusef, would you teach me how to play chess?"

Yusef draped his arm around me. I finally knew what it felt like to have a boyfriend.

"You wouldn't stick with it."

"How do you know? I stuck with swimming last summer. I learned the front crawl."

"Chess is a serious game, it takes a tough mind to really stay on top of it. Girls don't play chess. Y'all ain't got the concentration. Y'all'd be daydreaming about clothes or what color fingernail polish to buy and the other player would be saying 'Checkmate.' "

"Ha, ha, very funny. It just so happens that I wouldn't be daydreaming about what color nail polish to buy because I use clear."

"That's one of the things I digs about you, Stevie, you funny, you really funny." Yusef smiled as we turned up my street.

Actually I was dead serious, I thought.

We stood in front of my house and Yusef handed me my books. He reached over and pressed his lips on mine. I swallowed. It was the first time a boy had ever kissed me. I liked feeling his mushy lips up against mine.

"Jean Eloise!" I turned around. Oh, shoot, I said to myself, it had to be her. Mama was standing there holding a bag of groceries. She looked like she was fit to be tied.

"What were you two doing, entertaining the neighbors?"

"Mama, this is Yusef Brown, he's in my class, he plays chess, his uncle graduated from Morehouse College."

"Humph." Mama frowned.

"Nice to meet you, Mrs. Stevenson, can I carry that bag for you?"

Mama didn't crack a smile. "No thank you, Jean Eloise can carry it." Mama shoved the bag at me.

Before we could get in the house good, Mama started preaching, chapter and verse.

"I'm not going to stand for it, Jean, I'm not going to have it. If you're doing this at thirteen, what will you be doing at sixteen? You're not even allowed to date yet."

I started putting the groceries away. "Mama, it was just a kiss, and besides I didn't even know he was gonna do it. *He* kissed *me*, Mama."

"I didn't see you putting up a struggle." Mama pointed her finger. "And you better be glad it was me who caught you. If your Daddy had driven up and seen that, he would have lit into you right out there on the sidewalk. So you just better count your blessings. We work too hard to let riffraff come along and drag you down," she continued, helping me with the groceries.

"Yusef isn't riffraff. I told you he plays chess."

"Don't hand me that cat fat. The negro doesn't even look like he knows a chess from a checker. Humph, he'd like to play with your chest," Mama said from the refrigerator.

"Oh, Mama."

"Oh, Mama, nothing. Look, I wasn't born yesterday. I know riffraff when I see it! I smell a rat, mark my words!"

"Mama, you don't even know Yusef." I sneaked a couple of butter cookies as I put the box in the cabinet.

"Look, I don't have to know the nigger! I can look at him and tell where his mind is. Got that cigarette behind his ear, he's not fooling anybody. You need to stay clear of him."

"He just walked me home. Dog!" I groaned between bites of cookie.

"That's how it starts."

"Why don't you all just send me to a convent now so I won't have to suffer through four years of high school." I poured a glass of milk to wash my cookies down.

"Get smart with me, will you? You're not too big to be whipped, don't you forget that! Just because I carried that bag of groceries four long blocks, don't think I don't have the strength to wear you out. I'll do it if it takes my last ounce of energy."

I stuck my mouth out as I watched Mama put the eggs on their shelf in the refrigerator.

"Here I am the vice president of the Block Club Association," she continued. "I wouldn't stand out there in broad daylight and kiss your father, and I'm a grown, married woman. And you know how Mrs. Joseph and Miss Pugh stay up in their windows. Don't think they won't talk. They'll know more about what's going on in my house than I do."

"Mama, it was just a kiss."

"Don't talk back to me. Don't hand me that 'it was just a kiss' mess. It starts with a kiss. And I'll tell you one thing, Miss Smarty, you make your bed hard, you sure will have to lie in it. If you want to avoid a lot of heartache and suffering, you'll play ball with me. I expect more from you than the boys, plus you're the oldest. If anybody has to set an example, you do."

"It's not fair for everything to be on me 'cause I'm a girl."

"Life isn't fair, child. I'm telling you how it is. Nobody much cares what a man does. No matter how low a man stoops, he

coffee will make you black

can always get up, brush himself off, put on a clean set of clothes, and he's still Mr. Johnson. A woman has to consider her reputation. You think those busybodies in the window are gonna run to the phone and talk about what Mrs. Brown's son did? No indeedy, they're gonna be talking about Mrs. Stevenson's daughter, that hoe, that slut! When they get finished you would've been practically doing the do out on the grass! I know people. No matter what a man does, he can always get somebody. Baby, they got women who want to marry murderers on death row! It is still a man's world and don't you forget it. I'm telling you this because I want you to be somebody. And I won't stand to let anybody drag my only girl through the mud, not as long as I've got some fight left in me!"

"Mama, I've finished putting the groceries away. Can I go watch TV?"

"Okay, but you remember everything I've said."

"Yeah, Mama." I headed to the cabinet and got a handful of butter cookies.

"Give me a couple of those cookies." Mama stretched her hand out, forgetting about her diet.

chapter 10

I was sitting in my favorite swing at recess, just letting my feet drag through the wood chips. I didn't have the heart to swing.

"What's going on, Sally Sunshine?"

I looked up and saw Carla standing in front of me.

"Yusef asked me to go with him," I mumbled.

"Well, can't nobody 'cuse you of dancing in the streets."

"There's a catch."

"What's the catch? You gotta give up Roland?"

"Very funny. He wants me to pee with him."

Carla sat down in the swing next to me.

"Wow, I knew Yusef Brown was cool, but I ain't know he was this cool! Wow, Stevie, I knew you was square but I ain't know you was this square."

"Shut up, Carla, seriously. I told him I had to think about it.

I would be lying if I said I wasn't kind of scared. I wanted to get your opinion, okay?"

"Stevie, sometimes you have to get over being scared. You can't stay a baby forever. Look at it like this, it's just a body function, it's natural. You pee all the time. He pee all the time. The only difference is y'all will be peeing together." Carla looked at me like she'd just finished describing one of the most romantic things in the world.

"Would you do it?" I asked her point-blank.

"Sure, if Tyrone asked me, I'd do it in a minute." Carla snapped her fingers. "Just like that."

"Sure you would, like fun." I tried to call her bluff. "I never heard of you peeing with Tyrone or anybody else for that matter. You've never done it before, have you?"

"Maybe, maybe not."

"You would've told me, wouldn't you?"

"I don't tell you all my business." Carla tried to sound grown-up.

"Well, I bet you and Tyrone never peed together before."

"Who says it would've had to have been with Tyrone?"

"If you'd done it with some other boy, I'd know about it, wouldn't I?"

"Maybe, maybe not."

"Oh, stop being so doggone mysterious."

"Look if you must know, I have peed with a boy before, okay?"

"Who? What's his name?"

"You don't know him."

"Yeah, me and nobody else. How old were y'all, three and four?"

"No, I was twelve. It happened summer before last; I was visiting my grandmother in East St. Louis. You think you're the first girl some boy ever asked to pee with him? Folks been peeing together all over East St. Louis, way before you was born, not to mention the South."

I took a deep breath. Maybe I was making too big a deal out of it. I had to admit when I squeezed my legs together and thought about peeing with Yusef I got an excited feeling. Scary, yes, but exciting just the same.

"Well, how was it?"

"How was what?" Carla asked.

"Peeing with that boy in East St. Louis?"

"It ain't something you can really put into words, it's something you gotta experience for yourself." Carla started swinging.

"Carla, he wants us to do it after school tomorrow, behind his house." I started swinging alongside Carla.

"Stevie, you've come too far to turn back now. You this close to being Yusef's lady." Carla held her thumb and finger real close together.

"Okay, I'm gonna do it, Carla. I'm just gonna go head and do it!"

"Do it, do it, do it till you satisfied!" Carla laughed.

I started swinging faster. I wanted to see how high I could go.

I usually hated the fact that I always had to be the one to wash the dishes because I was the only girl. Mama and Daddy wouldn't hear of my brothers having to so much as rinse out a glass. But tonight I was kind of glad that everyone was out of the kitchen, leaving me to my dishes and the thoughts running through my head. I started cleaning off the table and thinking about peeing with Yusef tomorrow.

"How many times have I told you not to throw away my glass!" Daddy shouted. I jumped as he grabbed my hand over the sink. I watched the thin brown stain almost disappear.

"I thought it was empty," I said softly. There couldn't have been but a drop, I told myself. My wrist was hurting where Daddy was holding it. I was afraid to move it because I might drop the glass in the sink, and if it broke then he would really get mad.

Mama stood in the doorway. "You know your father wants the last drop of whiskey. Just leave his glass alone. I don't care if it looks empty or not, just leave his glass alone."

Daddy let go of my wrist and grabbed the glass out of my hand. He walked over to the cabinet and poured himself another drink.

"I'm sorry, Daddy, I really thought it was empty." He ignored me, which I took to mean that he accepted my apology. I could get back to thinking about peeing with Yusef, now.

I squeezed some Joy into the dishpan and filled it with water. There was the exciting, scary part about letting Yusef see what was up under my panties and me seeing his dick. But what was also going through my head was, what if we got caught or what if my parents found out? I tried to picture it in my mind. I could see Mama now; she'd probably have to lie down for a week. She would say over and over how if anyone had told her I would've done something like this, she wouldn't have believed it. If it had been one of the boys maybe, but not her Jean Eloise, named after her favorite grandmother, may her soul rest in peace. Then she would grab a belt. No, it was June, she'd send David out to pick her a switch. As she hit me, she'd shout, "Six summers of vacation Bible school down the drain! I'm gonna beat you till I beat the devil out of you. I'm gonna whip you till I can't whip you no more. I'm gonna beat you till I drop!" Then we would both collapse and I would be glad, because at least after hitting me she would feel better. Then she'd be able to pray for the Lord to show me the way.

If Daddy had been there and whipped me instead, I could picture him just going off, beating me to the ground with his belt, leaving welts on me, like he did on Kevin and David last month when they forgot and left their bikes in the yard, and somebody could've come by and stolen them. But maybe if Daddy had had a few drinks, he might be in such a good mood that he wouldn't let anything spoil it, not even me peeing with Yusef. Then Daddy might just go to bed or go back out into the street. Then Mama would cry and ask God what she'd done to deserve a no-good husband and a wicked daughter. Mama would say that if she had to stay on her knees the rest of her life she would. "Lord, just give me the strength to get through this," she'd pray.

I looked up. I had practically finished washing the dishes. I squeezed out some more Joy and started on the last pan. I couldn't believe I was gonna actually pee with Yusef. Mama always said the devil was powerful. Probably God would forgive me quicker than Mama. Didn't seem like peeing with somebody all by itself would keep a person out of heaven. What with all the worse things people did, like murdering and raping folks. Didn't we sing in church, "There is a balm in Gilead to heal the sin-sick soul, there is a balm in Gilead to make the wounded whole"?

My stomach was in knots and Yusef Brown was forever smiling at me from across the room. I had told him this morning that, yeah, I would pee with him today.

I hadn't done doodly squat all day. I was gonna have to do homework over the weekend. I would have to tell Mr. Cox I had been sick and that's why I hadn't turned in the assignments. I just hadn't said anything at the time, I'd say. I had it all figured out in my head.

Aside from being scared, I was excited about seeing Yusef's thing. Oh, forgive me, God. Me, an alto in Faith's Junior Choir, me, with almost perfect Sunday-school attendance. I wondered if there was really hope for a wretch like me. I would have to remember to ask Mr. Berry, the junior choir director, to let us sing "Amazing Grace" as soon as he could fit it in.

"How come you so quiet?" Yusef asked, as we walked between the bushes and his brick apartment building. I hunched my shoulders as Yusef opened the metal gate leading to the backyard.

"Just down these steps; see, there's a drain by the basement door."

I glanced at the backyard. It was all dirt, not a blade of grass, and there was a lot of old toys and junk lying around. It smelled like somebody had peed in it already.

"Don't worry, ain't nobody here." Yusef put his hand on my shoulder. "It's gonna be fun, you'll see."

It was hot, even for June. I squinted as Yusef pulled me toward him and kissed me. I felt a little weak and dizzy, like I was in a dream. Yusef started to unbuckle and unzip his pants. I squatted and reached up under my dress. I grabbed hold of my cotton panties. They felt heavy and wet on account of the heat, I supposed. I couldn't help but look at the bump in Yusef's underwear. We're just gonna pee, I told myself as I pulled my panties down from my waist.

"Stevie, Stevie, hold up."

I stopped and looked up with my panties hugging my thighs under my dress. It was Carla; I recognized her voice.

I wondered if my mother had gotten wind of what was going on and that's why Carla was here.

"Carla, what do you want?" I asked as she came through the gate. Yusef looked like he didn't know what to do, standing there in his Fruit of the Looms.

"I gotta tell you something. . . . I ain't never peed with that boy in East St. Louis! I ain't never peed with nobody!"

"Carla, you mean you lied to me?"

Carla nodded. "Stevie, I'm sorry, I was just talking smack, that's all."

I pulled my panties up and Yusef pulled his pants back on.

"What you talking about, girl? Don't nobody care about what you done, or ain't done." Yusef frowned. "This here ain't got nothing to do with you."

Carla ignored Yusef, "Stevie, don't go through with it if it ain't you, girl. I was wrong to push you into it."

Carla hadn't peed with anybody, she was admitting she'd lied. She was sorry she'd pushed me into peeing with Yusef. I couldn't believe Carla was saying all this stuff. I had never seen Carla look so concerned.

"How you know it ain't her, maybe it is her," Yusef growled.

A lot was going through my mind. I remembered when we were at Riverview last summer and I was scared to go up on the roller-coaster ride and how Carla had waved to me down on the ground. It seemed like I was always looking up at her. She'd gotten her period a whole two months before I'd gotten mine last year. For once, I felt like I could have something happen to me first. I would be the one to tell her how it felt. I was the one going up on the roller coaster, she was the one left on the ground. It was the first time she couldn't call me "chicken."

"Carla, it's okay, I'm still gonna go through with it. It was okay when you'd peed with somebody and I hadn't. I'll tell you how it was." I smiled. Carla's mouth dropped open like she didn't know what to make of me.

"Well, if you ain't gonna drop no draws, Carla, you can take your tail out of here," Yusef said.

"Forget you, Yusef Brown. Stevie, I'll wait for you out front."

"Stevie, you back here? It's me, Roland."

"Oh, shoot. Carla, you the only one I told. You tell anybody?"

Carla shook her head, "I ain't told a soul, I swear 'fore God."

"You better get that nigger out of here, now this shit done got ridiculous!" Yusef shouted.

We all stared at Roland standing at the gate.

"Roland, what are you doing here?"

"Stevie, I just couldn't let them do you like this, I went back and forth in my mind, but I just wouldn't feel right, not telling you."

"Tell me what? Do me like what? How did you know I was back here?"

"I ain't told you," Carla said to Roland.

"I hear your mama calling you, boy. So why don't you take your narrow ass outta here?" Yusef moved toward the gate.

I was confused. What was Roland talking about? Somebody had to have told him I was back here unless he followed us.

"Roland, you should leave, this has nothing to do with you.

And I don't appreciate you following me, getting all up in my business," I said.

"Stevie, don't pee with him," Roland begged.

"I ain't gonna tell you again to get your black ass off my property, nigger!" Yusef looked like he might hit Roland any second.

"Wait a minute," I shouted. "How did he know we were gonna pee together if nobody told anybody?"

"Stevie, I heard them talking about it in the john, they didn't see me. I would've been here sooner but Mrs. Verducci kept our class after school. And I had to do some detective work to find out where Yusef lived. They're hiding in the basement, at the window," Roland pointed.

I looked up. I could see some heads bobbing up and down, and heard laughing. I turned toward Yusef, who was cracking his knuckles. I felt my eyes filling up with tears.

"Yusef, how could you do this to me?"

"Yeah!" Carla cut in.

"Look, I don't know what you talking about, he's just trying to get next to you hisself. Ain't nobody in there stud'in you, they in there looking at baseball cards."

"Tyrone ain't up in there, is he?" Carla twisted her head.

I knew Yusef was lying: I could feel it. He hadn't looked me in the eye once.

"I hate you, Yusef Brown!" I pushed past him with Carla at my side.

"You ain't nothing, bitch! You think you something, but you ain't shit! And I better not catch you, you four-eyed faggot!" Yusef shouted at the three of us as we headed toward the street.

I couldn't understand why Yusef had blabbed to his friends and done what he'd done to me. I never understood before how somebody could hurt you unless they hit you. But what Yusef did hurt me worse than the slap I felt when I dived into the pool and forgot to tuck my head.

We had reached my block. "I'm okay," I told Carla and Roland as I wiped my face off with my hand. "I've gotta look like I just came from the library. Thanks, Roland, that was really nice of you. I'm sorry you had to be in the middle of this. I hope Yusef doesn't mess with you."

"It's okay, Stevie. I just couldn't see anybody doing you like that, because basically you're a very nice girl. And don't worry, I'm not that scared, although I'm glad it's Friday."

"He'll probably be cooled off some by Monday." Carla nodded.

Roland waved and headed toward his street.

"Stevie, Yusef done you dirty and had the nerve enough to call you a bitch. Did you hear him say you wasn't shit?"

"Look, Carla, I don't want to hear another word about whether anybody asks me to dance or not at the Graduation Tea, okay? At this point I don't care if I have to hold up the walls or dance with Roland or even end up dancing with Willie Jean, for that matter, okay? I just hope they have some good food, that's all!"

"You right, Stevie, sho you right, I ain't saying nothing else. Although you do have a whole week. Hey, a lot can happen in a week. If I was you I'd. . . ."

"Shut up talking to me, Carla." I cut her off and walked up my front stairs.

And if I wanted to play basketball next year, I didn't want to hear anything about that either, I told myself as I went into the house.

I sat alone in the kitchen with a glass of milk and a handful of Oreo cookies, thinking about what had just happened. Yusef Brown had done a job on me; he had really done me dirty. If it hadn't been for Roland, no telling what would've happened. My throat felt tight and my eyes began to fill up with tears, as I pictured myself standing butt naked in front of Yusef with his friends watching and laughing. I hated cold-blooded people.

I wished Grandma was here and I could crawl into her lap like back when I was younger, and feel like everything was going to be okay. But now I was too big for Grandma's lap and besides I couldn't tell her how Yusef had shamed me.

I remembered Roland and felt bad about the way I had treated him. He had risked everything for me. Roland had risked everything to be himself.

The next day I was on my way out to the playground at recess time. I had kept to myself this morning and hadn't crossed paths with Yusef. There had been a few whispers in the coatroom, 'cause like Mama always says, some people thrive on mess. But nobody had the nerve to get up in my face about what had happened.

Melody caught up with me as I headed toward a big rock in the corner of the playground near the swings.

"Stevie, girl, I got something to tell you if you can keep it to yourself!"

I wasn't in the mood for any foolishness. But Melody looked excited, and besides, she wasn't the foolish type.

I sat down on the smooth rock and looked up at Melody. I shaded my eyes from the sun.

"Stevie, you won't believe what happened! Girl, you know how Carla always says payback is a dog!"

I nodded as Melody sat next to me on the warm rock and folded her legs. She pulled at her blue checked tent-style dress so nobody could see her panties. I smoothed out my denim skirt and crossed my legs, just in case.

"Okay, Stevie, you know how you told me on the phone you were worried about what Yusef Brown might do to Roland?"

"Yes, so, did Yusef jump on Roland?" I asked, feeling scared.

"No, remember, I said payback is a dog. Well Yusef got the big payback!"

"What?" I couldn't help but smile.

"Dig up, Stevie."

"Okay, shoot," I said, surprised that Melody had become so cool.

"Okay, I was working in the office today like I do every Monday morning, putting teachers' mail in their boxes, right."

"Cut to the chitlins, Melody."

"Okay, but don't you want me to clean them first?"

I smiled; she had a point.

"Okay," Melody continued, jumping up and talking with her hands. "Who would come stepping in to see Mr. Davis, in a tight miniskirt and a red shell top, but Yusef Brown's mama!"

"For what?" I asked.

"She had an appointment with the principal. He called her into his office. Next thing I knew, I heard Mrs. Brown begging, 'Please let my baby graduate!'"

I raised my eyebrows. "Then what happened?"

"Well, Mr. Davis must've turned her off cold. 'Cause, baby, then Mrs. Brown proceeded to call Mr. Davis a white-ass motherfucker!"

I gulped; this was something. Yusef Brown wasn't graduating, and his mama had cussed the principal's behind out!

"What did Mr. Davis say?"

"He ran her out of his office. You should've seen her face when she left. Her liquid eyeliner was running into her powder, her face was full of sweat and tears. If she hadn't been Yusef's mama, I would've felt sorry for her. Especially 'cause while she was waiting for Mr. Davis she told me her 'frigerator broke down and one of her sons got shot two days ago and was in what they call stable condition, not to mention her no-good, two-timing husband had left her."

"Wow!"

"Anyway, when Mrs. Brown left, Mr. Davis turned to me and said, 'I'm sorry you had to witness that. It's people like her who give the Negro race a bad name. It's people like her who make it hard for the rest of you.'"

"So, Stevie, don't worry about Roland. Yusef's got enough of his own problems. I don't think he'll be stuttin' Roland now."

"Wow, Melody, thanks for telling me. I gotta go. I gotta ask

Carla if she wants to trade sandwiches at lunch," I mumbled, jumping to my feet.

I was at my seat, recess was over. It was almost lunchtime. I watched Yusef cleaning his desk out of the corner of my eye. He was trying to act cool, but his hands were shaking as he threw stuff into the green metal wastebasket. Everybody had been whispering about him in the coatroom. I still don't know how they found out. I just told Carla and she'd promised not to tell anybody. I couldn't help but feel sorry for Yusef, now that I knew his brother had been shot and their refrigerator had broken down and his daddy had cut out. I mean I couldn't be too cold; I still planned to join the Peace Corps.

chapter 11

I sat at a long table between Carla and Linda, munching on little chicken-salad sandwiches, green grapes, and chocolate cake. I couldn't believe how good the gym looked, the waxed floor and the crepe-paper decorations and balloons made you forget how funky the place usually was. All the girls were decked out in pastel-colored chiffon and other dressy materials. The boys had on their best suits and white shirts and ties. Every girl's hair looked freshly done. Even girls like Patrice who had "good" hair had made a date with a straightening comb before the Graduation Tea.

Mrs. Cunningham stood in the middle of the room with her hair down and wearing a lilac colored, lacy dress. She had been promoted to assistant principal last September, and was about to make a speech.

"Good afternoon, class of nineteen sixty-seven."

"Good afternoon, Mrs. Cunningham."

"It was the best of times. It was the worst of times. It was a tale of two cities." Mrs. Cunningham's voice sounded strong and clear through the microphone.

"Ladies and gentlemen, that is as true today as it was in Charles Dickens' time. We live in the richest nation in the world and yet some of our children go to bed hungry. Dr. King is preaching love and yet many still practice hate. They say we have a generation gap. Your music is too loud, your hair is too long, your skirts are too short, and we are sending nineteen-year-olds to a place called Vietnam. Some of them aren't coming back or are coming home in body bags."

Mrs. Cunningham paused and looked around at our faces. I felt a lump in my throat. I knew that everyone was thinking about Michael Dunn's older brother, Donald, who had recently been killed in action. I glanced in Michael's direction and saw Calvin put his hand on his shoulder. Michael's eyes were clouded with tears. It seemed like a long time ago when Michael had asked me if I was a virgin.

"We still have prejudice and discrimination," Mrs. Cunningham continued. "Dr. King's dream has not been realized. Our cities have exploded in the summertime. And yet you young people have opportunities that your parents only dreamed of. You can make it if you try. You can do anything you set your minds to. But I bet more of you can tell me what the number-one record is this week than what year the Magna Carta was signed." Mrs. Cunningham stared us down.

Peaches jumped up out of her seat and shouted, "What you want, baby, I got it, ooh. What you need, you know I got it, ooh. All I'm asking for is a little respect!" Peaches gave a few claps and sat back down. Lots of kids giggled and some applauded.

"All right, settle down, young people, I hope you will channel that energy toward making the world a better place. I know you'd rather hear Aretha Franklin at this point, but in closing, I'd just like to congratulate you and say that you've earned it. And I hope that whatever you become you will strive to be the best. Whatever you do, bad or good, will always reflect on your

entire race. Remember that and make us proud. Good luck, and
may God bless you, class of 1967!"

Mrs. Cunningham grinned as we clapped loudly, partly because we were proud and partly because we were glad she was
finished.

I felt a little nervous as I sipped frappe and stared at the dance
area. What if no boy asked me to dance, how could I not feel
like a loser? I almost hoped that no one would ask Melody or
Linda to dance. I felt guilty, but they say misery loves company.
I figured Carla, Patrice, and Tanya would hardly get a chance
to sit down.

"Tell It Like It Is" was playing. Oh, no, I thought, why start
with a slow song? I waited for Tyrone to walk over and ask
Carla to dance. Carla was ready in her pink chiffon dress and
matching dyed shoes and purse. I was no small potatoes in the
turquoise rayon Empire-style dress that Mama had made from
a Vogue pattern.

To my surprise, Tyrone continued to laugh and talk with his
friends. No boys made a move to ask anybody to dance. Only
the girls stared at the dance floor or looked around the room
desperately.

"They just 'shamed to slow dance," Carla said.

Oh yeah, that explains it, I thought.

"All right, 'I Heard It Through the Grapevine'!" Patrice
shouted, snapping her fingers and shaking her head.

Tanya stood up and danced at her seat, practically drooling.
But not one boy seemed interested. They were too busy joking
and giving each other five and getting more cake.

"Look, there go a couple dancing," Linda said, sounding
hopeful. I was surprised to turn and see Roland dancing with
Willie Jean. Even Carla looked jealous. She couldn't knock
them because at least they were dancing.

"Respect" came on, and I decided to take matters into my
own hands. "Melody, Linda, Patrice, Tanya, Carla, let's do a
line.' To my surprise the other girls followed me onto the floor.
Denise and Gail wanted to know if they could join in. I nodded,

willing to let bygones be bygones. Soon practically all of the girls and some of the boys were dancing in lines. "Jimmy Mack" was playing, but everybody had formed a circle. I peeked through to see Roland come out of his blue suit jacket and get down. The way he was wiping up the floor, you would've sworn he was James Brown, Jr. It was like watching Clark Kent turn into Superman. If a square like Roland Anderson could become the life of the party, then anything could happen, I thought.

Graduation had come and gone. "Pomp and Circumstance" had made Mama cry. I had gone to Riverview with my crowd to celebrate. I'd had enough money and enough nerve to ride the roller coaster twice. Carla had teased me, saying I was nigger rich counta I had $10 in my pocket. I'd given Carla a dollar to ride the bumper cars again, and that had shut her up.

It was only eleven in the morning but it was already hot. You could tell today was going to be a scorcher. Me and Grandma were alone in the kitchen playing checkers. I was wearing shorts and a halter top and she was in her slip. There was no breeze except for the little metal fan blowing in our faces. Daddy was at work, David was out collecting for his paper route, Mama had gone to the post office, and Kevin was in the living room watching TV.

"You study long, you study wrong," Grandma said as I stared at the checkerboard.

I didn't pay Grandma any attention, she would say anything to win. I carefully picked up one of my black plastic checker pieces and moved it a space forward.

"Well, Merry Christmas, you finally moved. And I'm still gon jump you." Grandma snatched my checker piece and slammed hers on the board.

Grandma thought she was slick. She usually was, but I was

determined to beat her for a change. I studied the board. Grandma had jumped me and left herself wide open to get jumped twice!

"How do you like them apples?" I laughed, holding up two of her red pieces.

Grandma wrinkled her forehead and wiped the sweat off her face with a paper towel. "That's okay, you ain't winning this game. 'Cause it's many a slip between the cup and the lip."

Mama dragged into the kitchen waving an old church fan. She was wearing a white sleeveless blouse and a pair of beige shorts. She looked good; she'd lost ten pounds recently. Grandma glanced up at Mama after moving her king.

"Thought you got lost. Did they have a long line at the post office?"

"No longer than usual, but you won't believe what I saw! I mean I thought I had seen and heard everything, but this beat Bob's tail."

"What did you see, Mama?" I looked up from the game. When Mama said something beat Bob's tail, she was as close as a Christian woman could get to needing a drink.

"It was spray-painted on the side of a building. It said BLACK IS BEAUTIFUL, in big, bold letters!"

"Black is beautiful?" me and Grandma repeated.

"Yes, 'Black is beautiful.' Have either one of you ever heard such a thing before?"

Me and Grandma shook our heads.

"I didn't think so," Mama said, fanning herself.

"Black is sho-nuff beautiful! Crown me, Grandma!"

"Jean Eloise, stop acting silly, this is serious. I've been asking myself over and over, What would possess a person to write something like that?"

Grandma crowned me, but she was quiet, probably because she was losing.

I turned away from the game. "Maybe he just got out of the insane asylum," I teased.

Grandma winked at me and smiled.

"Jean, I hadn't thought of that, maybe that explains it," Mama said, walking toward the refrigerator.

"Oh, Evelyn, Jean was just pullin' your leg."

Mama shook her head as she cracked open a tray of ice.

" 'Black' is supposed to be a fighting word. I've heard, 'Black get back,' 'I don't want nothing black but a Cadillac,' and 'Coffee will make you black.' "

"What does 'Coffee will make you black' mean, Mama?"

"The old folks in the South used to tell that to children so they wouldn't want to drink coffee. The last thing anybody wanted to be was black."

"I never told my children any mess like that," Grandma cut in. "I told y'all, 'The blacker the berry, the sweeter the juice.' "

"Well, anyway, getting back to the wall, I wasn't the only one who noticed it. I saw plenty of folks peeking out of the corners of their eyes, like they were being drawn by a magnet. Seemed like people were just making excuses to parade past that wall," Mama said, sucking on an ice cube.

"Lord have mercy! I never thought I would live to see the day when 'black' would be called beautiful! It makes me damn proud!" Grandma shouted.

"Well, you know I don't condone your cursing, or folks defacing property, but I have to admit that when I saw BLACK IS BEAUTIFUL on the side of the A&P like that I couldn't help but feel . . . well, sort of proud myself."

"Mama, Grandma, times are changing, I've heard some people say 'black' instead of 'negro' or 'colored.' "

"Jean, you can tell your children stories about what it was like, once upon a time when we were negroes," Grandma said, her eyes twinkling.

"I'll tell them everything," I promised.

"You two don't think this stuff is going to catch on, do you?" Mama asked between sucks on her ice.

"Hey, everybody," Kevin yelled from the living room,

"there's somebody black on TV!" Me and Grandma fell out laughing.

"See Mama, what did I just get through telling you?"

Mama looked scared and excited at the same time. Maybe like a virgin, I thought.

PART TWO

fall
1967

.

fall
1968

chapter 12

I was actually in high school! I changed classes every time the bell rang. I only had one class with Carla and that was Art. Southside High School took up a whole city block. There was even an enclosed campus just for the seniors.

I'd looked out of the girls' bathroom window yesterday and watched them standing around looking cool. The seniors were royalty as far as I was concerned. I'd seen a girl hugged up with a boy in a purple-and-gold school sweater against the big willow tree in the center of the campus. Carla had already told me that was where couples liked to go and kiss.

There was a big difference between grammar school and high school. At my elementary school you had to bring your lunch from home. But at Southside you could buy a hot lunch for thirty-five cents or cookies, potato chips, and soda pop from the canteen in the back of the lunchroom.

In the school hallways, some of the monitors were middle-aged women instead of students. They got paid to ask you where you belonged this period. They also worked in the attendance office. You had to go there and get a pass if you were late to your first class. There was even a security guard.

At Southside, we had a school band, clubs, sock hops, football and basketball teams, cheerleaders, the whole bit.

This morning, the window had been open during my Spanish class. We could hear the cheerleaders practicing their cheers while we struggled to say, "como está usted" and "bien, gracias."

I recalled the cheers better than my Spanish lesson. "Two bits, four bits, six bits a dollar, all for the Bobcats, stand up and holler! Went to the river, yeah man, started to drown, yeah man. Started thinking about the Bobcats, yeah man, and I just couldn't go down. Went to the railroad, yeah man, had my foot on the track, yeah man, started thinking about the Bobcats, yeah man, and brought my big foot back, yeah man!"

It was exciting to be one of the three thousand or so students at Southside High. But right now I felt small and lonely, as I searched for my study hall. And even though I looked cool in my turquoise velour top and my straight skirt, hoop earrings, and fishnet stockings, I was afraid to ask anyone for directions for fear that they would send me the wrong way because I was just a freshman.

"Stevie, hey, Stevie."

I turned around, smiling, glad to hear my name called in the packed, noisy hallway.

It was Roland, wearing a white shirt and tie and a navy sweater. He was overdressed even for the first week of school. But I was glad to see a familiar face.

"Hi, Roland."

"Stevie, where are you headed?"

"I'm trying to find my study hall."

"I've got study hall this period too. Is yours in room 256?"

"Yes, but I'm not sure where that is."

"Follow me, I know where it is. It's by the Boys' Gym."

"I'm glad I ran into you."

"So, Stevie, what are you going to get involved in?"

"Carla's already planning to join the Pep Squad. She says then she'll have a better chance to become a cheerleader."

"Sounds like a good strategy. But what about you, Stevie? I didn't ask you about Carla."

"Okay, if I get up the nerve, I'll join the Drama Club."

"You always said a good Easter piece at church as far back as I can remember."

"Thanks. Well, what about you, Roland? What do you want to get into?"

"I'm seriously thinking about joining the Afro-American Club."

"The Afro-American Club?"

"Yes, it's new this year."

"I know. But if I were you, I'd check into it before jumping on the bandwagon."

"Why? What's there to check into?"

"Did you see those students who refused to stand for the 'Star-Spangled Banner' at the assembly this morning?"

"Yeah."

"And the ones who stood up but turned their backs and raised their fists."

"Yeah, they were cool."

"I heard they got suspended."

"That's more reason why I want to stand up to injustice."

"You could pay a price. It could keep you out of the Honor Society. It could keep you from getting a college scholarship. You never know. There's a girl in my Spanish class who wears her hair natural," I continued. "She's in the Afro-American Club. This boy named Donald yells 'nappy head' every time the teacher calls her name. A lot of students laugh. I feel for her."

Roland shook his head. "That's sad. The white man has really done a job on us. We'll never be free until we stop hating ourselves."

"Amen to that," I agreed, as we turned the corner.

I couldn't believe it. I was hip. I was cool. But I was alone. I wasn't even walking home with a square or two from my Honors English or Honors Algebra classes, but alone, all alone. I would've even settled for having Roland all over me like a cheap suit. Where was he when I needed him? I felt so embarrassed. Girls in twos and threes moseyed along past me as though I were invisible. Boys strutted in groups, jumping up to make imaginary baskets, not giving me the time of day. I couldn't help envying the couples strolling along with silly grins on their faces.

How could this have happened to me? Let's see, Carla was with Tyrone. She walked home with me on the days he was in band rehearsal. My tenth-period Biology class had been packed with sophomores. Most freshmen were enrolled in General Science classes. I hadn't known hardly anyone. That's why I was in this situation now.

I decided to enjoy the crisp fall air and take in the sights and sounds along my new route. A group of street-corner men sitting on crates asked me if they could walk with me. I shook my head and smiled.

I noticed that the same three Jehovah's Witnesses I'd seen this morning were standing in front of the Currency Exchange holding copies of The Watchtower.

A woman outside a phone booth yelled, "How long do it take to tell a nigger to go to hell?" The young woman inside, cradling the receiver and a crying baby, didn't bother to answer.

I looked down at the sidewalk when my foot stumbled over a large crack. I suddenly noticed that there was an incredible amount of old gum stuck to the sidewalk.

"Come on, baby, I'll let you have one for five dollars."

I looked up to see a red-eyed man who smelled like booze, showing me some gold chains glistening in the sunlight. I shook my head and said, "No thanks."

"Come on, baby! Two for eight! They charge you twice as much for 'em in Jew Town."

"Sorry, but I'm broke," I said, walking away. Even if I had five dollars, I wouldn't buy a stolen chain that probably wasn't even gold, I thought. I went back to checking out the gum on the sidewalk.

"Say, honey."

I turned around to see a petite, brown-skinned man with a face full of powder. As Mama would say, he had some "sugar in his tank."

"Yes," I answered, surprised.

"Peek in that window over there and tell me if you see a tall, fine-looking man. He's a redbone, darling. I know he's in there, 'cause I watched him go in. I want you to tell me if it's a high-yellow woman in there with him."

I hesitated. I couldn't believe this man. Then again it beat looking at old gum spots. "Okay," I answered mechanically. I peeped through the slit in the heavy red curtains of the Peek-A-Boo Lounge. I looked for a man with a reddish complexion. The tavern only had about six people in it. I spotted him, sitting at a booth across from a woman who looked to be high yellow from where I stood.

I turned around and looked at the smooth-faced man. "Does he have on a brown leather jacket?"

He nodded.

"Yeah, he's with a woman," I reported.

The man scrunched his face up. "Ted really acted like he cared! He really acted like he cared! I got half a mind to kill both of them!" he fumed.

"That wouldn't solve anything." I tried to sound calm.

"I hates a liar!" The man stamped his foot. "I hates a liar! He swore up and down that they was through." The man wiped his eyes, smearing his black eyeliner.

"My mother says all men are dogs. Some are just more doggish than others." I said, trying to make him feel better.

"Your mama is right, honey. I should kill the sucker!"

I wondered if he had a gun. Because this little man didn't look like he could even whip Kevin.

"No, you might end up in jail. And besides you wouldn't want to have that on your conscience, would you?"

"It wouldn't bother me one bit to have that on my conscience."

I swallowed.

"But Ted and that hussy ain't worth going to jail behind."

"That's true," I said, feeling relieved.

The man sniffed and threw his head back. "Besides, mens are like buses. If you miss one, there's always another one coming," he said, clapping his hands.

I smiled. "That's the spirit."

"Thank you so much, honey, you are a beautiful person."

"You're welcome."

"Well, let me go catch this bus," the man said, switching away in his tight polyester pants.

High school seemed a million miles away to me.

chapter 13

"**D**on't you think you're a little too old to be spying on people? You need to forget about that sissy!"

I ignored Carla and strained to see through the slit in the red curtains behind the plate-glass window of the Peek-A-Boo Lounge.

"Stevie, you as pathetic as that sissy you told me about!"

I was just curious. Every now and then I looked to see if Ted was in there with that hussy. So far, I'd never seen him again.

"Carla, come look!" I shouted.

"Girl, I don't have time to be . . . "

"Is that a white lady sitting up at the bar, or do I need glasses?"

". . . peeking through a window at some old sleazy white broad some nigger dragged in the Peek-A-Boo Lounge."

I looked at the slightly plump red-haired woman sitting alone, hunched over a drink, supporting her head with one hand. She turned and looked nervously toward the doorway. I was able to see her face. It looked strangely familiar.

"Stevie, if you don't bring your tail on . . . It's cold out here." Carla started down the street.

"Carla, it looks like Miss Humphrey!"

"Girl, you must need bifocals!" Carla teased. "Miss Humphrey wouldn't be sitting up in the Peek-A-Boo."

"Carla, it *is* Miss Humphrey, 'cause that's the same green blouse she had on in Art class under her smock today!"

"Okay, this I gotta see. Sho is Miss Humphrey, I can't believe it!"

"Carla, she's getting up, she's walking toward the door!"

"Let's go, Stevie." As we turned away from the window, we bumped into each other, and I dropped my books and papers. I bent down and began picking them up.

"Would you two like to come inside with me?"

I looked up, surprised to see Miss Humphrey just smiling back. Carla turned around a few feet away.

"Come on, you look like you could use a drink." Miss Humphrey helped me up from the sidewalk and then motioned to Carla. She walked toward us kind of stiff.

"But . . . but . . ." I swallowed. Miss Humphrey just pulled open the glass door and pushed us into the dark room.

"Hey, C.C., two Shirley Temples for my friends." The shapely woman with a blond afro behind the bar nodded.

I turned around on the high bar stool, sipping my drink, which tasted like a 7-Up. There were two men in leather jackets playing pool. One of them had a bald head, and he reminded me of Isaac Hayes. There was an attractive couple at one of the tables, and a sorry-looking man was slumped over the other end of the bar. James Brown was singing "Cold Sweat" on the jukebox. I started tapping my foot and began to relax a little. Mama never had to find out.

Miss Humphrey pulled a cigarette out of her pack.

"Can I have a smoke?" Carla tossed her head.

Miss Humphrey hesitated, then handed her one.

Carla doesn't smoke, I thought.

Miss Humphrey lit Carla's cigarette. Carla coughed and tried to pretend like she was clearing her throat.

"I call myself hooking up with this nigger and it looks like he's turning out to be jive." Miss Humphrey muttered like she was starting to get pissed.

I scrunched my face up. Miss Humphrey didn't talk this way in Art class. I hated it when white people tried to talk like they were black. And Miss Humphrey sounded so phony. I guess she thought she sounded cool.

"Maybe he's on C.P. time." Carla blew out smoke.

"Huh?" Miss Humphrey sounded confused.

"Colored people's time," I said, acting cool.

"Oh, yeah, right, colored people's time. At first I didn't hear you." Miss Humphrey tried to play it off.

"Miss Humphrey, the button on your blouse popped open," I said, trying to be polite.

"Look," Miss Humphrey smiled, "let me show you something."

She pulled at her bra strap, showing us a small tattoo of a rose right above her left breast.

"That's really slick," Carla said.

"Yeah, it's pretty," I added.

"Do you get it, though?" We shook our heads. "It's a rose, and my name is Rose. Get it now?" Me and Carla nodded.

Then the front door opened, and a big, tall, handsome man walked in. Miss Humphrey's eyes looked like they were gonna melt. She turned, almost falling off the bar stool.

" 'Bout time you brought your black ass on in here." Miss Humphrey sounded more loving than tough. But I still didn't like her saying "black," and a teacher saying "ass."

"Thanks for the drink, Rose." Carla was putting out her cigarette.

"Yeah, thanks." I was heading toward the door.

"Why y'all beautiful ladies leaving when I'm just getting here!" the man said, laughing. I smiled, feeling shy.

"You want us to stay?" Carla batted her eyes.

"Yeah, come on back," the man laughed.

"Okay." Carla grinned, turning around.

"Okay." I smiled, following them.

"I just love to be surrounded by beautiful ladies," the man said.

"What time did we say?" Miss Humphrey frowned, looking down at her watch.

"Be cool," the man said, smiling. "I couldn't leave the plant till three-thirty. I had to go through some changes, traffic and what-not," he explained.

"What's happenin, mama?" he yelled to the waitress.

"Nothing, cool," C.C. answered from the back.

"Okay, okay, you're here now. James Robinson, this is Carla Perkins and Jean Stevenson." Miss Humphrey pointed at us.

"Y'all can call me James," the man said.

"You can call me Stevie."

"You can call me anything." Carla put her hands on her hips.

"Let's get a booth," Miss Humphrey said, grinding out her cigarette.

"I've got to visit the little girls' room," Miss Humphrey said after we ordered drinks.

"How come you with a white woman?" Carla asked as soon as Miss Humphrey was out of earshot.

James started clearing his throat and hemming and hawing. "I ain't with a white woman; me and Rose are just messing around," he explained.

"Well, how come you messing with a white woman when my sisters are sitting at home?" Carla wanted to know.

"Look here, the white man used black women during slavery and beyond."

"You just using Miss Humphrey?" I asked.

"Let's just say I'm a brother trying to get over, that's all. Hey, when the revolution starts I'll be right there on the front line,"

James insisted, patting his afro. "Rose is just a nice side dish, that's all," he explained.

"Don't you like Miss Humphrey?" I asked, still confused.

"I like what I'm gonna get." James smiled.

"You too cold," Carla said, grinning, "but you a bona-fide brother. At first I thought you was like my Uncle Willie. He told my Uncle Melvin, 'Man, you need a white woman to go with that car.' See, my uncle had just drove up in a brand-new Cadillac. I thought maybe you had a brand-new car too. Maybe you'd take us for a ride in it."

"No, Carla, it ain't even hardly like that, I'm driving a sixty-two Chevy. But that's a good one: 'You need a white woman to go with that car,' " James said with a smile. "I'll have to remember that. You need a white woman to go with that car." He laughed.

We all laughed, but I didn't feel happy.

I was drinking my second Shirley Temple, wondering if Miss Humphrey really liked James. "Sip it," Carla whispered in my ear. I looked across at James and Miss Humphrey and noticed that they were sipping their drinks. I stopped drinking and commenced to sip.

"I wish we were all somewhere really nice." Miss Humphrey smiled.

"Like where?" Carla asked.

"I wish we were all lying on a beach in the warm sand. The sun would feel so good against our skin."

"Don't nobody need a tan but you." James snickered.

"The sky is so blue, you can see just a few puffy white clouds," Miss Humphrey continued, closing her eyes. "Everything is peace and love and we're feeling groovy. You can smell the ocean."

"Do we have to go to school there?" Carla wanted to know.

"Just take it all in. We're in the school of life."

"Can I get y'all anything?" C.C. came out of nowhere.

"Just sink in the sand deeper and deeper on down." Miss Humphrey rolled her head back.

C.C. looked at Miss Humphrey like she was crazy.

James shook his head, "You might need to get this one a straitjacket, but I'll have another beer."

"Another bourbon please, and how about some goblin punch for my two trick or treaters?" Miss Humphrey kept her eyes closed.

"We're too old to go trick or treatin'," Carla said, groaning.

"Yeah," I agreed, "we're in high school."

"I got some hot cider," C.C. said.

"Rose, you were really trippin' there for a minute," James said, after C.C. left.

"No, I wasn't, I was just talking about something beautiful." She belched.

"Well, are you back to reality now?" James asked.

"Love is my reality." Miss Humphrey pounded the table. "I know what's beautiful; I'm an artist. These girls are beautiful. They think they're tough, but they're just innocent babies. Especially this one," Miss Humphrey reached over and held my face between her hands. "She has the soul of an artist." She still had sense enough not to reach for Carla.

Miss Humphrey pressed her forehead against mine. I wanted to tell her to get out of my face. I could smell the alcohol on her breath.

"I'm not a baby," I said. "I just turned fourteen."

"I'm twice your age," Miss Humphrey said. "You know you've got a long time to be an adult, but only a short time to be a child, remember that. So enjoy it while you can." Then Miss Humphrey kissed my forehead. I wanted to escape. I felt so embarrassed, plus I had to pee.

"Rose, leave the girl alone!" James commanded. "This ain't the Haight Ashbury, this is the South Side of Chicago. She ain't no flower child. Can't you see you're making a fool of yourself?"

"Excuse me, I have to go to the bathroom." I split the scene.

"Don't turn cold like the world," I heard Miss Humphrey

shout behind me. "There's no more toilet paper," she added loudly.

I sat holding a paper towel inside the bathroom stall.

"Stevie, it's me." Carla handed me a roll of toilet paper under the door.

"I'm glad it's you and not her." I sighed.

"Girl, I didn't know she tripped like that. I swear I'll never understand peckawoods. The broad really needs help."

"Carla, I didn't know what to say."

"She knew better than to get all up in my face like that," Carla yelled from inside the other stall. "I would've asked that honky what her problem was. I would've jumped bad, do you hear me?" Carla tapped her foot against the cement floor. "What are you doing in there, are you constipated?"

"No, I'm reading. Faye loves Bobby," I announced.

"That's nothing, Debbie digs Dick." Carla laughed.

"Well Cathy is a hoe."

"Shoot, Michael is a dog."

"Let's space this place soon," I said, flushing the toilet.

"Don't worry, we're at the library, remember? I told Rose our mamas think that. Let's just wait awhile, I think things might get juicy. Besides, James is what you call easy on the eyes." Carla laughed.

"Okay, till six," I said, combing my hair in the mirror.

When we returned, James had his arm around Miss Humphrey. Me and Carla slid into the booth.

"I know we've seen each other three times now, but I'm not sure I want to wake up next to someone who doesn't really care about me," Miss Humphrey was saying.

The conversation had definitely gotten juicy, in my opinion.

"Now all of a sudden you're trying to act so prim and proper. Like you're so deep," James complained.

"I'm not prim and proper, but I'm not superficial either," Miss Humphrey insisted.

"The hell you're not. I know what you see when you see me, Miss Lady."

"What do I see, since you know so much?" Miss Humphrey lit a cigarette and moved away from him.

"We got minors present, besides you know what you see." James raised his eyebrows.

"Don't let us stop you," Carla said eagerly.

I was ready to hear the dirt too.

"This is almost the end of nineteen sixty-seven," Miss Humphrey reminded him. "These girls aren't that sheltered."

"I thought they were innocent babies," James said sarcastically.

"You think all I see is a nigger with a big black dick, don't you?" Miss Humphrey blurted out.

James started to choke on his beer. Carla's eyes opened wide. Miss Humphrey had a strange smile on her face. I stared down at my cider.

"You've really shown your behind now." James grunted.

"No, I haven't," Miss Humphrey shot back. "Not yet, I haven't. You wanted to get real, well, I got real," she added.

"You got vulgar," James said.

"So tell me in nice language what you see when you see me, James."

James cleared his throat, "I see . . . I see a dizzy, insecure person, that's what I see."

"Does that rate higher or lower than a piece of white pussy?" Miss Humphrey asked calmly.

"No comment," James said angrily.

The air seemed full of electricity.

"You know I don't care if you see me as insecure or dizzy," Miss Humphrey said, taking a drag off her cigarette.

"You don't?" Carla sounded surprised.

"No, because you can still care about an insecure person, in fact you can care about a dizzy person," Miss Humphrey explained. "So, James, do you care about this dizzy, insecure person, as you put it, or not?"

"What do you mean by 'care'?" James asked, staring at his beer bottle.

"You know, like when you care about somebody," Carla chimed in.

"Just liking somebody," I explained.

"Yeah, do you like me?" Miss Humphrey bit her bottom lip.

"This is too heavy. I mean, next you'll be wanting us to sign papers." James pretended to laugh.

"Do you care?" Miss Humphrey laid on each word.

"I care about everybody," James said, gulping his beer.

"Okay, so you don't care, and you don't have the guts to admit it, or else you do care, and you don't have the guts to admit that, either." Miss Humphrey sounded mad.

"I've got all kinds of guts. I ain't scared to say nothing!" James insisted, scratching at the beer-bottle label.

"Well, then, say it!" Miss Humphrey shouted.

"Maybe he's trying to be nice," I blurted out.

"What do you know about it?" Miss Humphrey turned toward me, ready to attack.

"Nothing," I said, feeling scared.

"Rose, don't you know what time it is?" Carla asked.

"What's time got to do with it?" Miss Humphrey said. She sounded irritated.

"She means like wake up and smell the coffee," I explained. Yikes, Miss Humphrey looked at me again.

"Yeah, he's just a brother trying to get over. Look how the white man used black women during slavery," Carla said. James let out a sigh like he wanted to shut Carla up.

"How do you know this?" Miss Humphrey looked dead at Carla.

"I know my history." Carla smiled.

"I mean about him, he told you this, didn't he?" Miss Humphrey looked at James.

"She's just speaking in generalities." James continued scratching away at the label.

"He's been talking about me, hasn't he?" Miss Humphrey turned toward me again.

"I didn't say anything." I stuck my mouth out.

"You've got ears. Did he say he was using me or not?"

I looked at Carla; her lips were sealed. I looked at James; his mouth was open.

"Answer me, young lady!" Miss Humphrey sounded like we were in school. I remembered she was still my teacher.

"Look, he ain't said nothing really," Carla cut in. "She just don't want to get in y'all's business."

"Look at me, young lady, and answer my question." Miss Humphrey stared at me.

It was scary looking at Miss Humphrey, although she wasn't a bad-looking person. Her green eyes looked watery like a river, and I felt sorry for her. But I still didn't say anything. I glanced at James and he put a finger to his lips.

"I saw that. Don't play me for a fool!" Miss Humphrey yelled at him.

"Stop pressuring the girl," James said.

All eyes were on him now. I was glad to be out of the hot seat.

"If you want to know the truth, I guess I *don't* really care about you. Is that so terrible? So what if I am a brother trying to get over? I thought all you wanted was a good time too." James sighed.

It was so quiet at our table you could've heard a rat piss on cotton. Then the jukebox started playing "When a Man Loves a Woman," which I thought was kind of bad timing. Still nobody said anything. Miss Humphrey stared into her empty glass. Carla glanced around the bar. James was rolling the shredded label between his fingers. I thought this was a good time to go. But I was afraid to move, so I just held my hand above the lit candle inside the fishnet-covered glass container.

"Happy Hour is now over," C.C. announced from the bar.

Miss Humphrey stood up. "Girls, we'd better go. We've got a big day ahead of us tomorrow. We have to paint our masks, remember. Goodbye, Mr. Robinson."

"Nice meeting you," I said automatically.

"Bye, James," Carla smiled.

"Sure, bye y'all." James belched and started toward the bathroom.

I blew out the candle and dipped my finger into the soft, hot wax.

"Be careful, sweetheart." Miss Humphrey pulled my hand out gently.

"You can't take her anywhere," Carla teased.

"Forget you," I said as we walked toward the door.

"Forget you, forgot you, never thought about you!" Carla answered.

"Look, let's keep this between us," Miss Humphrey said once we were outside.

I nodded and Carla half nodded. I wasn't about to tell Mama, I thought.

"Miss Humphrey, I liked the part about the warm sand and . . . "

"Yeah, it's cold out here," Carla interrupted.

". . . the blue sky and smelling the ocean," I continued.

"Really, well, I'm glad somebody did." She sighed.

Miss Humphrey went to call a cab, and me and Carla headed for home.

"You and that stupid-ass ocean," Carla groaned. "Now you'll probably get a 'A,' and you can't even draw."

"I don't have to be able to draw; I've got the soul of an artist." I stuck my tongue out at her.

"You better just bring your butt on." Carla ran ahead.

I was still thinking about Miss Humphrey and James and smelling the ocean, but I brought my butt on anyway.

chapter 14

I was headed for the canteen in the back of the cafeteria to buy my usual Friday lunch of potato chips and a Coke.

Carla called to me as I passed the line of students who were buying hot lunches.

"Girl, come get in line. It's sloppy-joe time."

I looked surprised. Carla and I never had enough money left to buy hot lunches on Friday. "Carla, I don't have sloppy-joe money."

"Just come get in line, girl. I got you covered."

I was still confused, but I grabbed a tray and butted in front of Carla.

"So where did you get the moolah?" I asked as we navigated our full trays through the crowded lunchroom.

"Rose." Carla smiled.

"Rose who?" I asked, sitting down across from Patrice and Tanya.

"You know, Rose Humphrey."

"Miss Humphrey?"

Carla nodded.

"You got lunch money from Miss Humphrey!"

"I got over like a big dog." Carla stretched her hand out for me to give her five.

I barely tapped her palm. Patrice and Tanya looked interested.

"You just told Miss Humphrey to give up some cash?" Patrice wanted to know.

"Carla, I just hope you didn't mention my name."

"Stevie, Miss Humphrey's crazy about you; you were my ace in the hole."

"What's that supposed to mean?"

"When Miss Humphrey heard that you couldn't afford a decent lunch today, she took pity on your poor black ass and dug deep in her heart as well as her pocketbook and gave it up for you."

"Wow, so you used Stevie to get over," Tanya said, crunching on potato chips.

Carla nodded.

"I don't appreciate what you did. I don't want some white person feeling sorry for me, behind a sloppy joe and french fries," I said angrily.

"Don't forget the lime jello."

I ignored Carla. "Getting over isn't everything to me. My pride is more important."

"Stevie, pride ain't got nothing to do with it. It's all about getting over, am I right, y'all?"

"I heard that," Tanya agreed. "Pride don't pay no bills."

"Shit, if Carla can get over on a honky, ain't no sweat off your nose," Patrice insisted. "Help that white chick work off some of her guilt," she added.

"Probably thinks she's a revolutionary now." Tanya laughed.

"Black folks got to get over any way they can," Patrice insisted, stealing one of my French fries.

"Yeah, Stevie, so enjoy your sloppy joe. It's free."

I bit into the greasy sandwich. "Carla, there's no such thing as a free sloppy joe."

Mama said she couldn't understand why anyone would want to celebrate a slave past. I tried to explain to her that we weren't celebrating it, we were commemorating it.

But, despite Mama's strong objections, I'd made it out of the house with my hair in a zillion braids and wearing a potato sack for a dress. Carla stood next to me in the hallway with her hair tied up in a handkerchief. She wore a raggedy cotton dress and an apron. I pointed at a girl walking by, with a sign on her big stomach that read: "The master done it!" Carla giggled and ran off to catch up with Tyrone.

"What's happening, Stevie!" It was Roland, dressed in patched pants with suspenders. He turned around and showed me the rips in his shirt. It looked like they had been made by a whip.

I nodded approvingly.

"Plantation Day looks like it's gonna be a big success!"

"Yeah," I agreed, noticing that most of the students in the hallway were dressed like slaves.

"Stevie, the natives are restless. It's time to tell the truth about our history. We weren't a bunch of happy darkies down on the plantation."

"No, we weren't," I agreed.

"Well, what did you think of the Afro-American Club?"

"That was only my first meeting, Roland. You see I'm supporting Plantation Day, don't you?"

"Stevie, the Afro-American Club is really talking about changing things. We're on the move!"

"What if you don't get the things you want?"

"The head brother, Brother Jamar, says we'll use 'any means necessary'!"

"Wow!"

"That's a quote from Malcolm X."

"Oh."

"Stevie, you should check out the *Autobiography of Malcolm X*. I'm reading it now."

"I never even heard of that book."

"You've heard of Malcolm X, haven't you?"

"Of course, I know he was a black Muslim. I remember when he died. My mother said she'd miss hearing him speak on the radio. She didn't agree with anything he said, but she liked the way he pronounced his words."

"Well, you need to get hip to his message."

"Dr. King is my hero."

"You can have more than one hero, you know."

"Maybe so. Well, lend me the *Autobiography of Malcolm X* when you finish with it."

"Right on, Stevie! Brother Jamar says, 'It's time for a new generation of black men to rise up and seize control!' "

"That was the second bell! Where do you two belong this period?" the short matronly hall monitor demanded.

The day after Plantation Day, we were sitting in Art class. "I saw a segment on the news last night about people doing some really groovy ice sculptures up in Minnesota," Miss Humphrey announced. "Did anyone else see it?"

Some people groaned at hearing her say "groovy." Me and a couple of other students raised our hands.

"Wasn't it neat?" Miss Humphrey asked.

"Neat," a girl named Kawanda mimicked Miss Humphrey.

"Hey, Wally, where's the Beaver?" Desmond rubbed it in even more.

Poor Miss Humphrey, I thought. She wanted to be cool so badly.

Everett raised his hand. "Miss Humphrey, how do peoples know how to do sculpture?"

"Everett, someone asked Michelangelo how he knew how to sculpt David."

"What he say?"

"I cut away at everything that wasn't David. Wasn't that a neat answer?" Miss Humphrey said as the bell rang. "Wait, Jean and Carla, I have something for you."

Kawanda and Peaches turned around to see what Miss Humphrey was talking about. They stood in the doorway and watched her drag out a cardboard box from underneath her desk.

"What is it?" I asked, not sure whether to be excited or not.

"Yeah, what you got?" Carla looked suspicious.

Miss Humphrey held up a plaid pleated skirt.

"I can't wear these clothes anymore, they're too small. I would normally donate them to Goodwill. But I asked myself, why do that, when I have a couple of students in my classroom who can't even afford lunch?"

"Tell her y'all don't need her funky old clothes," Kawanda groaned, as she walked into the hallway. "For real," Peaches agreed as they left me and Carla alone with Miss Humphrey and the box of old clothes.

Carla appeared speechless for once. "Miss Humphrey," I swallowed, "I know you mean well, but we don't need your clothes."

"Look, there are some really nice things in here. Some of them have hardly been worn."

"Is you deaf? She told you we ain't need 'em."

"Carla, I find that hard to believe. Especially since the two of you can't even afford lunch."

"That was Carla's idea of 'getting over.' I tried to pay you back, didn't I?"

"And I told you that I didn't want to be paid back, didn't I?"

"Look, we ain't piss poor, or nothin'. We got money," Carla insisted.

"Miss Humphrey, the only reason we don't buy a hot lunch on Fridays is so that we can buy a forty-five or fingernail polish or a magazine, stuff like that," I explained.

"Don't you get allowances?"

"Yes," I said, "but our lunch money has to come out of it."

"My younger sister gets lunch money and an allowance."

"Bully for your younger sister." Carla frowned.

"Frankly, I think you two are letting your pride get in the way here."

"Pride ain't got nothin' to do with it," Carla shouted. "We just don't need charity."

"Okay . . . if you say so."

The second bell rang and we headed for the door.

"See, Carla, I told you there was no such thing as a free sloppy joe."

We were at our desks, reading our Early World History books. Our minds weren't on the feudal system though. Dr. King had been killed yesterday in Memphis, Tennessee!

I'd been sitting in the lunchroom earlier when several students picked up chairs and crashed them through the windows. Now, most people seemed to think something was about to jump off. You could feel it in the air. You could see it in the way people looked at Mrs. Christopher, the way two people had "accidently" bumped into her. And neither of them had said "Excuse me."

I wished I'd brought my radio to school like Gerald. He held a transistor radio to his ear.

"Look what I wrote on the front of my notebook," Patrice said, turning around.

"What?" I whispered.

"Black Power," she answered loudly.

"Right on!" I heard myself say.

"Quiet, girls," Mrs. Christopher said, looking up from her desk.

"They turning it out on the West Side," Gerald shouted. "They done started rioting!"

The room rippled with excitement, people turned away from their classwork.

Mrs. Christopher sighed and ran her fingers through her gray hair. How could this white woman on the brink of retirement possibly control us now, I wondered.

I wasn't ready to start burning and looting, yet I believed I was just as angry as those who were. We as a people had been dogged for too long.

I prayed that nobody would burn down my grandmother's chicken stand. She and my uncle had worked so hard; they took so much pride in Mother Dickens' Fried Chicken.

The door burst open, and a group of students rushed in. "It's Nation Time!" they shouted. A brother in a dashiki, with a teke around his neck and a big fro stepped forward. It was Roland!

Mrs. Christopher stood up and faced the group. "You can't just barge into a classroom like this! Where are your passes?" she demanded.

All eyes were on Roland. I wondered what would happen next.

"It's time for a new generation of black men to rise up and seize control!" he shouted, raising his fist.

"Fuck this white-history shit," a boy named Carl yelled, slamming his book against his desk. "Let's turn this mother out!"

"Control yourselves!" Mrs. Christopher shouted. "That is not what Dr. King stood for. How dare you people disgrace his memory!"

The fire alarms went off and the class rushed to the door. Mrs. Christopher plastered herself against the wall to keep from getting run over. Carl slammed the green metal wastebasket against the window. We heard glass splatter on the pavement below.

"The revolution has started!" Roland yelled as we ran out into the smoky hallway.

Smoke was everywhere; the trash cans in the washrooms and the hallways had been set on fire. I stood with a huge group of students outside the redbrick school building. The principal had stepped out earlier with a bullhorn, telling us to go home. A few students had thrown rocks, one had hit his pink bald head. I'd seen blood on Mr. Finklestein's face before he ran back into the building.

We faced a line of policemen in riot gear, who rubbed their nightsticks and yelled for us to disperse. The firemen unrolled their hoses while some students chanted "Let the motherfucker burn! Let the motherfucker burn!"

My heart pounded. I wondered if the police would shoot rubber bullets into the air.

"Patrice, we better go. Somebody could get hurt."

"There's way more of us than there is of them," Patrice pointed out.

"Sister, if anybody gets hurt, it's gonna be the pigs!" A brother I'd seen selling Black Panther newspapers shouted.

Suddenly, my eyes felt like they were being ripped out of their sockets. My throat burned. The spring air had a white tint to it. People were running and moaning.

"We've been tear-gassed!" somebody shouted.

I'd read about it and I'd heard about it. But I never thought it would happen to me.

After washing the tear-gas out of my eyes, I rode two buses to get to Mother Dickens' Fried Chicken Stand and into Grandma's arms.

An old man on the first bus, whose face reminded me of brown leather, had shouted that he was "tired of marching" and "the hell with nonviolence!" It was like the whole bus full of us black folks felt his anger, frustration, and pain.

Outside on the street, I'd seen older people standing around as if dazed. Young men were pacing around restlessly, like the lions at Brookfield Zoo.

"Where's Kevin and David? Are they okay?"

I nodded. "They're at home. I stopped there first. Our school was on fire!"

"I heard, I already called over there. They said the fire was under control."

"Grandma, I'm scared. I heard on the radio that they've already started rioting on the West Side. It could spread to the South Side. This neighborhood could be next. Everything you and Uncle Franklin and Aunt Connie worked for could go up in smoke."

"All black people are going to do is tear up our own neighborhoods. We never get angry enough to strike out at the white man." Grandma sighed.

Uncle Franklin was calling for a chicken sandwich and a chicken dinner.

"I'll take the orders out, Grandma.

"Here, Uncle Franklin." He didn't greet me with his usual smile. I looked at the knot of black faces around the little store. People looked as though they were mad enough to bite nails. The tension was so thick you could cut it with a knife. To add insult to injury, a man walked in with a white girl! All eyes were on them. The sisters' eyes narrowed like darts. I ducked into the back to fill another order.

"Grandma, a man just walked in with a white girl! She even has the nerve to be blonde."

"Those fools may as well be throwing gasoline on a fire!" Grandma shouted.

I shook my head and returned with two chicken orders and a couple of little sweet-potato pies.

Things had gone from bad to worse. The couple was wedged into a corner between the Coke machine and the plate-glass window.

"Was yo mama white? That's what I want to know!" A big dark-skinned sister with a short afro demanded.

Before the man could answer, another sister said, "Tell me he couldn't find *one* black woman. The bitch ain't even cute."

The white girl was shaking.

"Where y'all from?" a tall, light-skinned brother demanded.

"We live in Hyde Park. We're students at the University of Chicago. But I grew up here in Englewood though." He swallowed.

"Your behind grew up in Englewood?"

The man nodded. "I graduated from Englewood High."

"Well, nigger, I'd say you forgot where you came from. Think cause you in somebody's college you too good for your own people, huh? Y'all call y'all self slumming?"

"No, not at all. I just wanted Linda to taste Mother Dickens' fried chicken," he answered weakly.

"You spit on me while you were talking," a sister shouted.

"You spit on my lady!" the tall light-skinned brother insisted.

"I didn't mean to."

"What you mean you ain't mean to? You spit in the black woman's face when you come in here with your white hoe!"

"Keith, please, let's just go," the white girl pleaded.

Keith ignored Linda. "Man, you didn't have to call her a hoe."

"I'll call her a hoe anytime I get ready!" The brother grabbed a Coke bottle from the counter and raised it over Keith's head. "I wish you would tell me you don't like me calling that white bitch a hoe again, 'cause I'm a minute off your ass!"

Uncle Franklin looked up from the cash register. His face was tense, but he didn't say anything. I sucked in my breath. Keith's face was sweating and Linda looked white as a ghost. Everybody waited to see what would happen.

"Say!" It was Grandma's voice.

"Hello, Mother Dickens," a few people mumbled respectfully, turning and looking at Grandma.

"Let's have a moment of silence for Dr. King," Grandma said, holding up her hand. The man with the Coke bottle lowered his arm and looked at Grandma. People bowed their heads. A brother removed his cap. You could've heard a pin drop. I was amazed that Grandma could command so much respect at a time like this.

"Chicken sandwiches and dinners are on the house," she announced, after a minute. The tension had been broken for now.

Grandma pointed to the interracial couple. "Get her out of here while you still can."

"Mother Dickens, I wanted Linda to taste your secret recipe. Your fried chicken is the greatest!"

"Thank you, son, but this ain't the time or the place. Now don't make me chew my chitlins twice."

The couple scurried away. Some people don't have the sense they were born with, I thought.

I followed Grandma back into the kitchen.

"I sho hope that Dr. King was right, chile."

"What do you mean, Grandma?"

"He said he might not get there with us. But we as a people *will* get to the Promised Land.' "

A few days after Dr. King was killed, the sun shone brightly through the stained-glass windows of Faith African Methodist Episcopal Church. The choir stood solemnly in their blue-and-white robes.

"Let us pray," Reverend Sawyer said to the congregation.

I stood with Mama and my brothers with my head bowed.

"Let us pray for this nation and for those who've lost so much in the rioting on the West Side of this city, and cities across the entire country. And let's thank God Almighty that despite our outrage, despite our anger, despite our suffering, the citizens of the great South Side of Chicago did not despair; did not destroy our own communities. For violence only begets violence. Vengeance is mine, sayeth the Lord."

There was a chorus of Amens, louder than usual for Faith. We almost sounded like Baptists.

chapter 15

$\mathbf{A}$ lot happened the summer after my freshman year. Bobby Kennedy had been killed two months after Dr. King's assassination; the Chicago police had beaten the hell out of the demonstrators outside the Democratic Convention while they'd chanted, "The whole world's watching." Mama had said over and over, "I can't believe they're beating white kids like that." I wouldn't have believed it either if I hadn't seen it with my own eyes on TV.

The country was in turmoil, but right now I was irritated that there was never enough time to deal with my hair after my sophomore swimming class. I hurried down the hallway, trying to beat the second bell.

"Stevie, I want you to sign the Manifesto."

I recognized Roland's voice in the hallway.

"What manifesto?" I asked as he caught up with me.

"It's a list of demands."

"What are they asking for, Roland?"

"Sister, they're not asking, *we're* demanding!"

"Well, excuse me. So, what are *we* demanding?"

"We're demanding a black principal, a black vice principal, all black guidance counselors, a black school nurse and that we not sing the 'Star-Spangled Banner' in assemblies."

"Wow."

"We're demanding that we sing 'Lift Every Voice and Sing,' instead."

"The Black National Anthem?"

"You got it, sister."

I couldn't help but notice how much Roland had changed. He was dressed in jeans and a green army jacket and combat boots. Plus he carried himself differently, with much more self-confidence.

Roland held out a clipboard. "You ready to sign?"

"Let me think about it. There goes the second bell. Right now, I've got to go dissect a frog. I'll get back to you, though."

"What's there to think about? Stevie, you're either part of the solution or you're part of the problem," Roland yelled behind me as I ran toward Advanced Biology class.

The next day was a cool Saturday but the sun was peeping through the hospital windows anyhow. Daddy had forgotten his lunch, and I'd told Mama I'd take it to him since I didn't have anything better to do before my hair appointment. The housekeeping receptionist had said, "Just follow the arrow, your father is right around that corner."

I could hear hollering, so I peeped down the long hallway.

I saw Daddy in his gray uniform mopping the floor. A short white man in a light blue shirt and black pants was standing near him, yelling. I stopped dead in my tracks.

"My ten-year-old kid could've figured it out, it's that simple."

"But, Mr. Donaldson, sir, it's always been one part solution to four parts water."

"I don't give a goddamn what it's always been, Ray!" The white boss shouted. "Things change and you'd better learn to change with them. That's what's wrong with you people, you refuse to read. You have to learn to think independently. Otherwise you'll be taking orders for the rest of your life."

I stood patiently waiting for Daddy to go upside his boss's head with his fist. Who did this white man think he was? But Daddy was quiet, he just kept on mopping, didn't even look up.

"When you finish here, go help Pluto and Billy clean up that mess in Emergency."

"All right," Daddy mumbled.

"If I don't keep my foot on you boys' necks, all hell breaks loose," the white man said, all friendly like.

"Mr. Donaldson," my father said as his boss turned away.

"What, Ray?"

"Wednesday was my birthday. I was forty years old."

"Happy birthday, Ray."

"Mr. Donaldson, I'm not a boy." My father's voice shook. "I'm a man!"

The boss's face looked red even from here.

"It was just an expression. Jeeze, you people are touchy these days!"

I bent over the water fountain as Mr. Donaldson rushed past me.

I peeped around the corner again. I watched Daddy kick the metal pail, spilling soapy water onto the clean floor. I waited a minute and walked toward my father, careful not to track on his work.

"Here's your lunch, Daddy."

"Oh, thanks, baby."

Me and my father both managed to smile as though nothing unusual had happened.

At that moment I decided that I would tell Roland that I was ready to sign the petition. I would do it first chance I got on Monday morning. I had made up my mind. Grandma says that there's nothing more powerful than a made up mind.

*

Having my hair washed always felt good. It was the only part I liked except for the talking. I sure didn't appreciate having a hot comb dragged through my hair. And curling irons were nothing to get excited about either. Carla's mother and Mrs. Tibbs, the other beautician at Watu Wazuri, were yakking away as usual. Watu Wazuri means "beautiful people" in Swahili. The name of the storefront salon had changed with the times. But Mama still called the place "No Naps."

Mrs. Perkins was straightening my hair with a pressing comb. Mrs. Tibbs was at the shampoo bowl rubbing a perm into Mrs. Jackson's head.

"Lean forward, baby, so I can get your kitchen. You don't want no nappy kitchen. You want to look pretty for the Church Tea tomorrow, don't you?"

I answered, "My old best friend Terri's going to be there! She's moved back to Chicago."

"That's nice," Mrs. Perkins said mechanically. "Know how I used to leave my kids each a dollar on Saturday morning?" she continued.

"Uh huh." Mrs. Tibbs nodded.

"Guess what I left this morning?"

"What's that, Darlene?"

"I left a note telling them to clean up the damn house!" Mrs. Perkins answered.

"I heard that!" Mrs. Tibbs laughed.

"I ever tell y'all about the time I ran into Henry at Riverview?"

"No," me and Mrs. Jackson said simultaneously.

"I don't mind hearing it again." Mrs. Tibbs smiled.

"Okay. It had been over three years since Henry had walked off and left me with two babies and expecting Carla. The girls had begged me all summer to take them to Riverview Amusement Park. They'd seen the commercials on TV."

"I remember they used to advertise that ride where the floor would come out from under you," Mrs. Jackson interrupted. "Anyway, I saved up till finally I had enough money and me and the girls went to Riverview. Y'all remember them black mens that used to sit up in them cages?"

I remembered the black men, who until recently had clowned while people threw balls that they hoped would dunk them in the water. I'd never forgotten the humid summer evening when I'd watched a redneck white man with a pack of cigarettes rolled in his T-shirt yell, "The zoo wants you!" and "Take this, you baboon!" I must've been around six.

"Hold your ear down, so I won't burn it," Mrs. Perkins commanded and reached for the sizzling hot comb again.

I obeyed.

"Anyway, who do you think would be sitting up in one of them cages?"

"Who?" I asked, cringing, as I felt the heat from the hot comb hovering near my scalp.

"Henry-no-good Perkins, that's who! Marla and Sharla ain't remembered him. But me and him stared each other down. I held Carla up for Henry to see her. That nigger had the nerve to look disappointed when he saw he had a third daughter. For me that was the last straw."

"I know it was," Mrs. Tibbs sighed, "hard as your labor pains was."

"I bought me as many balls as I could carry."

"No, you didn't," Mrs. Jackson said.

"Yes, I did too! I threw them balls and dunked that nigger so many times till it wasn't funny! I had to call somebody to come pick us up. I spent my carfare drowning Henry's black ass. I ain't never seen or heard from the nigger since. I called down to Riverview and they said Henry had quit. Told them the job was too much." Everybody laughed.

"Look, Mrs. Jackson is laughing so hard she's crying," I said.

"I'm crying cause this french perm is killing me," she explained.

"It burns so bad cause it's got lye in it," Mrs. Tibbs said and

turned on the water. "You gotta pay a price for beauty, honey."
Mrs. Jackson threw her head back under the running water.
"Seem like black folk gotta pay more for everything," she
said, sighing.

I could tell by the look on Carla's face when she walked into
the beauty shop to pick me up that she still hadn't gotten her
period. Carla had done it with Tyrone a couple of weeks ago
while his mother and sister were at a revival. Although I'd
known that Carla and Tyrone had seen each other naked before,
and Carla had watched his thing grow right before her eyes in
her own basement, I had been surprised to learn that they had
gone all the way.

Carla's sister Marla had told her not to trip, that she couldn't
get pregnant the first time. But when Carla's period was over a
week late, I'd gotten worried. When Nurse Horn had visited our
gym class, every girl was allowed to write a question about sex
on a scrap of paper and put it into a box. I'd asked if a girl could
get pregnant the first time she had sex. Nurse Horn had read my
question aloud and answered, "Yes, she certainly can." I had
glanced over at Carla and she had looked down at her stomach.
Carla has been in an evil mood ever since.

Me and Carla were sitting on her junky bed listening to
records.

"Did I tell you Terri and them are practically rich?" I asked.
Carla didn't answer, she just leaned her head against the blue
wall and made a new Afro Sheen spot. "Terri's got an English
racer bicycle, a cashmere sweater, her own stereo, and guess
what?" Carla didn't guess, she just continued crunching on the
pork rinds sprinkled with hot sauce that she was eating. "And
they've even got a color TV!"

I stopped to breathe and to look at Carla's face to see if she
finally looked impressed. She didn't. Carla had her nerve, I

thought, glancing around the crowded room she shared with her sisters, Marla and Sharla, and their two kids, Malcolm and Lakisha. Here we were sitting on a saggy mattress that her niece and nephew had both probably peed on, and you had to constantly knock the old black-and-white TV in their living room to get a decent picture. Huh, Carla was probably eating her heart out, I thought.

"Me and Terri used to be best of friends," I reminded Carla. "I even had a crush on her big brother, Reggie. I used to daydream about growing up and marrying him. I was so sad when they moved away. I wonder if me and Terri will ever be tight again. You think we'll recognize each other? I can't wait to see her!"

Carla took a sip from her can of Mountain Dew. "I seen the heifer over a year ago. Her and her mama was coming out of Sears on Sixty-third Street."

"Over a year ago? Why didn't you tell me you saw her? And why is Terri a heifer?"

"I didn't know you was still trippin' on her. Besides they had they noses so high up in the air till it wasn't funny. You woulda swore they shit didn't stink."

"Terri said they'd been back awhile. Carla, are you sure it was over a year ago?"

"Yeah, 'cause I was looking for me some Easter shoes." Carla sucked the hot sauce off a pork rind. "I called the bitch by name."

I groaned, "So now Terri's a bitch."

Carla didn't answer, she just sipped her pop. Mama would never let me eat in my room, let alone in my bed. I'd seen Carla and her sisters sit up in their beds and eat Kentucky Fried Chicken! Mama would have a fit if any of us did that.

"Carla, that doesn't sound like Terri. We were best friends from kindergarten. We planned to join the Peace Corps together when we grew up."

"Stevie, I don't think your girl is Peace Corps material."

"Well, anyway, I'm still looking forward to seeing her."

"Be sure and let me know if your Terri finds it in her heart to give you the time of day."

"Why would the girl call me to say she had moved back to Chicago and that she was going to the annual Church Tea if she didn't want to be bothered? Answer me that, Carla."

"Why did it take the girl almost two years to let you know her black ass had moved back to Chicago? Answer me that, Stevie!"

"We lost touch, okay? She got busy and I got busy. So now we're about to be reunited, okay?"

"Sho you right, Stevie. Look, that day I ran into her, maybe my breath stank or I had forgot my deodorant, okay." Carla sucked in her teeth. "Uppity ass bitch."

Carla was just jealous, I reminded myself as the record skipped. I fished in the soggy paper bag and pulled out the last pork rind.

chapter 16

I couldn't believe it, me and Mama were actually sitting across from Terri and her mother, sipping on orange frappe and eating fried chicken and potato salad in a far corner of the church basement. I'd recognized Terri immediately, despite her stylish haircut and the fact that she was taller.

All of us were stepping. Terri and her mother were wearing matching gold-colored knit suits that set off their light-brown complexions. I had on a simple, but sophisticated, rose-colored linen dress. Mama was wearing a jade outfit, and my brothers were off running around somewhere in their blue suits. Grandma was all decked out in chiffon that was almost the same color as the orange sherbet she was mixing with ginger ale at the main table.

"Stevie, I would've recognized you a mile away. You look the same, except you've gotten rid of your ponytail, and you've got a shape now."

Terri wasn't straight up and down anymore either, I noticed. We both had some breasts and booty to speak of.

"Even with your perm, you look like the same Terri."

"Have you thought about getting a perm, Stevie?"

"I just always get a press and curl. Carla's mother does my hair. Carla's my best friend now. You remember Carla Perkins, don't you?"

"Barely." Terri sounded like she might not want to remember her.

"Carla said she saw you and your mother coming out of Sears last year, around Easter."

Terri hunched her shoulders like it wasn't something worth remembering, even if she did.

"We don't even darken Sears' door now," Mrs. Mathews jumped in, picking at her little plate of food.

"We're regulars at Field's these days," she continued. "That's where we got these outfits." Mrs. Mathews stood up and turned around so that we could take in her clothes. I knew Mama was envying her slim figure.

Grandma walked over and set a sweet potato pie on our table. I turned my attention to it.

"Did I hear you say Marshall Field's?" Grandma asked.

"Yes, ma'm."

"My, my, y'all must be eating pretty high off the hog these days."

Mrs. Mathews took a sip from her coffee and looked up at Grandma. "Mother Dickens, I've learned that expensive is the cheapest way to buy."

"I'm scared of you!" Grandma teased.

"By the way, Terri, is Reggie still cute?" I asked.

Terri frowned at me. "Thinks he's fine. He's six feet tall, the girls won't leave him alone."

"You see David's over there, grinning in some girl's face." I pointed.

"I still can't believe that's little David," Mrs. Mathews insisted.

"Little David is eating us out of house and home." Mama laughed.

"Where's your brother, Terri?" I asked. "I thought I would get to see Reggie."

"Reginald and Terrence are out on the golf course," Mrs. Mathews answered. "Reginald is caddying for his father."

"A black golfer, my, my, y'all sho have arrived, huh?"

"Mother Dickens, there are a number of black golfers at Washington Park these days. By the way, where is Mr. Stevenson today?"

"He's working," Mama answered.

"Is he still at the hospital?"

"Yes."

"Is he still a janitor?" Terri asked and then looked embarrassed.

Mama swallowed. "Yes, he's still a janitor. He applied to be an assistant supervisor in the housekeeping department, but he didn't get it."

"They gave it to a white man, right in off the street," I explained. "They don't even have any black supervisors."

"And they don't plan to have any," Grandma snapped.

"They seem to always be hiring at the post office," Mrs. Mathews said with a phony smile.

"I'll tell Ray to look into it," Mama said, without enthusiasm.

"Stevie, you never answered my question. Have you ever thought about getting a perm? Everybody has a perm these days."

"I guess the thought has crossed my mind, sure."

"You can get a perm," Mama cut in. "We can afford it."

"Half the girls at my school are wearing their hair in afros now. Even Carla has one," I said as Grandma handed me a piece of pie.

"You know, Madame Walker inventing the straightening comb was the best thing that happened to the negro next to Emancipation," Mrs. Mathews declared. She shook her head and put her hand out to keep Grandma from giving her any pie.

"We learned about Madame C. J. Walker in Afro-American History class. She was the first black woman to become a millionaire," I informed everyone.

"How could the straightening comb be more important than the freedom fighters and the Civil Rights Movement?" Grandma asked.

I glanced up at the banner on the wall, WE AS A PEOPLE WILL GET TO THE PROMISED LAND, and the picture of the late Dr. Martin Luther King.

"Yeah," I agreed. "And plus I think the natural looks good on some people."

"Well, I've yet to see it improve anyone's appearance," Mrs. Mathews said coldly.

Mama sighed, "I don't care for the natural look either."

"My Afro-American History teacher, Brother Kambui, says that if the white woman can wear her hair in its natural state, the black woman should be free to do the same."

"I thought the negro's name was Johnson."

"His name used to be Mr. Johnson, Mama, but he changed it because he said Johnson is a slave name."

"Honey, don't you listen to Brother Watusi . . ."

"Brother Kambui," I corrected Mrs. Mathews.

"Whatever, anyway you keep right on straightening your hair, honey. Men don't want to be running their fingers through a bunch of naps, trust me."

Mama nodded. "You sisters will be walking around here nappy-headed with rings through your noses and next thing you know Brother Kambui will be marrying some blonde."

"Brother Kambui is a revolutionary, Mama."

"Why do they let him teach at your school?" Terri sounded concerned instead of excited.

"Revolutionaries are the main ones who are talking black and sleeping white," Mama whispered.

"What's sleeping white mean?" Kevin had sneaked up on us.

"Never mind. Here, get a big piece of your grandma's sweet-potato pie."

"Terri, are you still planning to join the Peace Corps?"

"The Peace Corps? Why, I'd forgotten all about that. Boy, that seems ages ago."

"Remember, we were going to teach in Africa? We couldn't decide between Kenya and Ethiopia, remember? I've still got my application."

"Stevie, you haven't changed, you're still so . . . idealistic."

"Terri's dad wants her to major in Accounting when she goes to college. He says that's where the money is. And he's with the IRS, he ought to know."

"Mom, you know, I really want to be an airline stewardess and travel all over the world until I meet a rich man."

Mom? Since when did Terri call her mother "Mom"? What happened to "Mama"?

"Stevie, what do you want to be now?"

"Oh, I can't decide between a newspaper reporter and an actress. I'm in the Drama Club at school."

"Ray wants Jean to become a lawyer, he says *that's* where the money is." Mama probably didn't want to be outdone, I thought, because Daddy wanting me to be a lawyer was news to me.

"Today, you can be anything you put your mind to. The opportunities are there like they've never been before."

"Yes," Mama agreed with Mrs. Mathews.

"Hey, when I grow up, I'm gonna be rich," Kevin said, finishing his pie. "I'm gonna have me a place looking out over the ocean."

"Which ocean?" Terri asked.

"The one we got right here in Chicago."

"Boy, you know we don't have an ocean in Chicago!" Mama shouted.

"It looks like an ocean, I know it's not a sea."

"Kevin, you mean Lake Michigan," I said gently, not wanting my brother to feel like a fool in front of people.

"Oh, yeah, Lake Michigan," Kevin mumbled, staring down at his lap.

"A friend of Terrence's sells encyclopedias; you might want to invest in a set. If you don't live in a neighborhood with good schools, an encyclopedia set can make all the difference in the world."

"We have an Encyclopedia Britannica and a big Webster's dictionary," Mama snapped at Mrs. Mathews.

Grandma wrapped her arms around Kevin and turned toward Mrs. Mathews. "I hear y'all's area is pretty much all black now," she said, smiling. "It sure did change quickly, huh? Soon y'all will be right back in the ghetto again, huh?"

Mrs. Mathews cleared her throat. I knew Grandma's dig had gotten to her.

"So far we've been able to keep the lowlife out." Mrs. Mathews raised her eyebrows. "I pray that we can continue to hold the line."

Grandma cut her eyes at Mrs. Mathews. I knew that she wanted to read her chapter and verse, but she had to be polite since we were in the church.

"Kevin, baby, come help Grandma, I need somebody strong with muscles to carry the punch bowl to the kitchen."

Kevin jumped up and made a muscle like Popeye and followed Grandma to the main table.

"Mother Dickens, your sweet-potato pie is screamin'!" A woman in a fur stole shouted from across the room. "You put your foot in it!" she added.

"Thanks, Sister Little." Grandma beamed.

Telling a cook she'd put her foot in a dish was a very high compliment.

"I see Mrs. Little still looks and sounds like a Baptist," Mrs. Mathews said, sighing.

Mama nodded.

"Stevie, do you have a boyfriend?"

"Not really, Terri, do you?"

"Not yet, but I'm working on it."

I glanced over at Mama. "I'm not allowed to date until I'm sixteen. Let's see, I've got eleven months, one week and how many days, Mama?"

"Now, Jean Eloise is just being silly, she's not really all that boy-minded. I'm thankful for that. I'd hate to have a daughter who was boy crazy."

"Well, Terri Ann isn't boy crazy, I mean she likes boys, which is natural at fifteen."

Mama cleared her throat, "Well, Jean Eloise likes boys, I didn't mean to imply otherwise."

"Otherwise." The word hung in the air like laundry with too much starch in it, I thought.

"Your Jean gives every indication of being normal. I think it goes without saying that we both want the best for our daughters."

I let out a breath after being pronounced normal.

"I've always been impressed with Stevie, ever since she was a little girl," Mrs. Mathews continued. "I was particular about who my children associated with from day one. That's why I'm about to go out on a limb now."

"Thank you, Mrs. Mathews. I'm just sorry that Jean Eloise has never made another close friend that came up to Terri."

I frowned at Mama.

"Please call me Regina. After all these years we should be on a first-name basis."

"And call me Evelyn. Anyway, Regina, you were saying, about going out on a limb?"

"Oh, yes, you see, it's so important that young people don't get mixed up with the wrong crowd."

"And these days it's more important than ever," Mama added.

"Yes, well, to make a long story short, some of the girls in our area have formed a club . . . "

"It's called Charisma," Terri interrupted.

"Yes, well, the girls are meeting to plan the first get-together, and I don't see why Stevie couldn't be included."

Mama was grinning and nodding and Terri was smiling. Hey, maybe we could be tight again.

"Will the get-togethers be coed?" Mama asked.

"Yes, Evelyn, but the young men are all gentlemen. And there is always adult supervision. These are college-bound young people, all from good homes."

"Is Reggie going to be at the get-together?" I asked.

"Of course." Terri winked.

"Sounds good to me." I winked back.

"Regina, I like the situation that you've described. Who knows, I might just be willing to lower the dating age, under the right circumstances."

"Well then, it's set," Mrs. Mathews said, reaching for her handbag.

The program was about to start. A large woman in a flowery dress was calling for everyone's attention.

"You remember Roland Anderson, don't you, Terri?" I asked.

"Yeah, he was always on the honor roll, wore glasses."

"We've gotten to be friends."

"Well, the whole family's gone militant. Roland and his sisters and brother don't even come to church anymore," Mama whispered.

"Roland just loaned me *The Autobiography of Malcolm X*."

Mrs. Mathews shook her head, "And they used to be such fine people."

"Well, all good things must end. Stevie, Terri Ann will be giving you a call," she added.

"Cool," I said, smiling. "I'll walk you all to the door."

I stood on the church steps, waving goodbye and watching Terri and her mother pushing against the wind to get to their big, shiny car.

"Come on, Terri Ann, let's get out of here before dark. This is Boogaville, remember."

I could have sworn I heard Terri say, "I sure hope she doesn't tell anybody her father is a janitor." Or did the wind distort her words?

I stared at the setting sun. My stomach was in knots as I watched it change colors.

It was Sunday afternoon, and me and Mama were in the kitchen. I was washing greens in the sink and Mama was cutting up a chicken and listening to church services on the radio. The only music that could be played in our house on Sundays was gospel. "I'd Trade a Lifetime for Just One Day in Paradise," Mama sang along with the tenor on the radio. She would listen to Baptist services all afternoon, even though she was a Methodist. The singing and the preaching were powerful enough to make a body want to know the Lord.

David walked into the kitchen and headed for the refrigerator. He'd shot up recently. He was only thirteen, but he was taller than me and Mama. He thought he was cute, too, even called himself liking this silly girl named Antonia Wilson. Mama said David must be smelling himself.

"Jean, I ran into Carla buying a hoagie and I said, 'Hey, baby, what's happenin'?' And she said, 'Tell Stevie, I got it!' I asked her, 'Got what?' She said, 'Nigger, just tell her what I said, she'll know.'"

"Oh," I said, letting out a sigh of relief.

"What did Carla get?" Mama asked suspiciously.

"Nothing, Mama." I cut my eyes at David for not telling me in private.

"Humph," Mama grunted, "you're not fooling me. I wasn't born yesterday."

"Later, y'all," David said, after gulping down a glass of milk and grabbing a handful of cookies.

I dumped the wet greens into a big pot and began filling it with water.

"Jean, you know, this might be a good time for you to inch away from Carla."

"What are you talking about, Mama?"

Mama was shaking the breasts in a brown paper bag. Some of the flour was escaping and settling on her nose.

"Get rid of her, Jean Eloise!" Mama said, as cold as a gangster. "Carla was never friendship material, let alone best-friend material." Mama shook the chicken hard. "It's time to call a spade a spade."

I felt myself getting hot. I faced Mama with my arms folded and my mouth stuck out. "Mama, will you stop trying to run my life? Carla is my best friend and that's all there is to it."

"Look, Jean, it was one thing when you were younger, but you're in high school now. You're fifteen, you'll be sixteen next year. It's time to cut Carla loose."

"It's time to cut you loose," I mumbled.

"What did you say?" Mama shouted with her hand raised. "Say it again so that I can slap you!"

"I was talking to myself."

Mama threw the chicken breast into the pan of hot oil. She jumped back to avoid the splattering grease. "One day, maybe you'll realize who your real best friend is. I'm the best friend you will ever have."

"Mama, how come you hate Carla?" I asked angrily.

"I don't hate Carla. I've always been cordial. Besides, I don't hate anybody. You know that I'm a Christian. It's just that you're at an age now where it matters who your friends are. You lie down with dogs, you should expect to get up with fleas. Who knows what kind of doors will open up for you if you get in with the right crowd. What do you need with somebody like Carla dragging you down for?" Mama set the legs and thighs in the pan.

"Especially now that you've got Charisma," she continued.

I stirred the pot of greens. "Mama, the club has nothing to do with my friendship with Carla, unless she wants to join."

"You've got to be kidding!" Mama said, shaking the chicken wings in the bag. "They wouldn't let Carla join Charisma in a million years. You're only getting in by the skin of your teeth, you know."

I remembered Terri's remark about Daddy being a janitor. I wondered why she hadn't called yet, and if she ever would. The lump in my throat felt as big as the piece of salt pork floating in the greens.

Mama had called me to the phone and whispered excitedly, "It's Terri!" I had almost given up on her. It had been two weeks. I took the phone back to the ironing board in the dining room so Mama wouldn't be breathing down my neck.

"Guess what, Stevie? This is so cool you won't believe it." Terri sounded happy.

"What, Terri? You met somebody fine?"

"No, Stevie, but I'm working on it."

"I can't guess, just tell me."

"Okay, we all came up with this really cool idea. Charisma's having a party a week from this Saturday. Are you free?"

"Sure. Sounds good." I held the phone under one ear while I pressed Kevin's shirt.

"Now, here's the super-cool part. Okay, there's this one girl, Roberta, who's started wearing her hair in a natural. Anyway, none of the girls in Charisma have afros."

"Is it a rule?"

"You just don't do it in Charisma, okay? Anyway, this one girl, Beverly, has a brother, Alonzo. . . . Anyway, Beverly had this really cool idea that nobody should ask Roberta to dance on accounta her hair. Alonzo told the guys and they are all for it. Roberta won't know why everybody's avoiding her like dog mange. It'll be fun to see how long it takes for her to figure it out. See, Stevie, isn't it going to be cool?"

I sat stunned. This was the stupidest thing I'd heard in a long time. I was almost burning a hole in Kevin's cowboy shirt. I set the iron upright. I decided to think before I spoke. I didn't know if cussing Terri out was the right thing to do. I found my voice.

"Terri, I can't understand why anyone would want to do something like that to somebody. I mean, what do you all have against this Roberta?"

"We don't have anything against Roberta, she's just out of step with Charisma, that's all."

I folded Kevin's shirt. "Don't you think Roberta's feelings will be hurt?"

"I don't believe you, Stevie. It's only a joke!"

"I know, Terri, but why put somebody down for wearing her hair in a natural?"

"Stevie, Charisma is a social club, not the damn Peace Corps!"

"I know that Terri, but still."

"Stevie, this is nothing, you should see the dirt they do in sororities and fraternities. You need to talk to my cousin."

"What did Reggie have to say about your little plan?"

"Nothing, he was cool with it."

"Oh."

"Stevie, let's talk later. I've gotta run, I told Beverly I'd go shopping with her out to Evergreen Plaza. Stevie, think about getting a perm. You won't have to worry about your hair going back in the rain or when you go swimming. Besides, everybody in Charisma has a perm."

chapter 17

$\mathbf{M}$ ama walked into my bedroom grinning, carrying a brown paper bag. I was at my desk doing homework.

"I got you something, baby."

"What?" I asked, surprised. It wasn't my birthday, or Christmas.

Mama shoved the bag under my nose.

I stared at the small tubes.

"Toothpaste samples?" I couldn't hide my disappointment.

"No, silly, bleaching creams. I got them for free from a teller at the bank. You've heard me speak of Ivy, we eat lunch together. Anyway, her brother works at a company that manufactures these, and he gets free samples."

"But, Mama, you remember how that bleaching cream burned Aunt Sheila's face that time. She still has scars. I'm not going to have people pointing at me and whispering the name of some bleaching cream."

"Look, baby, this is some new, improved stuff. It's different from that mess your Aunt Sheila used on her skin." Mama reached into the bag and pulled out a tube. "Ivy's been using this and I swear she's two shades lighter!"

"Mama, being two shades lighter doesn't peel my paint. I'm happy with my color. If color means so much to you, why don't you use them?"

Mama sighed, "My life is behind me. You've got your life in front of you."

"Oh, Mama, please, you're not even forty yet."

I turned back to my geometry problems.

Mama stood over my shoulder. "Jean Eloise, you can't just think of yourself, you have to see yourself the way others see you. You've already got a strike against you with Charisma. You're from the wrong side of the tracks. You can't afford to be too dark on top of it."

"Mama, where have you been? Don't you know that black is beautiful?"

"I know that black is supposed to be beautiful, but you use these bleaching creams, just in case."

I looked up from the angle I was drawing. "Just in case what, Mama?"

"Just in case it's a fad and people go back to thinking the way they've always thought. Don't fool yourself. Deep down, black men are still color-struck."

"Some black men, Mama, not all."

"I bet the boys connected to Charisma are."

"Look, Mama, at this point, I can take Terri and the club or leave them. After what they said outside the church, and after hearing how they plan to treat this girl named Roberta."

Mama sat down on my unmade bed. She rubbed her hands nervously against her housedress. "What are you talking about? What did they say?"

"Mrs. Mathews told Terri they'd better get in before dark, because this was Boogaville. And Terri said to her mother that she hoped that I didn't tell anybody that Daddy is a janitor."

Mama hesitated for a moment. She had a sad look in her eyes. "Jean, you've got to act just as important as they do. Don't let where you come from, or what your father does hold you back."

"Mama, I don't want to act important, I just want to be myself. Besides, you don't understand. The club members got together and decided that no boy would ask this girl named Roberta to dance, just 'cause she's wearing her hair natural. Everybody has agreed behind her back to ice her. It's their idea of a joke."

"Well you know how I feel about the natural, but I don't agree with that. They should just be up front with the girl. Tell Roberta to straighten her hair or get out of Charisma."

I rolled my eyes and sighed. "Oh, Mama, what they're planning to do is just plain cold-blooded and it shows zero pride."

"Jean, I'm not condoning it, but who are you to talk about pride? Your best friend is Carla Perkins. What is she going to do for the race but have a bunch of babies on ADC?"

"Mama, you don't know that."

"Isn't her sister Marla pregnant again? Or is she just fat?"

"You mean Sharla?"

"One of them."

"Yeah, she is, but she's getting married."

"I'll believe it when I see it."

"Mama, I'd rather be friends with a bona fide sister like Carla than a snob like Terri any day. Me and Carla will be friends to the end."

"It'll be a dead end," Mama sighed. "If your father had spent half as much time studying as he did sitting in a tavern or at the bowling alley, he wouldn't be stuck in that dead-end job now. He'd have gotten promoted. Your father's problem is he makes the wrong choices."

Yeah, he married you, I thought. "Mama, you don't understand about the System and you don't understand about Charisma. I was making the wrong choice when I considered joining that stupid club."

Mama stood up, "How can you say that about Charisma? You need Charisma!"

"Mama, I don't want any part of Charisma any more than I want any part of these bleaching creams. And besides, they won't want me in Charisma because I'll be wearing my hair in an afro."

"An afro!"

"Yes, an afro."

"You're not going around here looking like a Ubangi!"

"Mama, it's my hair!"

"Well, I'll tell you one thing, I'm not paying for you to keep it up."

"It costs a lot less than a perm or even a press and curl, for that matter."

"I don't care if it cost ten cents, I'm still not paying for it!"

"Fine, I'll pay for it out of my allowance."

"If you want to throw your money away, Jean Eloise, and if you don't want to take advantage of opportunities to better yourself, then it's no skin off my nose. You deserve to end up a nobody, just like your father!"

I slammed my protractor down and stood up and faced Mama. "I'd rather end up like him than . . ."

"Than what? Say it so that I can knock you into next week."

"I'd rather end up like him than like you," I said clearly, looking Mama in the eye.

Mama slapped the side of my face, shaking tears from my eyes. I sat down on my bed and held my stinging cheek. I wanted Mama to take her bleaching creams and get out of my room. The hell with Terri and the club!

"If you plan on going around looking like a boogabear, Jean Eloise, then I'm through." Mama grabbed the paper bag and headed for the door. "I'm through, do you hear me?" She shouted from the hallway.

"Is that a promise?"

Mama let out a loud sigh. "And to think we used to be so close."

I could've said the same thing about Terri.

*

The barber finished trimming my 'fro, and sprayed Afro Sheen on it. He turned the chair around and I admired my reflection. My natural was big and bouncy, I imagined myself on a BLACK IS BEAUTIFUL poster. The girl in the mirror looked like somebody I wanted to get to know.

"How do you like it?" the barber asked, revealing a couple of gold teeth.

"I like it a lot."

"G'on girl, with your bad self, knock 'em dead," he teased. I felt proud as I walked out into the sunshine.

"What's happenin', sister?" a tall brother asked respectfully as he passed by.

"Not much, brother." I smiled.

"Mama, she's got a nice 'fro. Why can't I get my hair like hers?" I overheard a teenage girl say as I turned the corner. I smiled all the way home.

I switched on my bedroom light. A frown replaced my smile as I watched the culprit in Batman pajamas yawn and rub his eyes.

"Kevin, what are you doing in my room? In my bed?"

"I was looking for your diary, but this is all I found."

Kevin pointed to my Afro-American Poetry Book.

"Boy, did it ever cross your mind that maybe I don't have a diary?"

"Do you have a boyfriend?"

"None of your beeswax."

"If you have a boyfriend, then you should have some nasty stuff to write about."

"Believe me, as long as I have a nosy little brother, I will not keep a diary."

"Dog, what good is having a big sister if you can't read her diary?"

"Sit up, boy, and listen, I'm gonna read you a poem I wrote."
"You wrote it?"
"Yes, it's going to be published in the school paper."
I held the book in my right hand and wrapped my other arm around Kevin as we leaned against the headboard. Kevin reached up and felt my head.
"Your hair looks cool."
"Thanks." I smiled.
" 'What Good,' by Jean 'Stevie' Stevenson.

> *What good is a flower if it can't bloom?*
> *What good is expansion if you have no room?*
> *What good is a twig if it can't sprout?*
> *What good is a voice, if it can't shout?*
> *What good is life, if you can't be free?*
> *And what good am I, if I can't be me?*

Clap! Clap! Clap!
I looked up, surprised to see my father leaning against the wall in his bowling clothes.
"Look, Jean, Daddy's clapping."
"Girl, that was beautiful. And I like your new do, too."
"Thanks, Daddy."
"Jean wrote it. It's going to be in the school paper," Kevin bragged.
"Is that right?"
I nodded.
"A person who has a way with words like that is pretty special."
"Thanks, Daddy."
"I dream about everything you said in that poem. I just could never express it like you done," Daddy said with a faraway look in his eyes.
"A person with a dream is pretty special too, Daddy."
Suddenly, I felt proud to be a janitor's daughter.

PART THREE

fall
1969

■

spring
1970

chapter 18

"**S**he's sixteen years old, she's sixteen years old, she's sixteen years old, she's sixteen years old!" Mama, Daddy, the boys, and Grandma sang in a variety of keys.

I blew out the pink candles on the pink-and-white cake. Mama was still ramming pink down my throat. It didn't matter how many times I told her blue was my favorite color.

"Did you make a wish?" Kevin asked.

I nodded.

"What did you wish for, Jean?"

"Boy, you sho is nosey." Daddy rubbed Kevin's head playfully. "You is one nosy son of a gun," he teased.

Mama cringed at Daddy's grammar, but she just pulled the candles out of the cake.

"Come on, Jean, what did you wish for? Tell me," Kevin begged.

"It's personal. Besides if I tell you it won't come true." Actually I'd wished for a boyfriend, but I felt guilty that I hadn't wished for something like us winning the War on Poverty or at least the end to the Vietnam War.

Mama set a box in front of me. I pulled the pink wrapping paper and white bow off. It was a brand-new Smith Corona typewriter!

"Thanks a lot! It's super cool!" I hugged Mama and Daddy. "Just a couple of weeks ago, I was saying I wished I had a typewriter. This will help with my English paper on the *Canterbury Tales.*"

"Open mine," Grandma shouted, pointing to the huge box wrapped in white butcher paper with a big blue bow on it. I wondered what it could be as I tore into the paper.

"It's a new stereo! It has separate speakers and everything! Thank you, Grandma!" I hugged her. "You shouldn't have. But I'm glad that you did!"

"First, new bicycles for Kevin and David on their birthdays, and now this. Business must be booming," Mama said.

"Evelyn, what else am I gonna do with my little money?"

Kevin and David handed me their presents. David gave me *Aretha Franklin's Greatest Hits* and Kevin gave me Stevie Wonder's new album. Grandma must've tipped them off. I couldn't believe that Kevin had managed to keep his big mouth shut about the stereo. I was impressed. The boy was growing up; he was twelve now.

"Thanks, you all. I have to pinch myself to make sure this isn't a dream."

"You won't have any trouble keeping up with the Joneses now." Grandma smiled.

"This is better than having a party."

"I told you you'd come out ahead this way," Mama reminded me.

"Forget the Joneses," Daddy said. "I just hope we'll be able to put all three of you kids through college."

"I hope they'll get scholarships," Mama said, handing me the knife so I could cut the cake. "Our savings won't be enough."

David made a sad face. "A mind is a terrible thing to waste, y'all."

"You remember that and maybe you'll bring home a better report card next time," Mama said without cracking a smile.

"If I had came North ten years earlier, I could have got ahead quicker," Daddy said as I served him a big piece of cake.

"Yeah," Grandma agreed. "But you done well. You done real well."

"Mama, Ray, you make me want to scream, the way you're butchering the English language."

"Go ahead and scream," Grandma said. "Knock yourself out."

Mama ignored Grandma and began scooping homemade ice cream into little bowls.

"Ray, how can you talk about putting our children through college with the kind of example you're setting?"

Daddy swallowed, looking embarrassed. Grandma scowled at Mama. Kevin gave Daddy a sympathetic look. David shifted nervously like he didn't know how to react. Why couldn't she let the man eat his ice cream and cake in peace? I wondered.

"Tell your father what he should have said, Jean Eloise."

I was quiet. I didn't feel like siding with Mama so Daddy could look bad.

David spoke up, "Dad, you should've said, 'If I had come here ten years earlier, I would have gotten ahead quicker.' "

"That's what I said, 'If I had come here. . . .' "

"No, you didn't, Dad, you said 'If I had came . . .' "

"Don't you get smart with me, boy! Don't tell me what I said. I can't even open my mouth around here anymore."

"Evelyn, this ain't no English class. You're ruining the party," Grandma said, groaning.

"Good grammar is important. Like it or not, people judge you based on the way you speak. Now that's just the way it is."

"Well, it's my party and nobody's here to be judged. We're here to have fun. So everybody is allowed to butcher the English language all they want to," I declared.

"Right on!" Grandma clapped.

Daddy walked over to the cabinet and poured himself a taste.

Mama sighed.

"Happy sweet sixteen," he said, toasting me.

So far it had been bittersweet, I thought.

Uncle Craig had picked Grandma up and taken her home. Daddy had gone out to a tavern for a nightcap. Mama and the boys had cleaned up the kitchen after the party. *Gunsmoke* had just ended. Matt Dillon had gunned down the bad guys. Me, Kevin, and David were still in front of the TV set.

Daddy staggered in the front door, singing "Happy Birthday" at the top of his lungs.

Mama came out of the bathroom in her nightgown with cold cream all over her face.

"Ray, hush up! You should be ashamed for the children to see you like this."

Daddy ignored her. "Happy birthday, dear Jeanie, happy birthday to you!" He smiled, popping his fingers as he went down the hall.

Mama shook her head, sadly. "You see what alcohol can do to a person. Let this be a lesson to all of you. The key to getting ahead in life is not in a bottle. Mark my words."

"Mama, is Daddy an alcoholic?"

"Of course not, Kevin. You think I would be married to an alcoholic?"

"Dad just likes to have a good time," David explained. "Some people get happy in church, other people have a good time by drinking alcohol."

"How old are you? How old are you? How old are you?" Daddy continued to sing loudly from the bedroom. "I'm sixteen years old, I'm sixteen years old, I'm sixteen years old, I'm sixteen years old," he belted out.

My brothers covered their mouths to keep from laughing.

*

The next day I was sitting in the office of my guidance counselor, Mrs. Stuart. I'd seen her before but we'd never met. She was an attractive woman in her thirties with a caramel complexion. She wore her hair in a large afro and was a sharp dresser. I looked at the big clock on the wall. It was ten after two. Mrs. Stuart was ten minutes late. My homeroom teacher had told me that I needed to meet with her to plan my future since I had been accepted into the Junior Honor Society.

I was surprised to hear a white woman's voice.

"I'm tired of just being seen for my color." Nurse Horn sighed and ran her fingers through her short brown hair.

I watched as the school nurse followed Mrs. Stuart into the office. I'd been down to Nurse Horn's office with cramps a few times, so we nodded at each other.

"I want to be seen as an individual too," Nurse Horn continued. "I marched with Dr. King, I was arrested during Freedom Summer in Mississippi. Pamela, I'm not just any white person."

"Diane, do you think you deserve a medal?" Mrs. Stuart asked, folding her arms against her rust-colored suit.

"No, I don't think that I deserve a medal. But I am tired of black people who haven't paid half as many dues making judgments about me. I want to be judged by the content of my character, like Dr. King said."

"If you're black you don't have to march to pay dues, Diane. You pay dues just by breathing." Mrs. Stuart glanced at me. "Jean, sorry to have kept you waiting. I'll be with you as soon as I can."

"That's okay, I'm not in any rush."

"Pamela, how can things ever change if we don't get to know each other as people? What did we march for anyway?"

"I marched with Dr. King too, Diane. And I didn't march just so that black folks and white folks could be bosom buddies. I marched for equal opportunity and justice."

"Well, as long as the black teachers sit at one end of the teachers' lunchroom and the white teachers sit at the other end, what's the difference between today and the fifties? We may as well go back to separate but equal."

"Look, it was separate but it was never equal. Was it, Jean?"

I shook my head, remembering the picture of the two water fountains in my Afro-American History book.

"White people have made it quite clear that they don't want to live next door to us. Haven't they, Jean?"

I nodded.

"*Some* white people. I don't appreciate being lumped together with all white people, Pamela."

Mrs. Stuart continued, "All it takes is for one black family to move into a neighborhood, and the FOR SALE signs go up so fast it makes your head spin. And white folks have made it crystal clear that they don't want their children to go to school with us. Haven't they, Jean?"

"That's true," I agreed. Nurse Horn looked at me with her soft gray eyes. I didn't have anything against her, but the truth was the truth. What else could I say?

"*Some* white people, Pamela."

"Like Jesse Jackson says, 'It's not the bus. It's us!' So no wonder we need to separate to figure out who we are as black people. How much rejection can you expect people to take? Right, Jean?"

"Right," I answered. I mean, Mrs. Stuart had a point.

"So does that mean if I see you sitting with black teachers at a table and I join you, you will pretend I'm not there again?"

"When I taught at a white school over on the Northwest side, I had to sit alone. I had to eat alone . . . no one gave me the time of day. Sometimes I felt like I was invisible."

"Is that how you want me to feel?"

"Look, Diane, if you come into the teacher's room and I'm alone, you can join me. Otherwise, wait for an invitation, okay?"

"I'm supposed to forget you're black on one hand and then, on the other hand, I'm never supposed to forget you're black. Is that it?"

"That's what we have to do. Isn't that so, Jean?"

For an odd moment, Nurse Horn and I exchanged glances.

chapter 19

I grabbed a handful of junk out of the locker next to mine. It had been vacant since the beginning of the school year. A tall stranger, wearing a navy pea coat, stood in front of the locker holding a briefcase and a combination lock.

"I'm sorry, I didn't know it had been assigned to anybody. I guess I'll never get the Good Housekeeping seal."

"That's okay." He smiled. He was cute; he looked like Jermaine of the Jackson Five. Fine as he wanted to be with his bronze skin and big 'fro.

"Hey, haven't I seen you before?"

I smiled. "Aren't you supposed to ask me what my sign is, instead?"

"No jive, I'm being for real. It's your eyes, they're so pretty, I know I've seen you before."

"Well, it's possible. This *is* my third year here, I *am* a junior."

"I'm new, I just transferred in. I'm a senior. My name's Sean."

"You're a senior," I repeated respectfully.

He nodded.

"Where did you transfer from?"

"Leo High School."

"That's a Catholic boys' school."

"Yeah, I noticed." Sean frowned.

"Why did you transfer your senior year? That must really be hard."

Sean shrugged.

"So, how come you're starting over a month into the semester?" I asked.

"I went back to Leo and I just realized it wasn't my bag. I didn't want to be around nothing but dudes, and besides, I was tired of the whole Catholic trip. I'm ready to have some fun this year." Sean smiled.

"Won't you have to go to confession?"

"Hell no! I'm not Catholic."

"What were you doing in a Catholic school then?"

"Lots of black folks who aren't Catholic send their kids to Catholic schools."

"That's true, my old friends Melody and Linda go to Mercy High School and neither of them are Catholic. They go to Faith A.M.E. just like I do."

"I know who you are now! You denied me!"

"Denied you! Denied you what?" First I thought Sean was jive, now I wondered if he was crazy. Although he didn't look "off," you never could be sure.

"I was Jesus Christ!"

Sean was definitely off, I thought. I started to back away from him.

"Come back, Peter. You were my disciple."

"Oh." I smiled, a light finally going on in my head. The Easter play. "I remember you too, Sean! It's just that the last time that

I saw you, you were carrying a cardboard cross and you had ketchup dripping down your face."

"That's right. 'Father forgive them, for they know not what they do,' " Sean said.

"Before the cock crows three times, I will have denied him," I recited.

"You didn't stumble once, even back then."

"My mother said that me and you were the only ones up there who enunciated." I laughed.

"I remember now, all the girls wanted to be Jesus's mother or Mary Magdalene, the prostitute. But you volunteered to play Peter. That took guts."

"I was looking for a challenge. Neither of the Marys had much of a speaking part."

"You were great."

"Thanks. My mother made my costume. Two robes, the outer one was striped and the other one was solid maroon. She even made a turban out of the striped material."

"You were lucky to have a mother who would buy material and make a costume just for a Sunday-school play."

I remembered that all of the other kids had been draped in things like sheets, towels, bathrobes, and bird-cage covers. "I guess I was sort of lucky. So are you coming back to Faith?" I asked.

"We're United Methodists now. My uncle's church."

"Oh."

"By the way, what is your name? And your sign, while you're at it."

"Oh, I'm sorry. Jean, but you can call me Stevie."

"That's right, I remember now."

"And I'm a Libra." I smiled.

"I'm a Gemini. Hey, you're not hooked up with anybody, are you?"

"No, not really." I flashed on Roland for a minute, but I reminded myself that we were just friends. He'd never made a move or anything.

"Good then, let's say we go get a milkshake after school is over?"

"Well . . . "

"Come on, don't deny me this time," Sean smiled.

"All right," I agreed. I'd always been a sucker for dimples. Besides, my birthday wish might come true, I thought.

I had been rolling around in my underwear on the cot like a wild woman. Now I wrapped myself around the hot-water bottle and held it like a baby. Thanks to it and my Midol tablets, cramps were no longer kicking my ass. Throwing up had made me feel better, too. I remembered that Tyrone had promised to make a stink bomb in chemistry lab this afternoon. I couldn't wait to see the look on Mr. Eversly's face.

I sat up and blinked in the November sunshine that poured into the school nurse's sorry office. Nurse Horn was bent over her desk reading something, so I checked out the posters on the tired green walls. I studied the four food groups and yawned at the picture of the Red Cross nurse with the silly smile on her face. The posters got old quick.

So I started thumbing through a fashion magazine. Nurse Horn wasn't skinny or glamorous like the ladies in the pictures, but she wasn't fat, and she was attractive in her own way. She wore her hair short, not so short that she looked like she was about to go into the Marines, but probably too short for most men's tastes. I wondered if Nurse Horn would've found a husband by now if she wore her hair longer. She was pretty old not to be married; she looked every day of twenty-five, as Mama would say.

"How's the patient?" Nurse Horn turned around, smiling.

"She'll live, I guess."

"You guess? You seem a whole lot better."

"Yeah, I was seriously considering a sex-change operation."

"You'd have to go to California for that."

Nurse Horn walked toward me, and I noticed for the first

time that she wore a white terry-cloth bathrobe instead of her nurse's uniform. She felt my forehead like my mother did, first with the back of her hand and then with her palm.

"Jean, you'll be fine."

"How come you're in a bathrobe? What happened to your uniform?" I asked, pointing to the white dress draped over the heater.

"Oh, Crystal Jones vomited on me this morning."

I made a face. "Yuck!"

"All in a day's work. I keep this robe handy for just such emergencies."

"Crystal Jones threw up on you this morning. Morning . . . morning sickness," I whispered excitedly.

Nurse Horn raised her eyebrows like she knew she'd let the cat out of the bag.

"I didn't say that." She tried to pretend like I was totally off base. "And I shouldn't have mentioned Crystal's name to you at all." Nurse Horn let out a sigh as she shook the thermometer down and walked toward her desk.

"You didn't have to; the word is already out. This just puts the icing on the cake. Some folks say it's Calvin's baby, but Carla says Dwayne was Crystal's main squeeze a few months ago."

Nurse Horn turned around and faced me. "Shush. I don't want to hear another word about it. This is not some sort of game. You're talking about a person's life. And I won't listen to you make light of some poor girl's misfortune." Nurse Horn's eyes narrowed, and I could tell she wasn't jiving. I started getting dressed and Nurse Horn sat down at her desk and began writing out my pass.

"I'm supposed to tell you that a young man came by while you were asleep."

"Sean, that's my boyfriend. Isn't he cute?" I pulled on my corduroy pants.

"I believe he did say his name was Sean."

I stuck my head through my turtleneck.

"Actually, Sean is what you call fine, *and* he's a senior." Shoot, plenty of girls wished they could get next to Sean. Out of all the girls, I'm the one he asked to go with him. It was like a dream. I was Cinderella and he was the prince. I put on my boots.

"You're not in love, by any chance?" Nurse Horn turned around at her desk.

"I guess you could run a train up my nose," I answered.

I stood behind Nurse Horn waiting for her to give me my pass. But she just sat there staring out the window like she was in a daze.

"Did I say something wrong?"

"It's snowing. It's the first snow of the season."

"Yeah, but I bet it won't stick. I hope it does." I watched the puffy white snowflakes drift slowly to the ground. "How come you seem so sad? Will you have to shovel it?"

"Just reflecting." Nurse Horn turned around and looked at me and then went back to staring out the window.

"In a few months we'll all be sick of it." I tried to force a laugh.

Nurse Horn turned and looked at me again, but a smile was nowhere near her face. She made no move to give me the pink slip of paper on her desk.

"Jean, I guess I'm a little concerned about you now, frankly."

"Concerned about me, why? What are you concerned about me for? Hey, I'm not the one who's pregnant."

I didn't know where Nurse Horn was coming from; why was she tripping on me? I didn't want her putting me in the same boat with Crystal Jones.

Nurse Horn looked me dead in the eye. "Not yet, at least you're not pregnant *this* month."

I felt myself getting all hot around the collar, and I jumped back and put my hands on my hips. "You've got no right to say that. I've known the facts since I was twelve."

"Do you know that if you play with fire you're going to get burned? Do you know that fact?" Nurse Horn stood up and faced me with her arms folded.

She looked silly standing there all stiff, staring me down. Who did she think she was? I was even about an inch taller than her. "Who says I'm playing with anything?" I raised my eyebrows and folded my arms too.

Nurse Horn cleared her throat. "I didn't say that you were."

"Well, why are you all up in my business then? I came down here to get well, not to catch hell." I wished it was time for chemistry and I was learning how to make a stink bomb, instead of dealing with this mess.

"I'm sorry you see it that way."

How was I supposed to see it? I wondered. Why was this woman all over my case? Here I finally had a real boyfriend and I couldn't even enjoy it. Nurse Horn was acting like I was a baby or something. I turned sixteen almost two months ago. I was the only sixteen-year-old virgin left on the whole south side of Chicago, according to Carla.

"Look, even if I *was* doing something, how could you help me? Could you get me the pill without my mother knowing?"

"The only pills I can give you are aspirins, you know that. But I can help you determine what you want out of life."

"Maybe I don't want to determine what I want out of life. Maybe I just want to live."

Nurse Horn shook her head. "I just know what can happen, and I'm concerned, that's all."

"I don't need your concern; just because I said I have a boyfriend, you start getting on my case." It hit me that Nurse Horn was probably jealous of me because she was an old maid. But that still didn't give her the right to jump on my case.

Nurse Horn started pacing with her arms folded. "I just don't want you to end up another statistic."

"A statistic! Oh, please!" I threw my hands up in the air. "First of all, my name is Jean 'Stevie' Stevenson, not Crystal Jones. And second of all, you need to be concerned about the

statistics of your finding a husband, steada worrying about me."
I was surprised to hear that come out of my mouth. I bit my
bottom lip and felt kinda sorry about what I'd just said, but it
was too late.

Nurse Horn walked toward me with her face all scrunched
up, pointing her finger at me. "Shut your mouth, young lady,
because right now I feel like slapping you!"

I'd never seen Nurse Horn lose her cool, but I took a few steps
backward just to be safe. "Oh, yeah, you hit a student and you
might get fired, not to mention that I'd hit you back." I tried to
sound tough.

"Jean, you're skating on awfully thin ice." Nurse Horn
pointed her finger up in my face again. I was scared and mad at
the same time. Nurse Horn had her nerve talking about smack-
ing somebody. What did she think this was, *Gone With the
Wind?*

"You don't have to point your finger up in my face. My
mama ain't dead."

"Okay, Jean, you had to push it. Get your things and get out
of my office now! I want you out of my sight!"

My mouth flew open. This lunatic in a bathrobe was actually
calling herself throwing me out of the nurse's office. I stuck my
hand out for my pass. Nurse Horn knew I'd get stopped in the
hallway without it. She started waving her arms in the air all
dramatic like. "Just go over there and sit down." I wished the
woman would make up her mind.

Nurse Horn glanced up at the clock. "This period is halfway
over anyway; I don't want you to leave with things like this."
She let out a big sigh. "I'm going to make us some peppermint
tea. I got it from a health-food store in New Town."

I plopped down on the cot and watched Nurse Horn fill up
the teapot and plug it in. I had never even tasted peppermint tea
before. Nurse Horn was really a trip, I thought. One minute she
was going off on me, and the next minute she was making me
tea. It wasn't like we were in England or some damn where.

I sat across from Nurse Horn, staring into my cup and breathing in the peppermint steam. Nurse Horn leaned forward, holding her cup with both hands. She took a sip of her tea.

"Jean, perhaps I was a little unfair to you, and I apologize. It's just that I see girls get into trouble year after year and sometimes I get frustrated. In many ways, it was easier when I was in high school back in the late fifties. At least there weren't as many pressures. We certainly weren't in the middle of a sexual revolution."

They barely had TV back in the fifties, I thought to myself.

Nurse Horn continued, "Why, I remember my best friend and her boyfriend getting suspended from school for wearing look-alike sweaters. The administration didn't think it was appropriate."

I rolled my eyes in shock. I was glad it was 1969, but I didn't say anything. I just let Nurse Horn speak her piece.

"It's part of my job to care about students, but I'm also a person. I don't just shut my feelings off every day at three-thirty P.M." Nurse Horn sipped some more tea.

I finally looked up at her. I realized that I never even thought of Nurse Horn going home. I guess I never pictured her outside of this office, at least not without her uniform on. But I had to admit that Nurse Horn probably was a person. I drank some tea.

"I feel that there is something special about you. I know that you try to act tough, but I remember the first time that you came down here: you were just a scared freshman."

I was surprised that Nurse Horn could remember the first time I'd ever come down here. I couldn't even remember that myself. And it was hard to picture myself as a scared freshman. "A scared freshman, I'm a mighty junior now. Are you sure you don't have me mixed up with somebody else?"

"Positive. I know that you can be sensitive. Maybe that's why I was so hard on you, because I think you have a lot of potential."

I could hardly believe Nurse Horn was saying all this stuff. I took a big drink of tea. "How do you know I have a lot of potential?" I belched. "Scuse me, or is that what you tell all the girls?"

Nurse Horn smiled and set her cup on the floor. "No, but it's what I'm telling Jean 'Stevie' Stevenson."

"The only time you see me, practically, is when I'm throwing up or rolling around in pain."

"Well, I saw you in the school play, and you were almost as dramatic."

"You saw me in *The Effect of Gamma Rays on Man-in-the-Moon Marigolds?*" I was surprised that Nurse Horn kept up with things outside of her office.

"Yes, I did, and I was quite affected."

I had to admit that I had been good. Carla had said, "Girl, you played your heart out up there on that stage."

"Thanks," I said to Nurse Horn, feeling shy all of a sudden. "We wanted to do *No Place to Be Somebody* or *Nobody Knows My Name*, you know, something really happening. But Mr. Turner was too evil to check them out."

Nurse Horn looked embarrassed, like she didn't want to go along with bad-mouthing the drama teacher. I slurped my tea.

"So are you trying to tell me that you think I'm special out of all the jokers that come down here needing medical attention?"

"I wouldn't put it exactly in those terms."

"When did you first notice that I had potential? When you saw me in the play or the first time that I threw up?"

Nurse Horn picked a piece of lint off my arm.

"Sometimes you just have a feeling about someone. You can't always explain it logically."

"Like Carla liking Tyrone counta he's bowlegged and got curly hair?"

Nurse Horn smiled and looked at me with her soft gray eyes.

"Well, not quite. I care about you and I want you to have a good life."

I swished some tea around in my mouth, thinking. Nobody had ever told me that they wanted me to have a good life before—a good day, yes, but not a good life.

"If this was a TV show, this is when they'd play the music."
I sighed.

"What music?"

"You know the kind of music they used to play when they found Lassie."

Nurse Horn pinched my cheek playfully. If I hadn't just made sixteen, I would've wanted to bury my face all up against her terry-cloth robe; she looked so warm and cozy.

I set my cup down on the floor. "Nurse Horn?"

"Yes, Student Jean."

I laughed. "Okay, Miss Horn; Miss Horn, I'm sorry about the stuff I said about you needing to find a husband."

Nurse Horn looked at me like everything was cool.

"And I'm sorry about making light of some poor girl's misfortune, too."

Nurse Horn leaned over and hugged me. I felt myself get all stiff. Wait a minute, I wanted to say. Nobody hugs me 'cept my grandmother. I'm sixteen years old; my mother doesn't even hug me. What if somebody walks in here and sees us all hugged up like we're in a Hollywood movie? But it felt kinda good, and the terry cloth was brushing up against my face and everything, so I just broke down and wrapped my arms around Nurse Horn and hugged her back. Then I began to inch away because I didn't know how long was too long to be hugging on somebody.

"Nurse Horn, I mean, Miss Horn, about Sean, you see with Sean I've barely got my big toe in the water. I want to swim out there in that ocean of love, but in some ways I want to stay safe on the shore."

Nurse Horn rested her chin in her hand like she was taking in everything I was saying. Then the bell rang so loudly I jumped.

I started grabbing my stuff together. "Thanks for the tea and all." I handed her my empty cup. "It's been real, but I gotta get to chemistry. Tyrone's gonna show us how to make a stink bomb."

Nurse Horn frowned. "Well, promise me you'll talk to me if you need to."

"Okay, I promise."

"And watch your nutrition and exercise regularly, and you won't get such bad cramps."

"Okay, less junk food and more sex." I grinned. Nurse Horn pretended to hit me. I backed away, laughing.

"Just kidding, now can I have my pass?"

"Here, and stay out of that ocean."

A warm feeling went through me as I stumbled into the mad rush of students in the hallway. I was glad that Nurse Horn wasn't married. I would hate to have to think of her going home to take care of some husband. Instead, I pictured her all curled up at home in a terry-cloth bathrobe, sipping peppermint tea and smiling to herself because she was thinking about me. Damn, I felt like running outside and tasting a snowflake steada going to chemistry and making a stink bomb.

chapter 20

Me and Carla were walking to school. We had just decided she should tell her new boyfriend, Ivory, to buy her the Temptations' and Smokey Robinson and the Miracles' new albums for her birthday. Carla's mother had given her a choice between a new stereo and a birthday party after Carla told her about my new box. She'd chosen the stereo. Carla finally had her room to herself. Marla and Sharla had both moved in with their boyfriends. They each had a girl and a boy now, but neither was married.

"There's Nurse Horn's car, the blue one," I said, pointing as we passed the faculty parking lot. "Carla, don't you think Mustangs are hot?"

"I already done told you that I want me a red Firebird. And you done showed me Nurse Horn's stupid car before."

"Well, have you checked out Nurse Horn's new pants uniform? And have you seen her new white earth shoes?"

"Stevie, I don't give a flying fuck about Nurse Horn or her car or her uniform! Do you hear me?"

"Dog, Carla, why you got to curse?"

"Cause you should be trippin' on the prom, steada her white ass, that's why."

"I *am* trippin' on the prom."

"So, when you gon get your dress? Don't wait till the last minute now."

"Carla, the prom is still almost two months away."

"I thought you said your auntie was taking you shopping?"

"She is, we're going Clean-Up Week to Carson's. My Aunt Sheila's got a charge there."

"Carson Pirie Scott, go 'head, girl!" Carla gave me five. "Who woulda thought you would pull a senior? Stevie, I'm jealous, girl; you should be so excited!"

"I am excited, okay?"

"Okay. So now, what the fuck are earth shoes?"

"I like the way you dribble," Sean teased me as I headed down the alley behind his house later that day. I jumped up, dripping with sweat, and made my basket. Sean grabbed the ball, slam dunking it and swinging on the rim of the hoop outside his garage door.

"It's getting late," I said, glancing up at the purple sky. The wind was kicking, but it felt good after working up a sweat. I breathed in the cool night air mixed with sweet-smelling funk. Yeah, we were sweaty, but neither of us stunk, I told myself.

Sean held me close as we snuggled, lying down in the back seat of his brother's '63 Buick in front of his house.

"Stevie, I like that you can shoot some hoops."

"Most girls wouldn't be into it, huh?"

"No, but I'm glad you're different."

"You are?"

"Yeah, I wasn't looking for the average bear."

"Me either, Sean."

"Stevie, I feel like this English writer Miss Porter told us about in class. I can't remember the dude's name, but anyway, he was at a dinner party and he heard this woman say she didn't care for any gravy. The writer dude said, 'Madam, I've been searching my whole life for someone who dislikes gravy. Let's swear eternal friendship.' "

"So I take it you don't like gravy?" I asked, smiling.

"Not really. What about you?"

"I'm not crazy about it either. But I can sho go for some pan drippings."

"I heard that!" Sean laughed.

"So, Stevie, how come you never went out for the girls' basketball team?"

"I don't know, I guess I got into the Drama Club and then I got on the newspaper this year, you know." I looked into Sean's dark brown eyes. "It really wouldn't bother you to have a girlfriend on the basketball team?"

"No, not so long as she was all woman off the court." Sean leaned over and covered my mouth with his luscious lips. I liked the taste of his tongue. I wondered what Sean would think if he knew that I daydreamed about Nurse Horn more than him— that my favorite daydream was of Nurse Horn rescuing me from drowning and giving me mouth-to-mouth resuscitation. And sometimes I just remembered Nurse Horn hugging me against her terry-cloth bathrobe, telling me that I had potential.

I kissed Sean back, trying my best to prove to him that I was definitely all woman. Sean's wet tongue teased my ear, sending shivers through my body.

"Sean," I whispered, "I like the way you dribble too, on and off the court."

Sean pressed against me and ran his fingers through my natural. I could feel his thing through my jeans. I knew that I couldn't allow myself to get too excited. Mama said that most boys won't go any farther than you let them. "It's up to you not to let them," she'd warned. I didn't stop Sean from reaching under my T-shirt and squeezing my breasts through my bra. I didn't want him to turn off completely. My job was to keep Sean interested without going all the way.

Sean ran his hand up and down my thighs. I couldn't help but feel excited. I held my breath while he tugged at my zipper.

"No, Sean, not here," I said, as he stroked my panties. "Anybody could come by and see us."

I sat up and Sean pulled his hand away and glanced around the deserted street.

"Stevie, I couldn't help it," Sean said hoarsely. "I just got really turned on. You said, Not here, well where? We've been going together six months."

"I don't know, Sean. Maybe I'm afraid that once I do it you won't respect me anymore."

"Stevie, I respect the hell outta you now and giving yourself to me could never change that."

"I don't want to end up like Patrice, having to go to a school for unwed mothers. Did you know that by the time she found out she was pregnant Yusef was already going with Gail?"

"Stevie, Yusef Brown always was a dog."

"Well, I tried to tell her that, but Patrice wouldn't listen."

"All Yusef does is hang out on the corner and sell weed." Sean sighed. "But, Stevie, not all brothers are about nothing. If I messed a girl up, I'd stand by her."

"But, Sean, there's just no way I could get pregnant. It would kill my parents. They're counting on me. And Mrs. Stuart says, with my grades, even if my SAT scores come back average, I can still get a college scholarship. She says our time has come. I couldn't face her if I messed up."

Sean held my hand. "I heard that, hey, I'm proud of you, baby. I don't want to be a daddy right now, either. I'm going to Chicago State in the fall, remember? I've got dreams, too."

"Thanks," I whispered in Sean's ear.

"For what?"

"For understanding."

"Oh."

*

The next morning me and Carla sat on the school's stone steps and faced a row of fudge-colored buildings. Carla held her big sweater together with one hand as she took a drag off her cigarette. I glanced up at the cloudy morning sky.

"So finish telling me about you and Seanny last night."

"Like I told you, Carla, I felt his thing up against me. And he touched me through my panties."

"And then what happened?"

"I told him to stop."

"You told him to stop! Why?"

"You know why, because I'm scared. I can't come up pregnant." I tightened the belt on my rain-shine coat. "I finally ended up giving Sean a hand job last night."

"Again!" Carla groaned, "I don't see why you don't just get on the pill like somebody with some sense."

I shrugged. We'd had this conversation before.

"Stevie, I know Sean is patient, but a man has needs, if you know what I mean."

"Yeah, I know what you mean."

"A man is only willing to be frustrated for so long, before he starts looking for a new prom date. Get my drift?"

"Carla, you don't understand. Sean is different."

Carla blew out smoke. "He ain't that damn different. He still a man. After a while them milkshakes begin to add up. Then it's payback time," Carla added.

"Carla, I wish it didn't have to hurt. It's hard to get excited over something painful."

"It don't be hurtin' no worser than bad cramps. You done felt them before."

"I don't look forward to cramps, Carla."

"Stevie, I got a idea. You smoke you a joint and do it when you high." Carla exhaled. "You will be feeling no pain then."

I couldn't help but raise my eyebrows. "Carla, you get high now?"

"Damn, Stevie, you lookin' at me like I said I shot heroin or some shit like that. It's just a little weed."

"You've smoked marijuana before! I can't believe you never told me."

"Look, I've only done it a few times, once with my sisters and twice with Ivory."

Ivory was Carla's fine yellow nigga, as she put it. He was tall, with a big 'fro and his rap had been so powerful that he'd stolen her away from Tyrone. Me and Mama had run into Carla and Ivory in K mart. Mama had taken one look at his lime-colored clothes and big hat and decided Ivory was about nothing. I had finally managed to convince Mama that Ivory's pants were avocado, but she still insisted that the "negro" was no good.

"Well, how was it?"

"It was cool, you get the munchies, you wanna eat a bunch of shit. And shit be funnier than hell."

"Wow, did you do it with Ivory when you were high?"

"Yeah," Carla exhaled.

"How was it?"

"Hot! Ain't nothing better than being high as a kite and getting it at the same time."

I didn't know what to say. I'd never been high and I'd never gotten it. I tried to picture it in my mind as the bell rang.

We were in gym class, jumping over a statue of a horse. Miss Bryant had a girl standing on either side of the horse, just in case. I stood in the line waiting to take my turn. I was still tripping on what Carla had said earlier. I wondered how it felt to be high. I had never even been tipsy. I had drunk a few sips of beer when they'd passed around a can on the bus after the homecoming game last year. That had been it. Maybe I should go ahead and do it with Sean. Carla said it wouldn't hurt if I was high. Maybe a glass of wine would be enough. Who knows? I might even like it.

I balled my fists and ran toward the horse. I grabbed each side of the saddle and lifted both of my feet to clear it.

"Jean, are you all right?"

When I stopped seeing stars, I recognized Miss Bryant's thin, worried walnut-colored face.

"Girl, your feet got caught, you hit your head up underneath on that metal part." I heard Tanya's voice. The group of brown faces and blue gym suits were all one blur. My head was swimming.

"Jean, can you walk to the nurse's office, or do you need for me to send for Miss Horn?"

I looked up from the thick cotton mat, unsure where my legs were.

"She looks monked up."

"Maybe her brain is damaged, huh, Miss Bryant?"

"She should sue the school."

"You mean the Board of Education, girl."

"Quiet, girls."

"Miss Bryant, you want me to go get Nurse Horn?"

"Yes, Rosita, ask her to come right away."

I heard footsteps and looked up.

I thought I had died and gone to heaven. Nurse Horn looked like one of the angels on the stained-glass window at my church. She felt the bump on my forehead and frowned. She explained, that, no, I hadn't lost my memory like the dude on TV. There were some sighs of disappointment and this one fool kept asking me what I'd eaten for breakfast. "Raisin Bran," I answered, as Nurse Horn put her arm around my shoulder and walked me out of the gym.

The cot had never felt more comfortable. Nurse Horn had propped two flat pillows under my head. She sat in a chair next to me, talking softly.

"Jean, I think you're going to be all right, but you should go to your doctor and have your head examined."

"Have my head examined." I smiled.

"Yes, just to be safe. Jean, all kidding aside, do get checked. You're starting to get two black eyes."

I sat up. "Two black eyes!"

"Don't get excited. Here, take a look." Nurse Horn walked over to her desk and returned with a large face mirror.

I stared at my reflection. My forehead looked like a cone and I had a wide black circle under each eye. It was like I'd been worked over by the mob.

"I can't believe I look this bad!"

"Just goes to show you, looks can go just like that." Nurse Horn popped her fingers and smiled. "Well, how do you feel?"

I tried to look as pitiful as possible, I wanted every ounce of sympathy I could get out of Nurse Horn. "My head hurts and I'm still a little dizzy."

"Well, the aspirin I gave you should help. I'll keep you down here for the rest of the afternoon. I want you to see a doctor tomorrow and maybe you'll be well enough to return to school on Monday."

"I don't really have a doctor. I'll have to go to the clinic."

"That should be fine." Nurse Horn looked out the window. "It's starting to rain."

"April showers bring May flowers," I mumbled.

"Jean, you haven't been down here since the first snowfall, remember?"

"I know. Who woulda thought it would wind up being a blizzard, remember?"

"Yes, I remember."

"My cramps haven't been bad lately. I took your advice."

"You've been staying out of that ocean?" Nurse Horn asked.

"So far, and I've been eating less junk food and exercising more."

"That's good, I'm glad. I'm sorry that you're hurt, but it *is* nice seeing you. I guess I've missed lecturing you."

"I've missed you too, Nurse Horn." Seeing her in the hallways every now and then hadn't been enough.

"Well, you can always stick your head in and say, 'hi,' you know."

"You mean you want to see me in sickness and in health?"

"Sure. I certainly don't want you to develop into a hypochondriac, Jean."

I smiled. I was glad she wanted to see me.

"Do you prefer to be called Stevie or Jean?"

"My friends call me Stevie."

"Well, I'd like to be your friend. So I'll call you Stevie, if that's all right?"

"Please do."

"Is there anyone who can come get you so you don't have to walk home today?"

"No. My father has the car and he's at work. Sean might be able to get his brother to give me a ride."

"If not, I can drive you home. It might be pouring by three-thirty."

I swallowed. Had Nurse Horn said she would drive me home? I could ride in her '67 Mustang with her! I forgot my pain for a minute.

"On second thought, I believe Sean told me Brian's car is in the shop. It's getting tuned up or something," I lied.

"Well, that settles it, then. I'll give you a lift."

I had no intention of arguing with her.

The doctor shone a flashlight in my eyes and told me to take some aspirin for pain. That had been it. Daddy said the school should pay my clinic bill, but Mama said it wasn't worth the red tape to try to collect ten dollars. They'd argued back and forth at the dinner table. It was settled when Mama sent me to get her checkbook. Of course, my brothers teased me no end about my shiners. And they were forever begging me to take off my sunglasses.

A week later Carla and I were at my locker.

"You think I still need my sunglasses?"

Carla shook her head. "Not unlessen you just want to look cool."

Sean walked toward us. "Hey, Stevie, let's say we check out White Castle ninth period? They gotta special going, ten burgers for a buck."

"I wish I could, Sean, but I'm booked."

"Booked? You gotta new nigger or something?" Carla cut in. Sean smiled but he looked worried.

"No, I've got to help Nurse Horn."

Carla shook her head at me before rushing away to catch up with Ivory.

"Help Nurse Horn? Help her do what?"

"Different stuff, Sean, file, type, clean up, whatever. I'm her student helper now."

"How did you get stuck with that?"

"I had to tell Nurse Horn what the doctor said. And while I was in her office, Barbara Taylor was in there."

"So."

"Anyway, Barbara was telling Nurse Horn that she couldn't be her helper anymore, accounta she's the new captain of the girls' basketball team, and they're in the finals and all."

"So, what's that got to do with you?"

"So I asked Nurse Horn if I could be her new helper. And she said, 'Great idea.'"

Sean frowned, "Why do you have to help her ninth period? Why would you want to be tied up at the end of the day?"

"Because that's when she needs me. Earlier she's more likely to have somebody sick in there."

"What if I need you?"

"Sean, you're being silly. You go to swim-team practice three times a week. You play basketball during most of lunch period."

"That's different."

"Well, I need service points for the Junior Honor Society.

Helping Nurse Horn two measly periods a week will cover it."

"I forgot about your needing service points."

"Sean, we can go to White Castle tomorrow."

"Stevie, tomorrow it will be too late. This is a one-day sale," Sean grumbled.

That's just too bad, I thought to myself.

chapter 21

I knocked on Nurse Horn's door.

"Come in," she said.

I was surprised to see her pacing in her white pants uniform. I just sat down on the cot and watched Nurse Horn do her thing.

"I came to this school because I wanted to make a difference. I could've been a nurse in a suburban school where everybody's Dad wore a suit and tie to work and their mothers all played bridge and tennis," she said, continuing to pace. "But I would've been bored to tears."

"Nurse Horn, are you through talking to yourself?"

"I'm sorry, I just had to let off some steam."

"Why?"

"I saw this semester's dropout list. Your name wasn't on it, but I recognized quite a few."

"Whose names *are* on it?"

"Never mind, they're just wasting their lives."

Nurse Horn faced me with her arms folded. "Stevie, I know that you're not getting a first-rate education here."

"You mean I'm not being prepared for Vassar?" I asked, looking down at my bucks.

"Don't get me wrong. We have some fine, dedicated teachers here. But even the best teachers can get worn down by over-crowded classrooms, a lack of supplies, poor equipment, not to mention the discipline problems. I know that you guys don't have the best shot. But it's the only shot you've got. And you need a high school diploma just to survive these days."

"Nurse Horn, Brother Kambui says, 'White people are raised to live, but black people are raised to survive.' "

"I don't care what Brother Kambui says, I care what you say, Stevie. I know that any black person who wants to get ahead is up against it. I'd be naïve to think otherwise. But the question is whether you're going to let racism stop you."

I looked up at Nurse Horn. "Twenty years ago my grand-mother was in Gainesville, Florida, cleaning toilets that she couldn't even use. Today, she owns Mother Dickens' Fried Chicken Stand and she's a success. And when my mother was the only black teller at her bank's downtown branch, people avoided her window. But eventually her coworkers voted her teller of the month. Now she's a loan representative," I said proudly.

I stood up and folded my arms. "My grandmother didn't let racism stop her, my mother didn't let racism stop her. And I'm damn sure not going to let racism stop me, either! Now, does that answer your question, Nurse Horn?"

Nurse Horn nodded and walked over to the sink and filled the teapot.

"I'm sorry I had to curse," I said.

"To Be Young, Gifted, and Black Is Where It's At!" We yelled and waved our fists. I took my bow with the rest of the Drama Club, ending our "To Make a Poet Black" Assembly.

"The Drama Club peed, girl! Y'all got down!" Carla stretched her hand out and I gave her five as we headed out of the auditorium.

"Right on, Sisters! Power to the People!" Roland greeted us with a raised fist at the door.

"Right on!" Me and Carla answered, raising our fists too.

"Who would've thought Roland Anderson would have become a tam-wearing, fist-waving black militant?" I asked Carla.

"Who would've thought he'd grow some behind?" Carla shouted above the noise in the crowded hallway.

I laughed.

"Stevie, come have a smoke with me."

"Carla, you know I don't smoke."

"I know, just come with me, girl."

"We've got Study this period."

"Damn Study, Mrs. Welles ain't even here today."

"Okay," I agreed, sort of looking forward to getting out.

Carla and I sat across from each other, on either side of the main school steps.

"Prom tickets go on sale next week," Carla announced after lighting a cigarette.

"Yeah, I know."

"I wish Ivory was a senior."

"How are you two doing these days?"

"He blew my mind last night!"

"What do you mean?"

"Girl, while we was fucking, he rubbed the top of my pussy with his thumb."

"Where?"

"It's a spot, like a little button," Carla said as she exhaled.

"The clitoris?" I asked.

"The what?"

"The clitoris. I read about it in this book called *Everything You Always Wanted to Know about Sex*." I had been walking around Hyde Park while Mama was at the dentist when I'd seen the book in a bookstore window. Hyde Park was the only neighborhood on the South Side where you were guaranteed to see something unusual, like hippies or interracial couples or pottery or a book like *Everything You Always Wanted to Know about Sex*.

"Well," Carla said, "you get a nigger to rub the clawtaurus the right way, honey, and it'll make you wanna slap the judge!" She stretched her hand out and I gave her five.

Carla blew smoke rings in the air. "Dang, Stevie, much as you read, seem like you'd wanna do more."

During the middle of tenth period, I returned to Nurse Horn's office with the stencils that she had given me. It was my third week of being her helper.

"You ready to collate and staple?" Nurse Horn asked without looking up from her desk.

"No, that doggone ditto machine was out of ink, again. They said it'll be a couple of days."

Nurse Horn sighed, "I wanted to have those handouts for tomorrow. But, oh well."

I nodded at Tanya lying on the cot, all doubled up.

"Tanya has a stomachache. She'll be all right. I just gave her some peppermint tea."

"Oh," I said, feeling kind of jealous.

It struck me how wavy Nurse Horn's brown hair was. It wasn't stringy like some white people's. And her breasts had felt soft and comfortable when she'd hugged me that time. Plus even Carla would have to admit that Nurse Horn had a nice behind for a white woman. And she had the softest gray eyes you could imagine.

"Stevie, you can type up my report for the district if you like."

"Is it urgent?"

"No, not at all. Why?"

"Because, look at that window. Aren't you tired of looking out of it? Wouldn't you like a clean window?"

"Sure, I didn't know that you did windows."

"I'm in the mood."

I'd found everything I needed in the janitor's closet. I couldn't believe how much clearer things were beginning to look as I washed away the layer of dirt. I couldn't wait for Nurse Horn to return from her break and see the sparkling-clean view of the faculty parking lot.

"Stevie! Stevie!"

It was Carla. She and Ivory were lounging up against a Volkswagen bug, smoking cigarettes. I waved my rag. Carla waved back and Ivory shook his fist playfully.

"Hey, what's happening, Aunt Jemima?" Carla shouted. She and Ivory fell out laughing. Ivory had the nerve to add, "Tote that barge, lift that bale!"

I glanced over at Tanya but she turned away. I wondered if she looked down on me as some white woman's flunky too. My view was suddenly blurred by my tears.

I wiped my eyes as Nurse Horn walked in with Miss Humphrey trailing behind her in a denim skirt and peasant blouse.

"Diane, you're a lifesaver."

"That's me, the human aspirin dispenser," she joked, opening the medicine cabinet.

"Well, maybe I can get rid of this headache before I have to hit the traffic."

"Good luck." Nurse Horn shook a couple of aspirins into Miss Humphrey's outstretched palm.

Miss Humphrey noticed me standing by the window.

"Jean, I've got your brother David in my class. He's a pretty good artist. But you were a real sweetheart."

"The window looks great," Nurse Horn cut in.

"Thanks."

Miss Humphrey got all up in my face and tugged at my cheek.

"Smile, honey chile," she said. I turned away and glanced at Tanya on the cot. She was facing the wall.

"I'm not in a smiling mood," I mumbled.

"But you look so cute when you smile."

I frowned even more. I wasn't in the mood to have Miss Humphrey up in my face. Why did white people want you to be all the time grinning for, anyway?

"I don't have to smile. I'm not on a plantation."

Miss Humphrey looked embarrassed.

"Excuse me," I said, passing by them carrying my rag and pail.

"You know, I've been offered a job in Vermont next fall. Maybe I should take it," I overheard Miss Humphrey say.

chapter 22

I stepped into Mother Dickens' Fried Chicken Stand, past the BLACK OWNED, BLACK OPERATED and KEEP A COOL SUMMER signs in the window. The same picture of the late Dr. King and the Kennedy brothers that hung above the takeout counter was on our living-room wall at home.

I needed to talk to Grandma. Carla and Ivory's comments had me all shook up. I needed to know if it was all right for me to be friends with a white woman, or if it was unheard of to try such a thing. I'd never known a black person who was really friends with somebody white. I'd heard of famous people like Sammy Davis Jr. and Leslie Uggams being buddy-buddy with white folks, even marrying them. But I wasn't rich or famous, and I also had my pride.

"How's my favorite niece?" my Uncle Franklin asked, revealing a gold tooth as he smiled from the cash register.

"Fine," I lied. "Your only niece is fine." I usually loved to joke around with Uncle Franklin, but today I was on a mission. I couldn't rest until I reached Grandma. My nose led me to the small kitchen. The smell alone was enough to set your mouth to watering. I almost forgot about my problems.

"What? Your mama ain't feeding you at home?" Grandma teased, looking up from a wire basket filled with golden fried chicken.

"I didn't just come here to eat, Grandma, I came here to see you."

"Well, you know I'm always glad to see my girl." Grandma smiled and handed me a wing.

"Thanks." I sank my teeth into the juicy meat.

I finished my chicken, washed my hands, and began helping Grandma by digging homemade potato salad out of a huge plastic container with an ice-cream scoop. I put a ball of potato salad and two slices of Wonder Bread on each paper plate while Grandma saw to the chicken.

"Grandma, could you ever be friends with a white woman?"

Grandma looked confused. "You mean really friends, not just 'hi' and 'bye' friends?"

I nodded. "Yes, really friends."

"Baby, white people are like actors, they don't feel things the way we do. If they really had deep feelings they couldn't have done half the dirt they've done and sleep at night."

"Aren't some of them different?"

"There might be that rare exception, that needle in a haystack. But generally speaking, getting close to a white person is just asking for trouble. Nine times out of ten, you'll only end up getting hurt. I wouldn't trust one behind a broomstraw."

Uncle Franklin stuck his head in to pick up an order.

"Did you ever trust one, Grandma?"

Grandma drained the fried chicken on a paper towel. She stopped and stared into space.

"Yeah, Kathy Jo."

"Who's Kathy Jo?"

"Once my mother was working for a family and I spent a lot

of time over there. I grew up with Kathy Jo. We even took baths together. That was common in the South. We couldn't sit together on the streetcar, but we could share the same bathwater. Figure that one out."

"Wow."

"The white man in the South is different from the white man in the North," Grandma continued. "In the South, a black person better not get too big, and in the North, a black person better not get too close."

"How's that, Grandma?"

"Kathy Jo's mother thought nothing of throwing her in the bed between me and my sister if she wanted my mother to keep Kathy Jo on a Saturday night. White folk in the South don't mind getting close to you as long as it's clear who works for who. White folk in the North don't care how big your house is, so long as you're not their neighbor."

"So, Grandma, did you trust Kathy Jo? Tell me what happened."

"Start mashing these sweet potatoes and I will."

Grandma handed me the masher. I started squishing and she sat down in a kitchen chair and started telling.

"It was Kathy Jo's tenth birthday and she was having a big party. It was all she talked about. For some reason I forgot that I was colored and thought that I would be invited. I dreamed about playing Pin the Tail on the Donkey and Musical Chairs and eating hot dogs and ice cream and chocolate cake. I bragged to my sisters and brothers that I was going to the party. Mama tried to warn me, but I wouldn't pay her any mind."

"Grandma, did you get an invitation?"

"Of course not," Grandma said. She stretched her legs out and I noticed her ankles were swollen again. Grandma had on a pair of Uncle Franklin's old house slippers. They kept her corns from acting up.

"I figured I ain't needed an invitation," Grandma explained. "Me and Kathy Jo was still sleeping together in the same bed sometimes. Well suh, my mother didn't ask Miss Mary if I could attend the party. She just let me put on my Sunday dress and go sashaying in there like I was rich and white, carrying my present. I'd made Kathy Jo a kite. She was nothing but a tomboy. The little white children looked at me like I was the boogey man, including Kathy Jo. Miss Mary turned beet red."

"What did you do?"

"I handed Kathy Jo the kite and asked her where she wanted me to sit. She took my present and told me to sit in the kitchen and they would call me if they needed anything."

"No, she didn't, Grandma."

"Yes, she did, chile. I looked into Kathy Jo's eyes and they were cold as blue ice."

"What did you do, Grandma?"

"I took back my kite and I took back my friendship."

"What Kathy Jo did was really cold, Grandma."

"I've never trusted a white person since. Oh, I might smile and act cordial, but I never let them touch the real me," Grandma said, pointing to her chest.

Grandma stood up and started adding eggs and sugar to the mashed sweet potatoes.

"So, Grandma, you think only a fool would try to be friends with a white woman, huh?"

Grandma laughed. "Chile, the only black women and white women who can be friends are hookers and bulldaggers."

"Bulldaggers?" I swallowed.

"Yes baby, bulldaggers, you know, funnies . . . lesbians."

"Lesbians." The word sent chills down my spine. I pretended to be cheerful as I poured the rich, orange mixture into the little tins covered with crust. But I felt scared and alone in the small kitchen with Grandma.

On Saturday, Mama decided to bake a pound cake for no reason. She was just in the mood. I was busy scraping the bowl with my finger.

"Mama, you want me to wake up Kevin and David so they can lick the beaters?"

"Jean, haven't you heard, let sleeping dogs lie?"

"Mama, are you calling Kevin and David dogs?"

"Just an expression. It's such a nice, quiet morning. The fewer people disturbing the peace, the better."

"I'll put the beaters aside for them, for when they wake up."

"That's a good sister."

I decided to take advantage of this time alone with Mama. I couldn't believe that I was sixteen and a half and still coming to her. But I knew that I was desperate for answers.

"Mama, me and Sean were arguing about homosexuality," I lied.

Mama looked surprised. She liked Sean. He was polite and intelligent, he came from a two-parent family, and he even had a decent grade of hair.

"Sean says they're sick and I say they're sinners. Who's right, Mama?"

Mama's face relaxed. She was probably glad that I was asking her to give the last word on a subject.

"Well, Jean Eloise, actually you're both right, they're sick sinners."

"Oh," I said, trying to hide my disappointment. I'd hoped that Mama might shed a little more light on the subject.

Mama shook her head as she set the cake in the oven.

"They're to be pitied. Every time I look at the ones in the choir, I say to myself, 'What a waste of husband material.' "

"So Mama, what about the women?" I tried to sound casual as I carried the bowl over to the sink.

"They're pathetic creatures, too. Remember Mrs. Huff who used to do my hair before she retired?"

I nodded.

"Her daughter Shirley is one, lived with her girlfriend right in her mama's basement. This close to where Mrs. Huff did hair," Mama said, holding her thumb and forefinger about an inch apart. "Shirley would come in demanding her dinner, just like a man."

"Mama, was Shirley like the husband?"

"Yes, and Cynthia was the wife."

"Does one always have to be the man?"

"Whenever you see a couple, it's like that: one plays the man and the other plays the woman."

I was confused. "Why didn't Cynthia just get a real man, if that's all she wanted?"

"That's why they call them queer, they don't do what a normal person would do."

"Mama, do you think Shirley and Cynthia were happy?"

Mama shook her head. "Women like that can never be happy. They live sad, lonely, tormented lives."

"Oh," I swallowed. My hands shook as I rinsed out the measuring cup.

"And on top of that, they're doomed to hellfire and eternal damnation," Mama said quietly as she opened the oven door to check on her cake.

Monday afternoon, I was in Nurse Horn's office, alphabetizing a stack of cards.

"Stevie, you sure are quiet today," Nurse Horn said, looking up from her desk. I ignored her comment, continuing to work.

"Are you feeling all right?"

"Nurse Horn, my grandmother says a black woman and a white woman can't really be friends."

Nurse Horn cleared her throat. "Well, I happen to disagree with your grandmother. One of my closest friends is a black woman." I knew she couldn't be talking about Mrs. Stuart. "We met in nursing school," she continued.

"Is she a prostitute?"

"A prostitute? Are you kidding? She's one of the best nurses at Michael Reese Hospital. Whatever gave you the idea that Allison might be a prostitute?"

"My grandmother said the only white women and black women who can be friends are prostitutes and . . . funnies."

"Funnies?"

"You know, homosexuals."

"Your grandmother is wrong, in my opinion. I know that it's not easy because this society is so . . . segregated. But I want you to know that it *is* possible for black women and white women to be friends in spite of that."

I let out a sigh of relief. "My grandmother's from a different time."

"Well, tell your grandmother the times they are a-changin'."

"Okay." I smiled. "I'm through with these cards. You want me to finish grading the health quizzes?"

"Good. Yes, look in my briefcase and pull them out."

I stuck my hand in Nurse Horn's open briefcase and grabbed the stack of yellow papers. I picked up the *Chicago Sun Times* and was about to ask Nurse Horn if I could read Ann Landers, when I saw it: a paperback book with two women in long dresses reaching for each other on the cover! The title of the book was *A Place for Us.* I flipped it over. "They lived together—in a world apart," it said on the back. I wasn't stupid. A chill ran through my body.

"Stevie, did you find them?"

"Yeah."

"Okay, use the top sheet as the key like you did before."

I stood staring at the book. My stomach started hurting. Nurse Horn had lied to me. I stuck the book back under the newspaper.

"I've decided to go ahead and do it with Sean," I announced. "Just get it over with."

"Get it over with? Sounds about as romantic as a dose of castor oil, if you ask me."

"I didn't ask you."

"I beg your pardon."

I faced Nurse Horn. She looked hurt. "Of course you would

be against it. 'Cause you just want me to end up a freak . . . like you!"

Nurse Horn just sat there with her eyebrows arched. I started grabbing my stuff together. I couldn't face her.

"Stevie, what brought that on?"

"That book of yours, that's what!" I said, and rushed out of the office.

chapter 23

Tonight was the night! After I did it with Sean there would be no doubt in anyone's mind that I was normal. When I had told Sean I was ready to go all the way, he'd seemed almost as happy as Carla had been to hear the news. Sean had smiled from ear to ear, but Carla had picked up her pompoms and shouted, "Two, four, six, eight, Stevie's doing it, before it's too late!"

I had just taken a long luxurious bath with Joy dish soap and rubbed Jergens lotion all over my body. I reached for my favorite jeans. I had on my lacy new bra and my best panties. I had told Mama that we were going to Old Town, over on the North Side, to look in the stores and get something to eat.

We were lucky. Sean's oldest brother, Walter, wanted to help him out. He'd offered the use of his pad, a one-bedroom apartment on the North Side in Belmont Harbor, four blocks from the Lake. Walter worked with computers, so he was doing well.

I was happy I wouldn't be giving it up in a cheap motel or the back seat of a car. We were going to do it in style.

I couldn't help but feel grown-up as Sean and I entered the high-rise apartment building. I was a little disappointed that there was no doorman like on the TV show *Family Affair*. But the building was still nice. Sean had told me that Walter paid $175 a month rent!

I felt proud to be with Sean, he was so cute in his leather coat. His turquoise knit top looked good next to his bronze skin. I could smell his father's Old Spice on him. I leaned my head against Sean's chest while we waited for the elevator. He put his arm around me. A middle-aged white couple stood nearby, glaring at us. I wondered if they knew what we were up to. The four of us rode up in silence. I tried not to let the couple's icy stares make me feel like we didn't belong.

"Da daaah," Sean said as he swung the door open.

"It's nice," I said, appreciating the cranberry shag carpet, the off-white furniture without plastic coverings, and the African masks.

"Brenda decorated it, that's Walt's fiancée. She probably cleaned up the place too."

Sean walked over and turned on the stereo.

I kissed Sean's sweet lips. He pressed back and sucked in my tongue.

Sean lit the candles and we sat down on the couch and kissed some more. Barry White was singing on the stereo.

"Baby, you ready to get down?"

I didn't know how to answer. I knew that I was supposed to be excited, but what was so exciting about having something pushed inside a hole? Especially if the hole was in your body. And I felt nervous about Sean expecting to fit his dick where I sometimes had trouble sticking a junior tampon.

"Sean, I'd be lying if I said I wasn't scared."

"Stevie, it's natural for a girl to be scared the first time. Here, drink your wine."

I took the glass.

"Don't worry, baby," Sean continued. "I'll steer the ship. This is your captain speaking." He clinked his wine glass against mine. Why rock the boat? I swallowed the red wine.

We were on Walter's king-size bed. Sean was lying on top of me and I could feel his thing, hard against my thigh through our clothes. I'd drunk half a glass of wine for the first time in my life. It had helped. I felt dizzy.

I lay still, holding my breath, while Sean rubbed his hands up and down my body. I let him undress me. I helped Sean with the hooks on my bra. He began sucking my breasts, which I liked. Sean unzipped his pants and took his thing out and started rubbing it against the inside of my thigh. I could've enjoyed it if I hadn't known what it was leading up to. But I reminded myself that I didn't have to enjoy it, I just had to get through it.

"Baby, you starting to get wet."

I felt embarrassed by the comment, but I couldn't deny the juicy noises my pussy was making as Sean's dick rubbed against it.

"Don't forget the rubber, Sean."

"Coming right up." Sean searched for his pants in the dim light.

I held my breath while Sean tried to push his thing inside me. I was reminded of Jesus saying it would be easier to get a camel hump through the eye of a needle than for a rich man to enter the kingdom of heaven. But I was determined to hang in there. I'd survived being at the dentist before, I could survive this, I told myself.

My body felt like it was being split in two! Had Sean forgotten I was a virgin? I knew that I had made a mistake. I really wasn't ready. It wasn't worth this amount of pain, just to have a boyfriend. And how long was this going to last? I couldn't take it anymore!

"Sean! Sean!"

"Yeah, baby, I knew you'd be calling out my name."

"Sean, stop!"

"Baby, I'm not finished yet."

"Well, I am!"

"Did you come?"

"What? Sean, just get out of me! You're hurting me!"

Sean pulled his dick out.

"Stevie, I was halfway to heaven."

"Well, I was in hell."

"Look, Stevie, you should've drank more wine. You barely drank half a glass."

"Because I didn't like the taste of it."

"It's good wine," Sean insisted. "It's Gallo. Bro knows his stuff."

"Sean, you know I'm not a drinker."

"But for something like this you might need a drink."

"I just didn't expect it to hurt so much."

"It gets better. It's important for a girl to relax."

"How can somebody relax when she's being tortured?"

"It wouldn't hurt so much if you weren't so uptight. You ain't got to be scared about getting pregnant. I was using a rubber. Maybe it hurt because I've got a big one," Sean added.

"You're lucky I'm not a witch, I'd turn all dicks into the size of my index finger."

"Stevie, that would be cold. You'd be sorry too. One day you'll be saying, 'The bigger the better.'"

"Don't hold your breath, Sean."

"Look, dig up, Stevie, drink some more wine and relax and we can try again."

"Sean, I don't want to try again. I could think of so many other things I'd rather do, till it's not funny."

I sat up against the rattan headboard and wrapped some of the sheet around me. I didn't know how I was going to face Carla. How could I ever explain this?

"What do you mean you don't want to try again?"

"Sean, I really wasn't into it."

"Well, you need to *get* into it! We've been going together over six months now. I've been patient, I mean, I've been nice. But, Stevie, I'm going to be eighteen in June. I'm not a little boy anymore. I have a right to expect to get some on a regular basis."

Sean lifted the sheet and wrapped his arms around me and pressed his naked body against mine. "If you want to see me beg, baby, I'll beg. Baby, I have no shame."

"You've got a powerful rap, Sean." I said as I felt his dick harden against my thigh.

"Stevie, I've got feelings for you deep enough to swim in."

"Sean, I'm sorry, you're the only dude I would want to do it with, but I don't want to half step."

"You ain't got to half step, baby, come on and be an all-the-way-woman."

What if it was no use? I thought. What if I just wasn't an all-the-way woman? Then I'd have to pretend on a regular basis. I wished I could just climb up in Grandma's lap and all of my problems would be solved.

"My rap's not powerful enough, though, huh?"

"I'm just not ready, Sean."

Sean jerked away from me and sat on the edge of the bed. He gulped down the rest of my wine. "When are you going to be ready, next week, next month? How long do you expect me to wait?"

"I don't know."

"Well, I'm not settling for a hand job on my prom night."

"Well, Sean, I can't make any guarantees."

"Well, then, I can guarantee you won't be my prom date."

"So are you saying that if I don't give you some, you won't take me to the prom? Is that what you're saying?"

Sean turned around and faced me. "Look, Stevie, it's time to shit or get off the pot. I don't want to push you. But I can't let you hold me back anymore, either."

"So much for your little rap about gravy, huh, Sean? You had me thinking that you were different."

"I *am* different, Stevie. Plenty of dudes wouldn't have stopped tonight. They would've just kept right on fucking you!"

I knew that I was losing my boyfriend, but I felt relieved. I realized that I had never been in love with Sean, just impressed with him. And that was a different feeling. It hadn't made me want to run outside and taste a snowflake.

I'd told Aunt Sheila to save her money, that I wasn't going to be needing that prom dress, after all. I'd explained to Mama and Aunt Sheila that Sean had dumped me because I wouldn't give it up. They had called him all kind of dogs. I figured that Carla would see things differently. I knew she'd be all up in my face, asking me how it was. So I beat her to the punch. I'd phoned Carla this morning and insisted that she come over. I'd refused to give her any details on the phone.

My lips had been sealed until we reached my basement. Daddy had paneled an area that we called the family room. I slumped back against the black vinyl couch.

"Sit down, Carla, you need to be sitting down."

Carla plopped down in the red bean-bag chair across from me. She leaned forward with her chin in her hands like she couldn't wait to hear the dirt.

"Well, how was it?"

"Carla, things didn't go according to plan."

"Well, what happened? Did his brother come home early or something?"

I shook my head. "I don't know where to begin."

"Start with when things started getting juicy."

"Okay, we were kissing and touching and stuff and Sean started undressing me."

"That was a good move, he relieved you of your threads. Did he tease you? Was you dripping wet?"

"My love came down, I s'pose."

"You s'pose?"

"Well, I got sort of scared when he pushed his thing inside of me."

"That's understandable, but you put that fear by the wayside and you let him make you his woman! Woooo!" Carla clapped her hands like she was in church.

"Not exactly, Carla. I sort of told Sean to stop, that it was hurting me."

"Knowing Sean, him being a gentleman and all, he eased up, and before you knew it, y'all was cooking with gas. That's normal, Stevie, it hurted me in the beginning too. But when you in love with a nigger, it's the sweetest pain."

"Carla, it wasn't sweet and so I didn't go through with it."

"Didn't go through with it! You really went and fucked things up now, didn't you!" Carla stamped her gym shoes against the floor. "Stevie, is you crazy?"

"Carla, why should I be tortured just to please Sean? Nurse Horn says that girls should wait until they're emotionally and physically ready before they have sex."

"Nurse Horn," Carla groaned. "I don't give a damn what that white heifer say. That's your problem, Stevie. You're choosing her white ass over Sean."

"No, I'm not. What do you mean by that, Carla?" I asked nervously.

"I mean you seem more into Nurse Horn than you do Sean sometimes. You think I don't be noticing how your eyes be lighting up when you talk about her. Well, it ain't natural, Stevie."

"Nurse Horn's just been nice to me, that's all. You're making it out to be something that it's not."

"Okay, fine, then what did Sean say after you acted a fool?"

I took a breath, glad that Carla had backed off about Nurse Horn. "Sean said he's taking somebody else to the prom."

"Serves you right. I don't blame Sean one bit."

"Thanks a lot, Carla."

Carla stood up and started pacing. "Stevie, you fucked up, but there's no need to panic."

"I did not fuck up."

"Drink you a glass of wine, smoke you a joint . . . "

"You know I don't get high."

"Whatever you need to do," Carla continued. "Put on your best panties and call Sean. Tell him to come on over here and sock it to you."

"No way."

"Stevie, you better wake up, girl, you lucky. You gotta decent nigga."

"*Had*, Carla."

"He's cute, he's a senior, he's willing to wear a rubber. You gotta *lot* to be thankful for, girl."

"*Had* a lot to be thankful for, Carla."

"G'on and get over the hump, Stevie. Let Sean bust your cherry and get it over with. Tell him you need a pair of heels or want a new album. Make him buy your ass stuff. You get over on him that way." Carla sat back down. "Ain't your mama taught you nothing?"

"Carla, that's just not me. I'm not into material things that much."

"Stevie, you sound like a white girl, like a white hippie."

"I sound like me."

"You don't care nothing about having no man, so long as you can grin up in that white woman's face. I got your number."

"She's got nothing to do with it."

"Stevie, you know you love you some Nurse Horn, g'on and admit it. You know you love her white ass."

I swallowed. "No, I don't, it ain't even like that."

"You a lie, Stevie, you love Nurse Horn's yesterday's drawers."

I felt the hairs on my neck stand up. "What are you trying to say about me, Carla?"

Carla struggled up from the bean-bag chair. She stood over me with her hands on her hips. I held my breath.

"Okay, fine, Stevie, I ain't trying to crack on you. But if I didn't know better, I'd swear you was funny."

Me and Carla were silent. She stared at the cobwebs on the ceiling. I became interested in the yellow wax buildup on the gray linoleum floor.

I bit my bottom lip. At least it had been said. Now it was out in the open, I thought, breathing in the musty basement air.

"Funny, me funny? Carla, I can't believe that you could say anything so ridiculous! Do I look like a bulldagger to you?"

Carla plopped back down in the bean-bag chair.

"I can tell if somebody's that way by looking in they eyes. The eyes is the windows to the soul."

"Oh," I said, turning away from Carla, my stomach churning. "Carla, you would still be my friend, though, if I was that way, wouldn't you?"

"You mean if'n you was funny?"

"We both know I'm not, but let's just say if'n I was."

"Naw, then."

"Naw, then what, Carla?"

"Hell no, I wouldn't still be your friend."

"Carla, are you saying that we wouldn't be tight anymore?"

"I wouldn't have shit to do with you, Stevie."

"You wouldn't give me the time of day?"

"You got it."

"Carla, I don't believe you. You're not serious."

"I'm serious as terminal cancer."

"That's really cold, Carla."

"It bees that way sometimes."

"But, Carla, we've been through thick and thin together!"

"I don't give a damn, Stevie. Hey, when Aries turn off, we turn off cold. Look, you ain't funny, so it don't make no never mind, do it?"

"It does make some never mind, Carla. I would stand by you if you were that way."

"Stevie, that's you. That ain't Carlene Zenobia Perkins."

"Carla, if you can't accept me for who I am, no matter what, then our friendship is really tired."

"It'll just have to be tired, then. 'Cause I ain't acceptin' nobody if they funny."

I felt hurt and scared, but I still wanted Carla to look into my eyes and tell me if I was really funny.

"Carla, look into my eyes so that we can put this mess to rest. In case you have any question in your mind."

My heart pounded, as I faced Carla. I held my breath as she stared at me. Carla turned away.

"Carla, could you tell I wasn't funny?"

Carla shook her head. "Stevie, if you one of them funny folks, I don't want to know."

I dared to breathe. "Well, I want to know."

"Well, I can't help you."

I'd seen a fear in Carla's eyes that I'd never noticed before. But it had always been there. It was like I was seeing Carla for the first time.

"Well, it's time I got a friend who *can* help me," I said.

Carla looked surprised.

"And another thing, Carla, good people come in all colors and types, just the same as bad people. But you're just too scared to find that out!"

I left Carla stuck in a bean-bag chair, with her mouth hanging open, in my own basement.

chapter 24

By Monday afternoon I'd managed to avoid making contact with Carla and Sean for the most part. I'd passed by Sean as he left his locker this morning. We'd both nodded, but neither of us had made eye contact.

A dude wearing an apple cap walked up to me. "Hey, sister, what's happening?"

He meant "sister," literally. It was David under the floppy cap.

"Nothing, brother, what's happening with you?"

"Not much, I just want to borrow your teke. I'm going to the Afro-American Club meeting this afternoon."

I felt the smooth, wooden sculpture hanging around my neck.

"David, why don't you buy your own?"

"Why should I, when I can borrow my sister's?"

"What are they going to be talking about at the meeting today, anyway?"

David hunched his shoulders. "You know Roland Anderson just got elected president."

"No, I didn't know that."

"Oh, and they gotta decide how to get rid of Nurse Horn."

"Get rid of Nurse Horn!"

"Calm down, kemo sabe, you signed the petition, remember? I saw your name on it."

I gulped. "That was umpteen years ago. Before I'd even met Nurse Horn."

"Well, all of the demands of the Manifesto have been met except getting a black school nurse," David reminded me.

"I have to stand up for Nurse Horn. She does a good job. Color has nothing to do with it."

"Good luck trying to convince a bunch of militants of that."

"Thanks."

"You gonna give up the teke or not?"

"No, I'm gonna need this teke. David, since when did you become a card-carrying member of the Afro-American Club, anyway?"

"Since this girl I like joined. Underneath that dashiki, Shantelle is a pussy cat," David smiled.

"Get out of here, fool. And you need to take off that stupid cap."

"Jean, watch what you say in there. Try not to embarrass me, okay. I don't want to have to disown you."

Roland looked more like a dark-skinned Malcolm X than ever. The squeaky voice, the tired glasses, and the pocket of pens were long gone. They'd been replaced by a print dashiki, stylish specs and a confident-sounding voice. As I watched him preside over the meeting, I couldn't help but be impressed. I also couldn't help but notice that membership was down. There were only about fifteen students in the room. But I reminded myself that the Afro-American Club still had a lot of power.

"There are far too many empty chairs in here." Roland

pointed around the study hall. "Negroes have fallen asleep, they think the battle has been won. They think that the struggle is over. But black people have only just begun to fight!"

"Right on! Brother Roland! Right on!" people shouted.

"There is a war going on, and I'm not talking about the one in Vietnam. There is another war going on, y'all. It's the war for political and economic justice! It's the war against poverty, racism, and police brutality. We can't afford to be complacent, y'all. Just because we have a black principal, a black vice principal, black guidance counselors, and we sing 'Lift Every Voice and Sing' at assemblies, doesn't mean the battle is won!"

"Preach, brother, preach!"

"Let's finish the job and get us a black nurse," a sister shouted.

"Shantelle, I'm going to take that up right now."

Did he say Shantelle? I looked at the light-skinned girl, whose hair wasn't even nappy enough to wear in an afro. Sometimes they were the most militant. I glanced over at David. He gave me a ridiculous grin and hunched his shoulders.

I listened as Shantelle took the floor.

"Not everybody wants a white woman taking their temperatures, feeling their foreheads."

"For real," a girl with a big 'fro agreed.

"I propose that as Afro-American people we demand someone who can understand our medical as well as cultural needs," Shantelle continued. "We need to push until we get a black nurse."

"I heard that," several people agreed, clapping.

"Any further discussion?" Roland asked.

"I have something to say," I spoke up, surprised that I could find my voice. I glanced at David. He pretended to be praying.

"I recognize Sister Stevenson." Having Roland smile at me and call me Sister Stevenson gave me a boost. I knew that my brown color and afro also gave me a certain amount of credibility.

I cleared my throat. "I signed that petition way back, because

I wanted change. I'm still for change, as long as that change is for the better. But since I signed that petition two years ago, I've gotten to know Nurse Horn. Now I'm her student helper. And Nurse Horn is somebody who cares." My voice almost cracked. I looked around the room. I seemed to have everyone's attention. "I believe that Nurse Horn would go beyond the call of duty for any of us. I know what her support has meant to me."

I tugged at my teke. "In my opinion, getting rid of Nurse Horn would be a loss, not a gain. That's all I have to say."

The room was quiet.

"What you expect her to say. She ain't nothing but Nurse Horn's flunky!" a girl named Brenda whispered loudly.

My throat felt tight and my stomach churned.

"I've known Sister Stevenson since jumpstreet. And she ain't nobody's flunky," Roland said firmly.

I let out a breath. The girl looked embarrassed.

"I've always known that Sister Stevenson had a strong mind and I've always suspected that she had a warm heart. Today, she proved my suspicions to be true. I don't know about y'all but if Sister Horn . . . "

"Sister Horn?" said a brother in dark glasses who looked like H. Rap Brown.

"Well, if Malcolm could go from calling them blue-eyed devils to calling some of them sisters and brothers, I can afford to slip every once in a while. Anyway, if Nurse Horn is all right by Sister Stevenson, she's all right by me.

"Any more discussion?"

"I don't have anything against Nurse Horn personally," Shantelle explained, looking at me apologetically. "I don't really know her. I just thought if everything was equal we should have a black nurse."

"Your point is well taken, but everything isn't equal," Roland said firmly. "We already got Nurse Horn, we know she's good. Who's to say that the next person we might get would be half as good, just because she's black?"

"That's true," Shantelle agreed.

I could've sworn I heard David breathe a sigh of relief. I relaxed. I'd won the battle.

I smiled at Roland. There was something really special about him. He smiled back at me. It warmed my heart. But I wondered if he'd still call me "sister" if I turned out to be a freak.

After the meeting ended, I got up enough nerve to knock on Nurse Horn's door. It was the end of the day, so I figured she'd be alone. I was afraid that she wouldn't want anything to do with me on accounta I'd called her a freak. But I needed to talk to her, I felt that she was my last hope to be understood. My heart was in my mouth as my knuckles tapped against the wooden door.

There was no answer. I knocked harder; my heart beat faster. Still no answer.

I tried the door; it was locked.

I rushed toward the main office to see if Nurse Horn had checked out.

My heart skipped a beat, there was Nurse Horn in her London Fog coat in front of her mailbox. I stood staring through the glass part of the office door. Nurse Horn turned around and headed toward me. My eyes fell to the floor. Suddenly she was standing in front of me. She was quiet. I was afraid to look up. My eyes were glued to the tan and brown floor tiles.

"Stevie, is there something you would like to say?"

"Uh, I'm sorry about what I said the other day." I looked up.

I moved out of the way to let Brother Kambui by. "About calling you a freak, and all," I whispered.

"Stevie, I care about you and I want what's best for you. I really don't have any other motives."

I turned and faced Nurse Horn. "Are you still my friend?"

"I'd like to be, Stevie."

I felt an urgent need to talk to Nurse Horn about everything. Stuff felt ready to bubble out of me like Buckingham Fountain.

"Nurse Horn, can we talk?"

She hesitated. "I have to run by the cleaners before they close.

I also need to go by the Coop Food Store. My cupboards are pretty bare."

I sighed.

"You want to come with me? If you don't mind going to Hyde Park, I can drive you home."

"Sure, I love Hyde Park."

"It's such a nice day. How would you like to talk while we walk along the lake?"

"Cool. Are you going to take the Drive?" I asked, trying to sound hip. It was much nicer to take Lake Shore Drive than the Dan Ryan Expressway.

"I always take the Drive; it relaxes my mind."

I leaned against the bucket seats while Nurse Horn put her cleaning in the trunk of her car.

She slid into the driver's seat.

"You know, I've never walked along the lake before," I said. "No?"

"I've been to Rainbow Beach; I've passed by the lake in a car. But I've always wanted to be one of those people who walked along the lake."

"I do it all the time in the summer. My uncle even has a boat out there. I've been sailing on it."

"Wow."

Nurse Horn and I strolled along Lake Michigan as the wind gently tugged at our coats. It was peaceful. There were a few bike riders, some people walking dogs, and a runner.

"I guess I don't know where to start. My mind is a mess. My biggest battles in life used to be with my mother. Those were nothing compared to this."

"What is it, Stevie? You sound like you lost your best friend."

"I may have." Not to mention my boyfriend, I thought. "Uh . . . I did it with Sean, sort of," I added.

"Well, you sounded pretty determined. I hope that you used protection." Nurse Horn looked me in the eye, but I couldn't tell if she was funny or not.

"We did. I even got my period yesterday."

"Is there a problem?"

"I didn't like it. It hurt. I told Sean to stop."

"Did he?"

"Yes, but he copped an attitude."

"Stevie, I can understand why he would've been frustrated. That's one reason why it's so important for girls to wait until they're ready. But so many of you seem to be in such a big rush these days."

"Is it normal not to like it, for it to hurt?"

"Stevie, some married women even consider sex a chore. A teenage girl who enjoys sexual intercourse the first time is the exception. I had a girl say to me once, 'I hope having a baby doesn't hurt as much as sex did.' "

"Wow, really?"

"Yes, really."

"Nurse Horn, me and Sean sort of broke up. He told me he was going to take somebody to his prom who was willing to give him some."

"You don't need that kind of pressure."

"That's true." I decided to put all of my cards on the table with Nurse Horn.

"Nurse Horn, I think there might be something wrong with me, though. I might be a disgrace to humanity."

"What do you mean? What are you talking about?"

I wondered if Nurse Horn was just playing dumb or if she really was dumb as a doorknob.

"You don't understand. I'm not normal."

"Not normal how?"

"I have unnatural desires!"

"Stevie, would you like to sit on that bench over there?"

I nodded, noticing how wobbly my legs felt.

"Honey, tell me what's bothering you," she asked after we sat down.

"I've daydreamed about you more than Sean," I blurted out.

"I fantasize about you holding me, hugging me against your terry-cloth bathrobe, telling me I have potential."

"That's really sweet, Stevie."

"Sweet? You don't think I'm sick?"

"No, I think you're wonderful."

"My favorite fantasy is about you rescuing me from drowning and giving me mouth-to-mouth resuscitation! Doesn't that make you nervous?"

"Yes, I suppose it does."

I took a deep breath.

"But only because I'm not that good of a swimmer," Nurse Horn said with a smile.

I looked out on the blue water. "But homosexuality is a sickness. It's a sin, too."

"Not all psychiatrists agree that it's a sickness. And the God I believe in is compassionate and merciful and cares more about how we treat each other than about who we love."

"I never thought about it that way before. But, Nurse Horn, I'm afraid of ending up without any friends, being an outcast. I want to have a normal life. I want to go to my prom next year."

"It's funny, my niece and her friends couldn't care less about the prom. At her school they might have to cancel it because of lack of interest."

"Really? Where does your niece go to school?"

"San Francisco."

"Oh, no wonder."

"I don't think you will end up without friends. If you stick with being Stevie, you'll always have a friend. And as cute as you are, I suspect that some nice boy will ask you to the prom next year."

"You think I'm cute?"

"I think you're very attractive."

"Thanks." I couldn't help but smile. "But what if I'm not normal? What dude would want to go to the prom with me if I'm not willing to give it up?"

"Stevie, having sexual intercourse is not a prerequisite for being asked to a prom. Nor for having a boyfriend, for that matter."

"You mean they're not all dogs. My mother says all men are dogs; some are just more doggish than others."

"Well, maybe that was your mother's experience. It doesn't have to be yours."

I leaned down and picked up a rock and threw it in the water.

"Honey, did it ever occur to you that your feelings might not be all that sexual?"

Nurse Horn had called me "honey" again. I threw another rock. I felt a warm glow as it made a splash.

"Not all attraction is sexual, you know," she continued.

"It's not?"

"No, it's not." Nurse Horn picked up a rock and threw it. "Do you know the difference between sexual feelings and affectionate feelings?" Nurse Horn threw pretty well for a girl.

I'd just assumed that because my knees got weak and I couldn't wait to be up in Nurse Horn's face my feelings were weird. I hunched my shoulders and let Nurse Horn have the floor. "Your fantasies sound pretty tame and innocent to me. Don't be so quick to label yourself. It's quite common for adolescents to develop crushes on teachers and other adults they admire of both sexes."

"Are you saying that I might not be a freak, that I might just be an adolescent? Is that your theory, Dr. Horn?"

"I'm saying that your feelings are natural and common and not necessarily all that sexual."

"So, Dr. Horn, what do you think? I'm just looking for a mother?"

"I didn't say that. But sure, maybe. Aren't we all looking for a little mothering?"

"Even you?"

Nurse Horn nodded. "Yes, even me."

"Yeah, I guess we all are, huh."

"Stevie, because you didn't enjoy intercourse the first time

233

doesn't mean you never will. And because you have a schoolgirl crush on me doesn't make you a homosexual. Okay? It doesn't mean that you are heterosexual either. Be patient. Relax, don't try to prove anything either way. See what happens. You're so young, you've got your whole life ahead of you."

A weight had been lifted off my shoulders. I felt closer to Nurse Horn than ever. I took my coat off and laid it on the bench. I ran in the breezy sunshine and did a cartwheel at the water's edge.

Then Nurse Horn and I sat on our bench and stared at the pale blue water that stretched as far as the eye could see. No wonder Kevin thought it was an ocean.

"Nurse Horn, were you this mixed up when you were sixteen?"

Nurse Horn nodded. "Stevie, if you're not mixed up at sixteen, there *is* probably something wrong with you."

"I suppose I'll have it all together by the time I'm thirty, huh?"

"I'm pushing thirty and I don't think I have it all together."

"You're that old?"

"I'm afraid so."

"You don't have it all together yet?"

"Not by a long shot. Stevie, it's like peeling an onion, there's always another layer."

An old, well-dressed white woman with a small, ugly dog leaned over our bench.

She looked directly at Nurse Horn as if I were invisible. "It's so wonderful to see you donating your time to help an underprivileged child. My daughter teaches the culturally deprived." The woman smiled at Nurse Horn and pulled her dog along.

Nurse Horn looked embarrassed. She was turning red.

"Culturally deprived! Underprivileged! Humph," I shouted.

Nurse Horn groaned. "She's the one who's culturally deprived."

I looked down at my Keds that Mama had been after me to

wash. "Do I look underprivileged?" I asked, trying to sound casual.

"No, of course not. If I had been sitting here with a white girl, she would've never said that."

"Yeah, I know."

"Are you hungry?"

I nodded. "What about the Coop?"

"I'm going to forget about grocery shopping until tomorrow. So come along, you underprivileged child, I'll buy you some pizza."

"Make it deep dish. I'm also culturally deprived."

I stood in a pay phone outside the restaurant. "Yeah, Mama, Nurse Horn is treating me to pizza in Hyde Park. Deep-dish, Mama."

"That's nice."

"She wanted me to call to see if it was okay. You know, I'm her student helper."

"Nurse Horn is white, isn't she?"

"Yes, Mama."

"Well, don't act ignorant, remember your table manners."

"Mama, we're having pizza, not filet mignon."

"I know. But when you're black, you're always being judged."

"Mama, just put the dishes in the sink, I'll wash them when I get home."

"That's all right, the boys can wash them."

I couldn't believe my ears. "The boys can wash the dishes? Do they even know how?"

"Well, if they don't, it's high time they learned. They can't depend on women to do everything."

"Boy, Mama, you sure have changed."

"This is a new day, Jean Eloise, it's nineteen-seventy."

"You're telling me, Mama."

"Jean."

"Yes, Mama."

"Don't forget to thank Nurse Horn. She doesn't have to do

this. It always pays to show appreciation. You never know when you'll need a white person."

"Okay, bye, Mama." She was still Mama.

The joint was jumping when Nurse Horn and I walked in. University of Chicago sweaters were outnumbered by jean jackets, some with peace signs on them. A singer was shouting on the jukebox.

"Who's that screaming?" I asked.

"Janis Joplin."

"Do you like her?"

"Yes, I have to admit she's grown on me."

"Oh," I answered, deciding to give Janis a chance.

We sat down at one of the little round tables in the dimly lit room. The pizza place reminded me of Italy, even though I'd never been there.

"Me and Carla fell out because she said that she wouldn't have anything to do with me if it turned out I was funny," I confided in Nurse Horn. "I had to read her."

"Read her?"

"Give her a piece of my mind. Tell her off."

"Oh."

"I told Carla if she couldn't accept me for who I am, regardless, our friendship was pretty tired."

"Tired?"

"Yeah . . . sorry, pathetic."

"Oh. You never know, Stevie, Carla might end up coming around. You might not be rid of her yet."

"Well, if she does, she'll come around on my terms. Do you hear me?"

"I hear you."

I stared as a waiter set a black skillet in front of a couple of hippies. The pizza was smoking; it smelled good as anything you could think of. So that's deep dish, I thought. The waiter twirled around toward us.

"Hi, Di, I'm ready whenever you are, darling."

The waiter was obviously a homosexual. Of course I felt sorry for him. He even had the nerve to have a little silk scarf tied around his neck. It was so unnecessary, I thought. Why not just wear a big sign?

"What can I bring you girls to drink?"

"I guess I'll have a Coke."

"Make that two Cokes, Dennis."

"No beer? We've got a new draft, no pun intended."

He didn't have to worry about going to Vietnam, I thought, cause they wouldn't accept him in anybody's army.

"Ha ha," the waiter laughed at his own joke.

Nurse Horn hesitated.

"Come on, Di, what's pizza without beer?" Dennis insisted.

Nurse Horn looked at me.

"You can have one beer, Di, I won't report you to the principal. Just so long as you don't get sloppy drunk," I teased.

Dennis laughed. "I'd love to see Di sloppy drunk. She never has more than one beer. She's sooo good."

"Okay, okay, I'll try it."

The waiter pranced away with our order.

"He's a trip, huh?" I said.

"Dennis is a sweet soul."

I decided to try to become more accepting.

"I still hope that I don't turn out to be like that."

"Like what?"

"You know, funny."

"Stevie, you can only become what you already are."

"Come again?"

"My yoga teacher says that you don't change, you just become more transparent."

"Is yoga where they stand on their heads?"

"That's one posture."

"So, you're into yoga?"

Nurse Horn's eyes lit up. "I'm a beginner, but it's great! We meditate at the end of each class."

"What's it like to meditate?"

"My yoga teacher says praying is talking to God but meditating is listening to God."

"Is your yoga teacher from another planet?"

Nurse Horn smiled, "Yes, Berkeley, California."

"Well, how do you become more transparent? Do you have to take LSD?"

"No, silly. Stevie, imagine a glass house covered with dirt, mud, and a lot of other junk."

"I'm following you."

"And you wash it clean till it sparkles."

"Right on."

"Well, the house hasn't really changed."

"It's clean."

"But the essence of what it is hasn't changed. It has just become more transparent. You can shine by becoming more who you already are. Am I being too deep?"

"No, I got it. I just hope the pizza is as deep as you are, though."

"Did I sound like a space cadet?"

"No, I can relate. I'm versatile."

"I thought that you marched to the beat of a different drummer."

I smiled. "Yeah, you can take me anywhere. You know Miss Humphrey told us something in Art class once. She said some dude asked Michelangelo how he knew how to sculpt David?"

"What did he say?"

"He just chipped away at everything that wasn't David."

Nurse Horn sighed. "That's beautiful, Stevie."

Dennis set our drinks down. While Nurse Horn was gazing up at the poster of the Leaning Tower of Pisa, I switched our mugs and took a drink of her beer. The bitter taste would take some getting used to. Nurse Horn sipped my Coke. She had a funny look on her face and sipped again. Nurse Horn looked over at me gulping her beer. I started laughing. She reached across and grabbed the mug from me.

"Psych! Fooled you, didn't I!"

"Stevie, if you think that was funny, you should see your mouth, it's got foam all over it." Nurse Horn smiled.

She leaned over and wiped the side of my mouth with her bare thumb. Nurse Horn's touch against my face reminded me of how cozy I used to feel up in Grandma's lap when I was young. But when her thumb brushed my lips, I had a different feeling, cozy and exciting at the same time.

My life might not turn out to be easy, I thought.

I just hoped that I turned out to be strong.

ABOUT THE AUTHOR

April Sinclair grew up in Chicago. She has worked for over fifteen years in community service programs, has directed a countywide hunger coalition, and has taught reading and creative writing to inner-city children and youth. She has read from her work in progress to large, enthusiastic, multicultural audiences in bookstores and coffeehouses in northern California for several years. April has been a fellow at the McDowell and Ragdale colonies. She is presently working on a sequel to *Coffee Will Make You Black*. April lives in Oakland, California.